ISLAND CAPTIVE

A DARK ROMANCE

JANE HENRY

Island Captive: A Dark Romance

Copyright © 2018 by Jane Henry

All rights reserved.

This is a literary work of fiction. Any names, places or incidents are the product of the author's imagination. Similarities or resemblance to actual persons, living or dead, events or establishments, are solely coincidental.

No part of this book may be reproduced, scanned or distributed in any form or by any electronic or mechanical means, including information storage and retrieval systems, without written permission from the author, except for the use of brief quotations in a book review.

The unauthorized reproduction, transmission, distribution of, or use of the copyrighted work in the training of Artificial Intelligences (AI) is illegal and a violation of US copyright law.

ISBN: 978-1-961866-44-7 (Alternate Cover Print Edition)

Cover Design by *Haya in Designs*

CONTENTS

TRIGGER WARNING

Content Warning:

Dear dark romance readers, please note this is a **dark romance** with the following content: primal play; non consent; dubious consent; kinky, sexual scenes including bondage, orgasm denial, and spanking; violence; explicit, graphic sex scenes; graphic violence; and punishment scenes. If you're still with me, I promise you're in for a ride and a guaranteed Happily Ever After.

"You had me at trigger warnings?"

Let's go.

Some monsters aren't born but made. And now, I'm stranded with one.

I was hired to apprehend a monster—a dom sentenced to life for the death of his submissive. I've seen what he's capable of, images that will haunt me forever. I swore I'd stop at nothing to make sure he stayed behind bars.

But then, our plane back to the States crashes.

We are the only two survivors.

And the monster will make me wish I'd gone down with the rest of them...

CHAPTER ONE

Nadine

HEAT RISES from the sunbaked earth as I pretend to be a normal civilian who isn't seeking the blood of an escaped convict. I lift a pile of limp green vegetables in my hand at the market and raise a brow to the man standing on the other side of the table. His beady-little eyes watch me touch his wares. He's charging twice what they're worth because I'm a white woman, so fuck that. My mission's left me edgy and irritable and I don't have patience for this bullshit.

There's no way he's going to negotiate with me. And I don't need this anyway, so I'm out of here. I place the greens back down on the pile and turn on my heel. "Have a good fucking day," I mutter under my breath, ignoring the way he pleads for me to come back and negotiate, loud enough we catch the attention of a few women and children nearby who watch me with wide eyes.

I catch the eye of my partner four tables out. With his dark complexion and eyes, he blends in better than I do with my pasty white skin. I could pass for a tourist. He, however, melds with the locals perfectly. Convenient when we need to ask questions, and hell do we have questions. Carlos shoots me a chin lift, a sign that we proceed as usual and meet in our rented apartment above the marketplace. He's gotten no more information than I have. I smirk. At least he's got an armful of vegetables.

If I hadn't trained myself to never let my guard down, to never truly relax even in my sleep, I might have missed him. But I know him as soon as he comes into my peripheral vision, because I've studied him with careful, mesmerizing precision.

I've spent countless, sleepless hours memorizing every inch of this man's physical appearance before I got on a plane to hunt him down. I've tracked him now for months, putting him back behind bars my primary life focus until all I could do was hone in on finding him.

I know that silvery scar that runs along his neck better than the back of my hand. I know that that black tribal tattoo peeking out from beneath his shirt is actually a full tat that covers every inch of his broad, muscled back and wraps around the front to his torso.

I know his name is Adrian Barone, though he'll be going by another name here. I know he grew up on the wrong side of the Bronx thirty-seven years ago, the oldest of six children raised in abject poverty until his father solidified mafia connections. I know he served three years of his life sentence before he escaped. I know his eyes are so dark they're nearly black, he has scarring on his neck, back, and legs, and that he has perfect vision. His blood type is A negative, and he still has all his wisdom teeth.

Before I'm done with him, I'll know the pitch of his voice, the way he smells, and the sounds he makes when he screams.

But first I have to capture him.

I don't let on that I've seen him. There's no way he expects me here, but it's best I keep my cool until Carlos is here for back-up. If I fuck this up, I'll never forgive myself.

I try to catch Carlos' eye, but Carlos is chatting it up with a beautiful, scantily-clad native sitting on a nearby bench. I'll fucking kick his ass. He makes a move, steps closer to her and nods, encouraging for her to continue her story. His back's to me. He might be making plans to meet her tonight for all I know, since the signal a minute ago meant he effectively dismissed me. I should be up in the apartment by now.

I pull out my phone to shoot him a text, walking as quickly as I can so I don't lose our man, but not fast enough that I arouse suspicion. I have to play this safe. He's walking in the opposite direction of Carlos, so there's no way I can grab my partner and get his attention.

I glance at my phone and watch the text stay suspended. Of course. Just when I actually need the damn thing to work, it's uncooperative. I shove my phone in my pocket and pick up my pace. Beyond the marketplace lies a cluster of buildings strewn with women and children, and soon when the men return from work, finding one person will become impossible.

I shoot one final glance in Carlos' direction. He's completely oblivious to me, the lovely little native practically sitting on his lap. Son of a bitch. I'll kick his balls when I get my hands on him.

I'm going in alone.

A small passel of children skips rope to my left. I skirt around them, but as I quicken my pace, one of them trips and goes sprawling. I yank the kid up by his armpits and steady him on his feet. "You okay?" I ask in English, nodding my head. *Yes, yes, you're okay, now get out of my fucking way.*

I practically shove the kid aside, and when I look up I see no trace of him.

Shit.

I break into a trot. I drop the fruit I bought at the stand, the sounds of the children squealing as they pick it up quickly fading. My pulse quickens, my lungs contracting as I inhale the humid air and try to run faster. I take a left at a building, then come to a screeching halt when I realize I'm at the top of a long, winding, spiral staircase that's dimly lit with one bare bulb. I catch a glimpse of him below, the light catching the silver of the scar on his neck and reflecting. He's below me now, still oblivious that he's being followed, but three staircases below the main marketplace, descending into the darkness of a staircase that leads underground.

No fucking way.

The spiral staircase ends in a courtyard ten feet or so below. Once he disappears down the cave-like stairs that lead to countless dank rooms and doorways, I'll never find him.

It takes me a split second to make my decision. With a surge of adrenaline that nearly makes me nauseous, I grasp the rail, heave myself over the edge, and jump, the screams of those who saw me drowning in the rush of air that surrounds me as I fall. I hold my arms and legs tight as I plummet, landing on my feet like a cat. Pain shoots through my heels and calves, but my mark was accurate: I'm within arm's reach of Adrian.

I use the momentary shock that registers in his eyes to my advantage and grab my taser. Just as he turns to run, I line up my target and pull the trigger. He freezes, jerks, and drops to the ground. I've trained for a full decade, and even though he outweighs me by a hundred pounds or more, I'm thin and lithe and vicious, *petite belette* my mama called me, little weasel. Even though he's on the ground and paralyzed, I kneel above him, not really caring that his head cracks on the stone hard enough to hurt but not injure.

The pictures I received in my file on Adrian arrived with the pictures of Lori Arsenault, the woman he murdered. They were vivid reminders of her mutilated, brutalized body that suffered torment before her life was taken from her. Those pictures haunted me in my sleep and followed me into the waking hours. Day and night, there was no escape from those images. The rope burns where he tied her wrists and ankles. Bruises along her thighs, back, and ass where he beat her. This is the son of a bitch who hurt her.

This man violated a woman who trusted him, brutalized her and then ended her life.

I don't always take jobs so personally, but the image of Lori Arsenault's brutalized body affected me harder than I anticipated. She came to America as a foreign exchange student. Like my mother. She hailed from Saint Paul de Vence, a little town south of Paris. My mother's hometown.

She isn't your mother, I tell myself. I mean, the girl was younger than I am. But I can't reason with the anger that fuels my need to hurt him.

This is not just a job to me.

I want to hurt him like he hurt her.

But I'm no bounty hunter. I work for the American government.

That isn't what makes me let him go, though. I could get away with murdering him and still, even now, be lauded as a hero. But no.

Death like that would be far too merciful. He needs to suffer before he dies.

So with a twist of my arm, I let him live, but take pleasure in watching him pass out, limp on the ground beneath me. Once I'm confident he's out, I reach for the pair of cuffs I keep on me, and quickly snap them on his wrists. Heaving with the effort of the takedown, I get my phone and squint at it, needing a signal. One bar flashes, then disappears. Fuck it. I hit *dial* and breathe a sigh of relief when the crackle of a ringer sounds.

"Nadine?"

"Meet me in the courtyard, ground floor," I breathe into the phone. "I've got him cuffed and uncon- scious." Stunned silence. Did I lose the connection?

"Carlos?"

"I'm here. Say that again?"

I repeat my command, but this time don't bother with formalities. "Fucking *move*."

OUR PRISONER HASN'T SAID a word to me since Carlos found us and helped me haul his huge body up. It was no easy task, but between the two of us, we managed to get him to the holding cell we'd prepared. The local police have several they've given us for our disposal. If we'd come to arrest a native, they'd have other things to say, but apprehending an American criminal is another story. They give us everything we need and send us on our way with reporters asking questions we wouldn't answer.

Though Adrian hasn't said anything, he doesn't need to. Carlos ran his specs and confirmed I'd apprehended the correct man. I knew I had, but you play it safe when you work for the government. So now that our criminal is safe and secured, we bring him back to the states for prosecution.

There are exactly five of us on this private jet: Me and Carlos, with Adrian between us, and the two pilots up front navigating us home.

I hate that I have to follow protocol. He's still subject to due process and shit like that, and I can't beat his ass when I bring him back. I wish I'd hurt him more when I brought him down. The bruising along his chin and forehead do little to sate my need for blood.

Here, while we're airborne, however, I'm subject to no such laws. Things happen in transport.

"We have five hours," I say calmly to Carlos.

Carlos blinks at me and raises a brow in silence.

"Five hours before we're responsible for the way we treat this piece of shit." Our prisoner doesn't react.

"Oh?" Carlos asks.

"We arrive in America and we can't punish him." When we get to Hawaii, there's a cell and a court waiting for him.

Carlos nods sagely. "True. But the pilots could know what we've done and report us."

"For doing what? Self-defense when in mid-air would hold up in court."

"I don't know," Carlos begins. "Jesus, no wonder your mom called—""

The jet plane lurches suddenly downward in a sharp descent that makes my stomach clench. I grip the armrests so hard my knuckles turn white. I blink, getting a grip, then breathe in through my nose.

Just a little turbulence, I tell myself, but the thought barely forms in my mind before we begin to plummet. It lasts just a few seconds but enough to terrify the fuck out of me. My skin is on fire, my breathing tormented like someone has a plastic bag over my head. I open my mouth to breathe but can't. I'm dizzy, I'm going to pass out, but no, I'm way too pissed off to lose my shit like this. With a vicious swipe, I unfasten my buckle and lunge toward the cockpit.

"Nadine. Get your ass back here," Carlos growls. I shoot him a glare for daring to use my name in front of a prisoner. I don't like prisoners to know my name. He ignores my anger, though. "Sit your ass down and buckle up," he says. "We've hit turbulence."

"No shit, Einstein," I retort. For fuck's sake. Who does he think I am?

I go to open the cockpit, forgetting for a moment that it's always locked from the inside once we take off. I can't get in there if I tried. I growl and turn back to the seats, my eyes momentarily meeting our prisoner's. I've avoided eye contact with him until now but it's as if I'm drawn to him by a magnetic force I can't control.

His eyes are narrowed on me, and when I look at him, he allows his gaze to roam slowly down the length of my body. I try to ignore the way it makes me feel. I hate him. I fucking hate him. He undresses me with his eyes, a lewd twist of his lips making me feel suddenly naked and exposed. He meets my gaze once more, cocks his head the side and raises his brows as if to say, "What now?"

Son of a bitch.

I won't let him fuck with me.

I spin around at the sound of the door to the cockpit opening. The pilot's eyes look at me, widened, and clears his throat. He's a short, portly guy with balding blond hair and large, watery blue eyes. "We have a rapid fuel leak," he says. "It seems the inspector missed something before we left. There's no other explanation for why we've lost fuel so rapidly."

It seems for a minute we're suspended in some sort of alternate reality. I can't quite comprehend what he's saying.

Losing fuel? We've lost fuel. *Fuck.* That means we don't get back to American soil at 3 a.m. as we'd planned.

Jesus.

"Do we have enough to get back?" I ask, knowing the answer already.

"No, officer," he says, shaking his head. "Nowhere near enough to get back to our take-off, and nowhere near enough to get to our destination. In fact, our only chances of survival are an emergency landing."

Carlos swears behind me. Our prisoner, however, begins to chuckle. He fucking *laughs*. I blink, trying to process this, and ignore his sadistic laughter, and for one ludicrous minute suspect he's done this.

I turn an accusatory glance at him, but he only laughs. There's no way. There's no fucking way he could have caused this.

"Emergency landing where?" I ask.

"We're figuring it out now," he says, turning back to the cockpit. I follow.

"*Christ*," I swear under my breath.

"The nearest island is far too small and forested to land on, so our best option is to land as close to the shore as possible."

Fuck. That means we're landing *in the fucking water*. Someone's put a rubber band around my lungs, as they're suddenly constricted, and I can't get enough air. The pilots don't even notice I'm there, as they begin emergency protocol. Gerry, or whatever the blond guy's name is, grabs his remote and pushes a button.

Gerry speaks into the radio, "Oakland Oceanic, Gulf Stream 563, Emergency."

A raspy response comes on the other end. For a brief moment I'm hopeful. He reached someone. Maybe they can reach us? Then I remember we're flying over endless blue in the Pacific, and nothing short of a miracle would get anyone to us now.

A response comes in a crackly voice. "Gulf Stream 563, state nature of emergency, souls on board, fuel on board, location and intentions."

"Gulf Stream 563 is 06 33 decimal 01 north, 162 36 decimal 05 west. We have five souls on board, one hour of fuel remaining and a rapid fuel leak. We are proceeding direct 08 39 decimal 14 north, 162 32 decimal 30 west. We will attempt a water landing on the south side of the island."

I wait for the response. We all do. But nothing comes.

Did they hear us? Has anyone heard our plea for help?

"Sit back down, please, officer," Gerry says.

"Did they hear you?"

His jaw tightens. "I have no idea."

For twenty minutes I sit and worry my fingers together, ignoring the stoic way our prisoner sits erect. Carlos mutters prayers in Spanish.

We don't talk. There's nothing to say. This plane is

going down, and whether or not we survive is out of our control.

"Is there anything we can do to prevent injury on impact?" Carlos shouts to the cockpit but the door swings shut.

I stare at the door, my hands on my hips.

"Sit down," Carlos growls. "For fuck's sake."

"Sit down? Have you completely forgotten your head?" I ask him. I don't wait for a response as I'm making sure we all have life vests. We won't need oxygen masks unless the cabin pressure drops, but they're supposed to deploy if that happens.

"Put this on him," Carlos says, shaking it at Adrian.

I glare at him, the image of the brutalized woman coming to mind. I'm supposed to help him? But then I remember. If I don't help him, he could die. And how will I see him punished if he's dead?

Carlos doesn't respond, so without a word, I pull a vest over my head, stark orange that lights up the inside of the cabin of blues and blacks. It looks so flimsy, way too flimsy to save anyone's life. There's a place where I pull to inflate it, but I'm not supposed to pull that until we hit water. I hand Carlos a life vest, but can't give our prisoner his, because he's cuffed.

I lean in, and ignore the way my hands shake, and my palms grow clammy when I draw close to him.

He's bigger, stronger, and more muscled than I remembered from the brief time I touched him. He's fucking huge, so big he could pick me up with one hand and snap me in two.

I'd like to see him try.

"Uncuff me," Adrian growls. It's the first time he's spoken. His voice is dark and gritty like gravel and pitch, carrying with it a scary, commanding vibe. "When we land, you'll need my assistance and if I'm the only other survivor and you can't find that key, you'll wish you had."

"Nice try."

I glare at him, bend down, and go to put his vest on, but as I do, he quickly turns his head. I jump, gasping, expecting him to bite me, and just about drop the vest when his tongue hits my wrist, lazily lapping at the tender skin. I curse, drawing back is if his mouth is fire, the wetness of his saliva on my skin making nausea roll in my stomach.

"You son of a bitch," I growl, and without thinking about it, smack my hand straight across his cheek.

"Nadine!" Carlos reprimands, looking at me sharply. Like I give a fuck? We're crash-landing a jet with a wanted murderer. It isn't time to be politically correct.

Adrian only shoots me a lewd grin, revealing

perfectly straight white teeth. I shiver involuntarily and toss the vest to Carlos.

"You lick *me*, I'll knee your nuts," Carlos mutters, turning to face Adrian. He puts the vest on, but Adrian only sits there meekly.

Son of a bitch.

The plane pitches down, and I stumble forward, smacking my head on the wall. I blink, trying to clear my star-filled vision, Carlos's voice coming from too far away as if he's in a tunnel.

"For Christ's sake, Nadine. Sit your ass down," he says. I make my way back but I'm falling, stumbling about the cabin like tumbleweed on a prairie, wild and reckless. Our prisoner's body lunges as far as he can go, as if he wants to reach out and catch me or something, but he's buckled in and cuffed, so there's no way for him to help me. I tell myself it's the fear making my brain irrational, imagining things that can't be. Finally, I fall into my seat and snap the buckle in place, craning my head to look out the tiny window. We're so close to the ocean now I can see the foamy flecks and the angry rocks below.

You're gonna die. This is it, I think to myself, closing my eyes and bracing for impact. I try to let the cadence of Carlos' jumbled prayers soothe me into a sort of acceptance of my fate, but our prisoner's lewd, raucous laugh makes it impossible.

This isn't the landing they planned. This isn't what we were supposed to do. We hit the water, the sound of wrenching metal and screams the last thing I hear before I lose all consciousness.

SO MUCH PAIN.

So much darkness, and so much pain. My head throbs as if I've been whacked with a baseball bat. One knee radiates pain so badly I wonder briefly if I've lost a limb. The thought makes my stomach clench, as I slowly, painfully, reluctantly regain consciousness.

My first thought is *I survived.*

The second thought is, *how badly am I hurt?*

And the third, did anyone else make it?

I try to open my eyes, but my lids are so heavy, it's as if they're pinned in place with super glue. I can't open them. My head throbs with a dull ache, and something warm and wet trickles down my face. The metallic smell warns me that it's blood. Mine, or someone else's?

I take stock of the pain I'm in. My head is killing, both internally and externally. Hot pain flares along my forehead, confirming that I have a head wound, but I can breathe. I focus on taking deep, cleansing breaths, welcoming the familiar rise and fall of my chest and shoulders with the effort of breathing. This is something I can still do. I may not be able to open my eyes, or speak, or walk, but I can breathe.

It's a start.

I try to grasp the threads of memory but it's hard when my head is throbbing and thoughts saunter in and out like wisps of clouds. Wet. Something is wet. Am I? Panic floods my gut as I remember we were crash landing in water. But no, I can still breathe. If I can still breathe, then I'm either not underwater or I'm dead.

Death shouldn't be this painful, though.

Should it?

My clothes are soaked, clinging to my body like cling wrap, my head heavy with damp hair.

I have to open my eyes. I must open my eyes.

With considerable effort, I open one of them. I'm on shore, and the wreckage of the plane is about ten yards from where I'm lying. Torn metal, smoke and small licks of flames litter the beach. The sun has almost set, the horizon a dark blue, and I realize with a shock that when that sun sets, I'll be plunged into darkness.

Then what?

I push myself up to sitting, taking inventory of my wrecked body. My left leg feels miraculously fine, but pain radiates near my knee on my right leg, and I realize there's something sticking out of my leg. It's a piece of metal, like shrapnel, wedged into my leg below my knee. If it's deep enough and I pull it, I could bleed out. Then what? Is anyone else here? With my stomach clenched in nausea and shaking hands, I reach for the metal that's torn right through my pants, crimson blood staining the torn fabric. A dry sob catches in my throat. I have to get to safety.

Is there safety here?

That's when my gaze falls on the unthinkable. It takes me a minute to make sense of what I'm seeing.

Plane wreckage isn't covered in blood-soaked fabric.

A body ripped asunder in the crash is strewn on the sandy beach in front of me, arms and limbs torn brutally apart as if ripped by cruel hands. I roll to my side and retch onto the ground, emptying the contents of my stomach until nothing but bile remains. I swipe the back of my hand across my mouth and fall to my back, wrecked. I can't look again. I recognized white, though, which means that body was a pilot's, and not Carlos or Adrian. Carlos was wearing regulation navy and Adrian in the clothes we found him in.

Something else caught my attention, though. I need to see again, so I open my eyes and look to the sandy beach, pretending the body parts washed on shore are part of the beach. I can't look again.

Out in front of me, stretching all the way to the waves crashing on the shore, lies a path where my body was dragged. I didn't land here, where I am now. Someone found me and hauled me out of the water while I was still unconscious, so I wouldn't drown. That would explain my soaking wet clothes and the fact that I'm here, on dry land, and breathing.

Someone else survived, then, or there are natives in hiding. Where did they go? Did they have to leave me here so they could rescue the others?

I push myself up to sitting again, ignoring the pain that flares in my leg, and scan the coast with gritted teeth. The task ahead of me makes nausea swirl in my recently emptied stomach.

I need to identify bodies. I need to know who I'm here with. I didn't become who I am by nursing my wounds and hiding in fear.

I push myself to my feet, but the pain in my leg is unbearable. I look down. The piece of metal sticking out is smaller than I thought at first, but it has to come out. When I pull it out, I'll bleed, which should cleanse the wound, but if I make a tourniquet, or even a bandage tight enough, I could staunch the flow of blood. I quickly undo the buttons on my top, take it off, and wrap it around my leg to form a loose loop above the wound. I'll leave it there to grab when the time comes. My hands shaking so hard I almost lose my balance, I grab the piece of metal and pull. My screams echo in my ears, the pain so intense my vision blurs. I throw the blood-soaked metal away, then quickly wrap my leg in the shirt. I watch as the bleeding slows. Temporarily I'm okay, but I won't be able to bear much weight on it. I'll need to rest it to heal.

In the dim light of the fading sun, I scan the coast.

Then my eyes fall on navy.

Carlos.

I whimper and drag my hand across my eyes, wanting to push this vision away. How do soldiers at battle deal with sudden, violent loss and devastation?

Get up, I tell myself. See if you can help him.

His legs lie at odd angles, broken beyond repair, white bone shining clear through one stretch of torn fabric. I kneel beside him, lifting his limp body in my arms. His eyes are open, staring vacantly to a place beyond. I know he's dead, but I need to prove it to myself. Gently, I place his body back on the sand where it falls with a soft thump, then pick up his arm and place my fingers where his pulse ought to be, where lifeblood should be flowing through his veins. No pulse. I turn away, the confirmation my partner's gone making sudden tears spring to my eyes.

But I don't cry. And I won't now.

I close my eyes tightly and give myself a moment to deal with the pain of loss, before I stand and look across the sandy beach once more. I don't have time to spare.

The plane lies in a heap of twisted metal on the shore, half in the water. I can see how one wing is completely blown away, and reason the wingtip must've hit a wave or rock, causing us to impact the water harder than we were supposed to. That wasn't the landing our pilots had planned. Ignoring the waves of pain that make me want to vomit, I stumble on unsteady feet toward the plane. And then I see it. One final body slumped against the window in the cockpit filled with water. Dead on impact? Drowned, pinned in the cockpit? I'll never know.

I fall to my knees as the memory of the pilot's last words come back to me.

We have five souls on board.

Including myself, the two dead bodies of the pilot and Carlos, I now have four.

I still haven't found our prisoner.

CHAPTER TWO

Adrian

I WATCH the bitch from where I crouch, hidden in the darkness of trees. I moved quickly while she was unconscious, ignoring the pain that pulsed against my skull. Still cuffed, miraculously tossed to the shore, the first thing I did was locate the man she called Carlos. I took the keys and uncuffed myself, putting the cuffs in my pocket. I'd need those later.

I walked out to the sea and did a quick scan of the remains. The co-pilot's body was torn to pieces, the impact of the crash likely killing him before he was dismembered. The pilot never made it out of the aircraft, unconscious against the window as water filled the small cabin. He likely drowned, if he wasn't already dead.

And then I saw her, her body slumped over the one good plane wing, unconscious. Bloodied, but breathing. I dragged her body to shore. Having another survivor will prove useful, no doubt. The fact that she's a woman will be even more convenient. She's a total bitch, but I know ways to subdue women. I'll punish her for the way she's treated me. Then make her obey me.

What happens after that will be up to her.

After looking her over to make sure she's breathing and has no life-threatening injuries, I leave her where she can see the remains of her comrades when she wakes. Good. Maybe it'll scare her a little. Take some of the fight out of her.

Hopefully not too much, though. I like a good fight.

After she's on shore, I go about getting whatever useful supplies we may need that I can salvage from the wreckage: a small store of food, first aid supplies, and bottled water.

It's a small island. I remember from being airborne seeing the coasts from above. Thousands of small, uninhabited islands litter the Pacific. There's no telling where we are now, but it appears we're alone. I'm guessing I could walk the whole perimeter in under four or five hours. Beyond the shore lies a man-made structure that piques my interest. Clearly, someone civilized was here once, but it appears no one lives here anymore. The small, clapboard building houses a sign,

U.S. SCIENTIFIC RESEARCH OCCUPIED 2010

FUTURE RESEARCH PENDING APPROVAL

Interesting.

I try to open the door but find it locked. I huff out a laugh. Strange to lock a door where literally no one would be around to get in. Still, I'll have to pick the lock and see if there are suitable sleeping arrangements inside. Possibly more supplies. Something to keep me out of the cold.

I frown, looking back at the shore. Something to keep *us* out of the cold, I suppose. There's no use letting her fend for herself if I need her. She'll prove useful to me, but not if she dies from hypothermia or some fucking savage animals. Natives, maybe? But my gut says we're alone.

My jaw clenches at the memory of the way she treated me. As if I were some type of monster who ought to suffer pain and torture. I shake my head.

We're all monsters. Every last motherfucker deserves no less than I've suffered.

She has no idea what I've seen. What I've done. What I've suffered.

They probably showed her the pictures, though.

I shake my head. Now isn't the time to dwell on this. I look at the flimsy lock on the shelter. I need to find something to pick it and do it soon before it's totally dark here.

I have to find the bitch before she hides somewhere or does something stupid and hurts herself. This is no rescue mission, though.

This is survival of the fittest.

CHAPTER THREE

Nadine

I SIT on a large rock on the beach with my back to the wreck for minutes. Maybe hours. My stomach churns with hunger, my head aches from lack of water and food. But it hurts to move. I'm still surrounded by their bodies, too weak and helpless to do anything about that. The smell of death hangs in the air. I wonder if I'll follow them.

I have no idea where I am, no idea how to reach anyone who could rescue me, and for all I know, the man whose ass I just arrested is somewhere hiding. A man I know is capable of brutal, devastating murder and wicked, unspeakable torture if it suits him.

There is no safe place.

But as I sit, something that should have dawned on me much earlier becomes crystal clear.

The large rock I'm sitting on has been getting smaller by the minute, and as I wallowed in misery and indecision, the tide has been coming in. The change to the beach is dramatic. Panic wells inside me and I get to my feet, suddenly not caring if he does see me. What's he going to do? Kill me? At this stage, that would almost be welcome.

When the tide rises further, I'll be submerged with literally nowhere to go but the cold, deadly depths. I need to get back to the shore. I could swim, but my leg is hurt and I have no idea what lurks in the depths.

A low, familiar chuckle makes the hair on the back of my neck stand on end. He's behind me. Oh, God. He's behind me. I turn and look over my shoulder to see Adrian, remarkably unscathed, standing by the trees. His arms are crossed on his bare chest, but it's so dark I can barely make out his expression.

"Quite a predicament you got yourself into there," he says.

Asshole.

"So you survived."

"Clearly."

I don't say anything else at first. I'm not sure what to say. I just arrested this man, hurt him, and allowed my hatred for him to shine through in every interaction we've had with one another. And now we're alone, on a deserted island, like some type of sick survivor show.

He nods his head and looks around me. "Were you planning on sleeping out there?" He asks, the mockery undisguised in his voice. I realize now it was a stupid thing to do, but I wasn't exactly playing with a full deck either. The trauma is affecting my brain.

His voice cuts through the thick, humid air like a whip. "I asked you a question."

He's no longer amused.

"Maybe," I spit out. "So why don't you just shut up."

He shakes his head, as the sun dips even lower in the horizon. "Better yet, why don't I leave you?"

He turns to go, but I feel like a kid whose mother just bluffed about leaving them in the damn store after they had a fit.

"No!" I shout. "No, please don't go!"

He turns slowly and eyes me. I'm glad I can't see his eyes in the shadows. His eyes scare me.

"If I rescue you, you'll pay for it," he says.

Cold fear clutches at my chest. "Pay for it?"

This man is sick. Twisted.

He releases a low, mirthless chuckle. "You think I'm going to rescue the woman who captured me? Humiliated me? Hit me? With no recourse?" He tips his head to the side and his voice hardens to granite. "I'm no fucking altruist."

"Fine, then!" I grit out. The water's risen so high now it laps at my feet, and panic sweeps across my chest.

I'll pay. I'll do whatever the fuck he wants right now.

He gives one quick nod, then reaches for something behind him. I can't see anything in the darkness, but I'm beginning to lose my mind with the fear of drowning. It's something... yellow? I squint my eyes and look. He has some sort of inflatable raft with him. It must be the rescue one aboard our flight that he managed to salvage.

What else has he gotten?

And how the hell is he going to make me pay for this? I push the thought out of my mind. I don't need to focus on that yet.

I watch as he puts the raft in the water, pulls out a sturdy plastic paddle, and comes toward me. When he reaches me, he stops and looks up at me. "Get in."

I shake as I step toward the tiny raft. He takes up two thirds of it. If I get in, I'll be flush up against his body. Nowhere to go.

The water hits mid-calf. I'm frozen.

"Get in the fucking raft or I'm leaving."

"And have another death on your hands?" I snap.

His black eyes narrow. "You're right. I wouldn't leave you. If you don't get in, I'll drag you in by your fucking hair, and once we get to shore I'll whip your ass. Your call."

He will. He fucking will.

"Three seconds," he says. "One."

He's given me no choice, but I'm no wallflower. I'll go with him but he's not gonna be the one in charge.

"Two." I'm the girl who leapt ten feet to catch him.

He lifts the paddles. "Three."

I fall into the tiny rescue raft. My knees hit his back and I circle my arms around his waist. My pulse is hammering, my breath ragged and uneven.

"Hold on," he orders. I am holding on. I don't understand his command until he starts pushing the paddles, water splashing hard. It isn't until we're five feet from the shore I see ripples in the water behind us, visible only under the light of the moon. Sharks?

The front of the raft scrapes along the sand. He throws the paddles on shore. "Go!"

I scramble out of the boat, ignoring the radiating pain in my leg. He follows behind me, dragging the boat. A smack hits my back, and the next thing I know I'm sprawling on the sand facedown. He fucking pushed me.

Before I can recover he's pushing my head down, sand scraping my left cheek. His hand holds my head in place, the calloused palm scratching along my cheek. I try to scream but sand fills my mouth.

His mouth comes to my ear. "How does it feel?" he asks. "You like being the one under me? Get used to it."

The familiar sound of metal on metal makes me freeze.

Shit.

He twists my arms so the tops of my hands are together just above my ass. With a cooperative prisoner we allow palms together. It's the uncooperative assholes who get cuffed like this, in a way that makes pain spike along my shoulders and neck. The cuffs click into place.

"My, how the tables have turned," he says with a mirthless chuckle. "On your feet."

He yanks me to my feet by the cuffs, sand cascading down my body. I stifle a scream. I won't give him the satisfaction.

I swallow sand, gagging from the gritty taste between my teeth.

"Don't like that taste, sweetheart? I'll give you something better to taste when you pay me back."

The pictures of the dead woman come to mind once more. The marks from the rope. Welts. Bruises.

He'll rape me. Whip me.

I wish I'd died along with the rest of them.

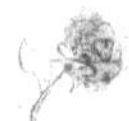

CHAPTER FOUR

Adrian

I DRAG HER WITH ME, enjoying the way she clenches her teeth and refuses to scream in pain.

I'll break her before we're through.

It's dark, but the full moon shines down on us, and I managed to find a small but powerful flashlight in the first aid kit. I hit the button and a beam shines out like a beacon, lighting our way. Something scuttles in the brush behind us, something heavy by the sound of it. She takes a step closer to me, then looks up at me, startled, as if she surprised herself. I'm her captor, after all. But I like the feel of her close to me like this.

She doesn't know it yet, but tonight she'll warm my bed.

She owes me.

If she wasn't so damn high and mighty, I'd find the girl pretty. She's a little younger than I am, with blonde hair, a thin, aristocratic nose, a full mouth with cherry red lips, and bright eyes rimmed in long, thick lashes. Her body is lithe and fit like a gymnast's, petite yet solid. I've taken my time checking her out thoroughly. She's a little on the small side—I like my women sturdy, able to withstand the way I like to fuck, long and hard—but she's gorgeous.

She's wearing nothing but a bra and pants, and I see her top has been fastened around her leg like a tourniquet.

It's really too bad she's a goddamned bitch.

I suppose I should cut her some slack. After all, she likely believes she was doing society a favor, tracking down a wanted criminal like me.

But she doesn't know everything there is to know.

"There were no other survivors," I say to her, as we draw near the entrance to the small house.

"No shit," she mutters.

Without thinking, I crack my palm against her ass so hard she stumbles forward, but my hold on her cuffs prevents her from falling all the way. She whips her head to look at me, but I don't bother meeting her eyes. She'll learn to watch her mouth, and the sooner she learns that, the better. That's only a taste of what she's got coming.

"So that's your plan," she mutters, clearly not subdued by the smack I just gave her. "I'll act like a little puppet, and if I don't, you'll smack me around? Brilliant." She purses her lips and rolls her eyes.

"Actually, it's a lot more entertaining if you fight me," I say, kneeling down in front of the lock. "And no," I say in a bored voice as she makes a step toward me. "You will not smack me with your cuffed hands and try to get away. I'm not a dumbass, you won't escape, and then I'd have to punish you tonight instead of waiting for the morning. And frankly, I'm a little tired."

She doesn't say anything but doesn't step any closer.

"It's an easy enough lock," she says. "One hair pin will do it."

Problem is, I don't *have* a hairpin.

I turn and look at her. She rolls her eyes to her hairline, and I realize her hair is tucked into a bun at the nape of her neck. It's not uncommon for female officers to wear this type of hairstyle. If her hair swung free or in a ponytail, an assailant could grab it, and gain the upper hand.

"Convenient," I say. "Since you need to lose the bun anyway."

I stand, then walk to her. She's about as tall as my shoulders, and when I stand behind her like this, she's small and vulnerable, like a cornered mouse.

Perfect.

I reach for her bun, and when my fingers touch her hair, she freezes, her body tensing, muscles contracted. I almost feel sorry for her. It's a fuck of a lot harder to submit when you're wound up this tight. But then I remind myself she doesn't deserve my sympathy. She deserves nothing but retribution.

"Hard to grab a bun, isn't it, sweetheart?" I ask, wrapping my fingers around the thick golden coil. I tug, and her whole head lurches back, but it's not as satisfying as a really fucking good hair pull. Still, I like the way she whimpers a little, and I love the feel of the golden silk between my fingers.

"How do you take this goddamned thing out?" I mutter.

She breathes out an exasperated sigh. "You pull the pins," she says. "They're tucked into the bun. I use six of them, every time. Just pull them out, one at a time."

I slide a finger under the bun until I feel the hard pin. The bun stays tight when I pull the first pin out, then wobbles a little with the second. With the third, it tumbles over my hand like gold, the fragrance of lilacs stirring my cock to life.

Forget the blow job I was gonna make her give me. I'll wrap this hair around my cock while I fist myself off.

I have fetishes aplenty. Apparently, I now have a hair one.

With a handful of pins, I go back to the lock. "Stay there," I order. I don't want her anywhere near me while I work.

"I could do this for you," she says. I don't bother to answer.

I kneel in front of the lock and wiggle the pin in, but this particular lock must have been fashioned differently than the ones I've picked in the past. "Son of a bitch," I mutter, but I can't trigger the damn release.

"Let me do it," she says behind me.

I ignore her until I'm panting from the exertion and cursing the motherfucking lock to kingdom come. Then finally, I turn to her.

"Fine. You'll get a shot. Obviously, I'll have to uncuff you, but it goes without saying that if you pull any tricks, you'll wish you hadn't."

She rolls her eyes.

I cannot wait to train this woman into obedience.

But right now, we need to get inside.

I pull the key out of my pocket, slide it into the cuffs, and release her. She swings her arms free but doesn't make a move toward me, just takes the pins from my hand and walks to the door.

She eyes the lock, frowning, then opens the pin and slides it in. Within seconds, I hear a faint *pop*. She stands with a satisfied smirk on her face and turns the knob. The door swings inward, and she walks inside. I follow, keeping an eye on her.

"Careful," I tell her. "This place hasn't been inhabited for what looks like years. You have no idea who or what could be inside."

"Whatever," she says with another eye roll. My palm literally twitches.

"Come here." I take her by the wrist and tug her close, pull her wrists behind her back again while she groans, and cuff her once more.

"For fuck's sake," she says. "I'm not going to do anything stupid. Do you really have to cuff me?"

I don't bother responding. Waste of breath.

I swing my flashlight around, until the beam lands on a light switch. I flick it, expecting nothing to happen, but bright fluorescent light immediately floods the entire room. We both blink in surprise, stunned at the blinding light for a moment. I shield my eyes, and shut the door, then turn to scan our surroundings.

The floors and walls are constructed of bare wood, as if the entire structure was put up quickly but no one could be bothered to finish it. The bulbs that hang from the ceiling are bare, wiring still showing in various places. It was a slapdash job, no doubt done by people who were on a mission or had limited resources to spare.

"Come with me," I say to her, taking her by the arm and marching her around the small interior. There's an office, with a chair and a desk and some type of computer equipment. I frown. If she can find a way to communicate with anyone using this, I could be fucked. I have literally no intention of ever trying to get rescued on this island. Why would I want to? So I could go back to a life of captivity?

I'll have to be sure that computer is disabled. We'll need to see how there's an energy source, though.

Just a few paces past the office is a small bathroom. I peek in. Everything is sparse stainless steel, with a prison-style metal toilet, tiny shower, and sink. I run the tap, but nothing happens when I turn it. I'll look into that.

"I wonder who lived here," she says softly, as if to herself. I look over at her, now basked in the glow of the vibrant overhead light and see she's more injured than I realized in the dark. One eye is nearly swollen shut, blood stains her lips and cheek, and her clothes are torn. "And how the hell there's light in the middle of nowhere."

"Likely a solar-powered generator," I grunt. I'm not sure how or why there's evidence of civilization here, but I'm not fucking complaining.

I look her over and shake my head. "You're a goddamn mess," I mutter, not wanting to give her the satisfaction of knowing I want to clean her up.

I'll do more than that before I'm through with her.

She scowls at me and doesn't deign to respond.

Behind her stands another open door. I head in that direction while she looks around us. Her lips thin, and she wears a grim expression on her face. The doorway opens to a bedroom. I feel along the wall until I find another switch, hit it, and a dimmer light floods this room. In here, there's one twin-sized bed with nothing but a sheet on top and two pillows, what looks like blankets covered in plastic, one window, and a small bedside table. It's not unlike the prison cell where I spent my time, except here one can roam free.

Looking at the bed, I'm suddenly overcome with exhaustion.

"Get in here," I order. I'm tired and hungry and about to share the bed of the bitch that tried to ruin my life. I'm not in the most pleasant of moods. She doesn't come, though. I inhale deeply, trying to calm myself. I'm going to train her. That will involve inflicting pain and punishment and seeing that she obeys my commands. But I want to be in control of myself when I do.

"I said," I growl out, exiting the bedroom. "Get *in* here."

But when I come to the main area, she's frozen in place, staring at something in the corner with wide, terrified eyes. Her mouth hangs open, her body rigid with terror. I whip my head around to look where she's staring and see a dark brown spider in the middle of a large web I somehow missed before.

"Get behind me," I order. I hear the slightest scuffle. For once she's actually doing what she's told. I look around me, trying to locate something I could use to capture the thing when it scuttles quickly away from us. Her high pitched scream makes my pulse spike. I kick my foot out, catch one leg, and the spider spins wildly out of control, the legs flailing in fight, but I'm bigger and stronger. I hit it with another vicious kick, then another. It smears on the floor and wall and she whimpers like a little child. When it's good and dead, I turn to her.

"Come here," I say gruffly. I take her by the arm and lead her to the bedroom. "We're calling it a night."

"I'm not sleeping in here. Are you out your mind? And if you think I'm getting in bed with you, you're sicker than I thought."

"Oh, honey," I say, shaking my head sadly as I draw her to the side of the bed. "You have *no* idea."

She blinks and looks around the room, then shivers. It's fairly warm in here, so I suspect she's shivering for another reason.

I sit on the edge of the bed, grab her arm, and pull her between my legs. Her body tenses and her jaw tightens, but before she can react, I bark out an order.

"I'm inspecting your injuries. You stand still and let me."

"Fuck you," she hisses. I'll teach her to watch that mouth, but not until I've inspected her to see she isn't badly hurt. The others died. She won't.

"Not yet, sweetheart," I say in a low growl, the vision of her laid out stripped on the bed with her head thrown back as she comes flashing in my mind's eye. I'm barely tempering the desire to whip her ass. "Get out of those fucking clothes," I grit out, angry at her for manipulating me into the slightest thought of her pleasure. "Now it's time to strip. I'll remove your cuffs first."

Her jaw drops, and she stares at me, dumbfounded.

I've had enough of this.

With a swipe of my hand, I grab her hair, fist it in my hand, and yank her head back, my other hand as secure as the cuffs around her wrists. "You will learn that when I tell you to do something you'll fucking obey. Now I told you to strip."

My reason is twofold: I want to inspect her body for injuries, to make sure there's nothing pressing I need to tend to before morning, and secondly, I want to humiliate her.

The added bonus will be sleeping in bed with her naked. She's bruised and bloodied, but my dick doesn't fucking care.

"If you rape me," she hisses out, "I'll find a way to murder you. Just so we're clear. If that's the end game, you might as well kill me now."

I huff out a laugh. "And end the cat and mouse game so soon? I don't think so, sweetheart. I need to toy with my little pet first."

I have to hand it to the girl. I've got her by the hair, at my mercy, and all I'd have to do is twist her neck just so to snap the life right out of her, and she's got the fucking audacity to threaten me.

I pull her close to me and sniff along her neck, letting my nose just graze the tender skin. Her breath hitches, her shoulders tighten, but she doesn't let out a sound. I nearly cradle her but for the vise-grip I have on her hair. Slowly, wordlessly, I run my tongue along her collarbone, tasting salt and fear. I want to devour her, brand her, until her every thought is of me. I don't give a fuck if those thoughts run to fear. She's mine, my plaything, and she'll pay for what she's done. The faintest lingering scent of lemon clings to her skin. This morning, which may as well have been years ago, she bathed in a feminine soap that clings to her still.

The reminder of this morning brings back the memory of my own brutal confinement in the hot, muggy holding cell they put me in. She bathed with luxury soaps while I crouched in the corner, watching the rats skitter in the shadows of the cell. My vision grows hazy with fury. I sink my teeth into her neck until she screams and writhes. I stop just before I draw blood.

I want her terrified, not injured. I keep myself aloof, pull back, and look into her eyes now wide with fear.

"You'll strip now," I whisper, letting the words drip on her skin like melted wax. "Or I'll strip you myself. My way will be quicker. I won't bother keeping your clothes intact. And then tomorrow, when I punish you, I'll add more strokes of my belt for your defiance."

She closes her eyes as if to block out her choices. As if I don't see straight through her when she shuts me out. I can feel her trembling. I can see the dark pink mark of my teeth on her skin, pulsing with the heat of pain and her terror.

"Fine," she finally whispers.

I release her and unlock the cuffs, then sit back. My body tenses. I'm prepared to defend myself should she be stupid enough to attack me again, but she isn't. She glares at me with undisguised hatred as she reaches for her bra strap and pulls it off. Her breasts swing free, full and pale, enough for a good handful. I smile, slowly appraising her dusky pink nipples. They're hard.

"Cold in here, sweetheart?" I ask, mocking her. She isn't cold.

"I hate you," she whispers.

"And doesn't that make two of us. I'm getting a little tired of your mouth, though," I say lazily. "No more talking. Talk again and I'll gag you." My voice cuts through the quiet like lighting. "Pants."

First, she steps out of her shoes. They tumble at the foot of the bed. Next, she fumbles with the clasp at her waist, unfastens it, but then struggles when she goes to remove her tattered pants. She's got a makeshift tourniquet on her leg. I look over and inspect her wound briefly, and in the dim light it looks superficial. I reach for the knife in my pocket. She freezes as I cut what remains of her pants, then I place her on her feet. "Take 'me off." She scowls at me, but unfastens then removes the remaining tatters of her pants. She wobbles on her feet, but stands before me now in nothing but a thin, bikini-style pair of black panties edged with tiny pink hearts. The delicacy of them seems incongruous with someone as tough as she is.

"Put your hands behind your back and present yourself to me," I order, before I remember that she isn't a submissive and doesn't know what it means to present herself to me. "Shoulders back, stand straight, knees slightly apart."

She opens her mouth to speak, but I raise a brow at her, reminding her that she's been instructed to be silent. If I need to punish her again, there will be no hesitation no matter how fucking tired I am. Gritting her teeth, she clasps her hands behind her back and pulls her shoulders back obediently, her breasts pert and full. I swallow hard. I'll fuck her, but it'll be on my terms. Right now, we're tired, dehydrated, and we both need sleep. There's more than training here that I need to do. We need to be able to see what our resources are, find water and food, and figure out how we'll sustain ourselves here.

I look her over in an almost utilitarian fashion, cataloging her injuries. There's a bruise on her shoulder that will turn an ugly black and blue before morning. She's scraped along both arms, but thankfully they're only superficial cuts. She has no injuries of concern until I get to her leg. When I do, I whistle softly. Fuck, I way underestimated this injury.

"That's one hell of a gash," I say. "Do you know what did it?"

"Yes," she grits out. "Metal like shrapnel."

"Oh?" I look at her curiously.

"Yeah," she states. "I pulled it out and tied my leg up to staunch the bleeding."

I nod and hope my face doesn't give away that I'm impressed. It's no small feat pulling metal from your own fucking leg. If I gave a shit about her, I'd feel bad about this injury. It must hurt like a motherfucker.

"I'll have to clean that," I say. "Make sure it's irrigated and disinfected." The kit I found in the supplies should at least have enough for this. She nods as I continue my inspection and sits on the bed while I fetch the supplies. I come back in with what I need, then irrigate and treat her wound. She sighs with noticeable relief when it's bandaged and cleaned. I don't want her to grow too comfortable with me, though.

I've looked her over for injuries.

Now my gaze roams over her body to serve another purpose.

I sit back on the bed and pull her onto one of my knees so she isn't putting weight on her leg anymore. "Your breasts are little," I say with disdain, though it's really only to make her squirm. They're actually perfect. "But they'll do." She lifts her chin as if being led to the executioner, the stoic set of her jaw making me smile.

I'm a sick fucking bastard, but I make no apologies for being this way.

I heft one full breast in my palm, then the other. She still doesn't react. Slowly, my eyes meet hers in bold challenge, I lean in and let my tongue graze along the sweet, tender skin of her nipple. Though her eyes don't betray her, her breathing pattern changes, becoming heavier and labored. My eyes boring into hers, I pull her nipple fully into my mouth and suckle. Her breathing stops altogether.

Slowly, I draw my hand between her thighs, just letting the top of my hand glide against the soft, vulnerable skin of her inner thighs, still sucking on the tender bud in my mouth. I keep my teeth away from the sensitive skin. I want her to know that I could bite her if I wanted to. I could have her screaming if I wanted to.

When the time is right.

But right now, she can't control her body's response to arousal. Even tired and injured and hungry, her body knows my touch can bring her pleasure. When I lick her nipples, her breathing intensifies.

I release her nipple and kiss the tender skin at the valley of her breasts. I want her to see I can be more than a brutal tormentor. I'll manipulate her into obedience more efficiently if I use more than vicious force. I listen to her heavy breathing, evidence she's turned the fuck on, and smile at her.

I release her breasts and pull my hand out from between her legs.

"You're a fucking asshole," she grinds out, likely embarrassed that she's turned on.

But I'm gonna train this girl, and her training won't wait.

Since I'm already conveniently sitting on the bed, it's an easy matter to turn her bodily over my lap. She bucks, but I hold her down with my left hand, then smack her ass with my right. She's tiny and frail in my grip, and even though I want to hurt her, even though I *will* hurt her, I'm aware of my strength over her.

I will not break her.

Not yet.

My palm slams against her ass so hard she arches, but I hold her in place and punish her with ten more biting smacks of my palm. Even though I only use my hand, I know how to wield it, know how to cup my hand so she gets the maximum impact. She needs a good round with my belt, and whatever other tools I can fashion for her training, but we'll get there.

Her real training begins tomorrow.

"Now," I say, as she wriggles over my knee. "Will you cooperate, or do we need to take this further?"

"For Christ's sake, let me go!" she hisses.

"Answer the question."

"Fine! Fine, I'll behave."

I smirk to myself.

I never said anything about behaving. I asked her to cooperate. It seems my little captive responds well to humiliating punishment.

Perfect.

With a nod, I stand her up. She glares at me and rubs her scorched ass and honest to God it's the first cute thing I've ever seen her do. I want to pull her onto my lap and tell her she's a good girl.

Fuck *no*.

She isn't my submissive. She's my fucking captive, and she will damn well learn her place. Any softness from me and I might as well bare my jugular for the kill.

It isn't going to happen.

"I'm going to clean you up and get you in bed," I say, ignoring my raging hard on and the scent of her feminine arousal wafting in the air. "Sit."

I show her where to sit, and without meeting her

eyes, cuff her wrists in front of her. She doesn't respond.

"Get in bed," I order. Without a word, she obeys, lying on her side. "You'll wear those cuffs until I remove them," I say. I strip out of all but my boxers, then pad noiselessly to the entry room. I lock the door and check the windows. I have no idea what creatures, if any, live on this island, and if there are any human inhabitants I sure as fuck don't want to meet them half asleep.

I shut off the lights, plunging us into darkness. It's warm in here, and suddenly, I'm exhausted. I climb into bed beside her, reach down, and lift the blanket that lies at the foot of the bed, covered in plastic. I yank open the bag, remove the blanket, and snap it open before tossing it over us. She pulls away from me, her body tight, but I'm having none of that shit. I rope an arm around her and draw her into me, letting her feel my hard cock against her ass.

She doesn't respond, though, and it takes me a minute before I realize that she's already asleep.

CHAPTER FIVE

Nadine

I WOKE SOMETIME in the middle of the night. Jerked awake by dreams of the plane crashing, screaming, and pain. Exhaustion pulled me back down into a restless slumber. I slowly come awake, noticing the sun peeking through the window. For a moment, I think that maybe it was all just a bad dream, but then I feel him behind me and I know this isn't a dream, though it's still very much a nightmare.

I close my eyes and try to steady my breathing, hoping that he won't realize that I'm awake. If I wasn't his captive, if he wasn't the man who fully intends on tormenting me, this would almost feel nice. Last night, with the lights still on, he stripped down to his boxers. It was the first time I truly allowed myself to look at him. My body had begun to respond without my permission, and in my sleep-deprived, traumatized brain I reasoned that if I was going to be stuck with this guy, I might as well enjoy what I could.

He's much taller than I am, muscular and strong. I know he must have spent some time lifting weights when he was imprisoned and then on the island, because the definition in his shoulders, arms, and in the defined planes of his abs is not accidental. This is a man who trains, and trains hard, not an ounce of fat on his muscled, chiseled form. He has a thick, dark beard that matches the color of his near-obsidian eyes arched with heavy brows. When he walked to shut off the light, I could see the way his back rippled, the full back tattoo. He's strength personified. I'm fully trained, but easily one hundred pounds lighter than he is, and at a very clear disadvantage.

So when his arm flexes around my waist, I'm not immune to the masculine feel. And I have to admit, in a moment of weakness, I almost like it. But then I remember who I'm with, and I need to get out of this bed. I've never slept with handcuffs on before, and it's really fucking uncomfortable. Despite the fact that I've had nothing to eat or drink for far longer than twenty-four hours, I need to use the facilities.

Oh, right. There *are* no facilities. There's a

makeshift bathroom that'll do when we have running water, but until then I'm screwed.

I try to wriggle out from under his arm, but my cuffed wrists prevent me from doing a very good job of it. There's a crick in my neck since I slept all night without moving, and my body aches all over. My head pounds from where I hit it. But not all the pain is from the crash.

My ass throbs from the spanking he gave me, and the place where he bit me feels bruised and tender. This man is an animal, and the worst part is that I know he's only just begun.

I know he's awake when I feel the length of his cock pressed up against my ass. "Are you awake, sweetheart?" he rumbles.

The "sweetheart" is pure mockery and makes my skin crawl.

"Yes," I say. "And I need to pee, so I'd appreciate it if you'd unfasten these cuffs so I can do my duties."

"Not sure why I need to uncuff you to pee," he says.

He presses his cock up against my ass, likely just to remind me he can before he rolls away and gives my ass an almost affectionate spank on his way out of bed.

Asshole.

"We have a lot to do today, so up we go."

He shakes his head. "Morning wood, even when famished and sharing a bed with the likes of you," he quips. "I need that shower working sooner than later."

Gross, my brain says. But another part of me is relieved. If he's referring to jerking off, that means he isn't thinking about raping me. After last night, I wasn't so sure.

He walks around to the side of the bed and tugs his pants on. I drag my eyes away from him, refusing to watch the way his abs ripple, and the way the dark line of hair trails down his chest all the way into his boxers.

He might look hot as hell, but he's a monster. A fucking monster.

Walking around to my side of the bed, he takes me by the arm and marches me out to the main room. He doesn't say much, just grunts and takes me outside, then points vaguely in the general direction of some bushes. "There are no thorns over there. Go."

I turn around and look at him, my mouth agape. "Go? Just go. Where you can see me?"

He shakes his head with mock sadness, crossing his arms. "I don't give a shit about your privacy. You might as well accept this now. But I'll give you two choices. You stay cuffed and I turn my back, or I take your cuffs off and I don't turn my back."

He doesn't trust me. I don't blame him. I have no intention of complying.

"Fine," I hiss out. "I'll stay cuffed, but don't look."

He smirks, and turns away ever so slightly, but he's still fucking *there*. However, nature calls, and I can't fuck around with this much longer. I turn away from him, trying to delude myself into believing that if I can't see him, he can't see me. I fumble with my panties and try to take them off, finally do what I need to, but it's all a lot harder with the cuffs.

"I hate these stupid cuffs," I tell him. "They're uncomfortable and not meant to be used long-term like this. They're *temporary*." Already the metal chafes against my skin, angry red marks visible when the cuffs shift a bit.

"I'll choose different restraints later, once we're settled," he says, which surprises me. No nasty comments or biting sarcasm.

I do, however, wonder exactly what he has in mind.

"We need to take care of the basics," he says, when he leads me back to our shelter. "Food, water, safety. You paying me back for saving your life." The corner of his lips quirks up. "Your training."

I choose not to respond.

His focus is on survival. Mine is, too. I don't know what this "training" is he refers to, but I'm not jazzed.

He leads me back into the room and to my relief, takes the keys out and uncuffs me. I run my fingers along my wrists, trying to rub away the ache and burn, but I sit on the bed obediently. My stomach rolls with hunger, my mouth as dry as sandpaper. With such little sleep, I'm feeling weakened. I need sustenance.

"Lay down," he orders. I welcome the bed beneath me, feeling suddenly tired. "Hands in front of you." I do what he says. I can't fight him. Not now. I'll wait until the time is right.

He kneels in front of me and pulls a large folded blade out of his pocket. I wonder where he got it from, but my thoughts are beginning to grow hazy and confused from lack of food. He pushes a button on the side and the blade springs open. Lifting my tattered pants from the floor, he makes quick work of cutting the fabric into strips. I don't fight it. The pants were useless at this point. They now lay in ribbons, which he inspects with a frown. Kneeling in front of me, he takes the strips and winds one over my wrists, not quite as tight as the cuffs, but tight enough that there's little room to move. When I'm good and secured, he stands, inspects his work, and nods.

"Good," he says. "That'll work better long-term than the cuffs."

My stomach drops. Long-term? God. The thought of endless days tied up as his captive makes my throat clench and tears water my eyes, but I blink them back quickly.

I'm no victim. I'll escape from him. And when I do, he'll pay for the way he's treating me.

He kneels down in front of me. "I'm going to gather up what we have for food and water," he says. "You're going to lie here like a good little girl. Understood?"

"Where the fuck am I gonna go?" I snap.

He reaches for my hair, but doesn't pull, just winds his fingers through it so the warmth of his hand is against my scalp before he brings his mouth close to my ear. "I said your training begins today, Nadine."

It's the first time he's used my name, reminding me there is nowhere to hide here.

"And the first thing you need to understand," he begins patiently, like a teacher instructing a small child, "is that you're no longer allowed to mouth off to me. You'll speak to me with respect or be punished." His breath is warm and tickles my skin, but it's the latent threat in his words that makes me shiver. "This is your only warning," he continues.

"For now, I'll allow you to get away with that comment if you say, '*I'm sorry, sir.*'"

I shudder, then his hand tightens in my hair, warning me.

"I'm sorry, sir," I say through gritted teeth.

"Good girl." He releases me and stands, crossing his arms on his chest and looking me over. "Roll over to your back so I can inspect your leg."

I felt hidden on my side. On my back, I feel more exposed, dressed in nothing but my underwear. But he doesn't look me over or touch me this time, just kneels and lifts my leg to inspect the injury. "Very good," he says. "No sign of infection or swelling, miraculously." He runs one hand from my calf up my thigh, his eyes on mine. Reminding me I can't stop him. He turns away from me and walks to the door. "I'll be back soon."

The door creaks open and closes. Bound like this, I have little choice but to rest and listen to the noises around me. A breeze rustles leaves through the window, and somewhere nearby I hear the murmur of running water. Is that fresh water? God, I hope we have a water source. Without one, death from dehydration is inevitable. Even if we found the resources from the plane, there's only enough for a few days. It's almost tranquil, lying in the bed like this, the early morning sounds around me lulling me to sleep. I've heard tell of people stranded on islands who were dying from dehydration try to use the saltwater to quench their thirst. It won't work, though. It will kill us.

At home, I've had two cups of espresso by now. What I wouldn't give for a cup right now. My mama made the best coffee I've ever had. *Une noisette*, espresso with a dash of frothy milk, ruined me on American coffee. She made it sweet and strong, and I grew up on it.

The memory of my mama is vivid and brilliant, stunning me with the sudden pang of grief at her loss. I can still see her sandy brown hair tinged in gray tucked into a loose bun at the nape of her neck as she rolled the dough for her homemade *galette*, singing softly in her pretty voice. We lived in a rented room, but the older man who owned the house let her use the kitchen if she'd bake for him. As a child I could sit and watch her in the kitchen for hours, stirring the pot of bouillabaisse then checking on her bread rising.

"You'll go somewhere, some day, Nadine," she'd say. "You are fierce and determined."

And I did. I watched as illness stripped the fire from her eyes. At twelve years old, I took to picking up odd jobs whenever I could to pay our meager bills so she wouldn't have to worry about them.

And now, when I close my eyes and wait for Adrian, I wonder.

Is this what she felt? Hopeless and weak, waiting for certain death, with no hope left in front of her? I hate the thought.

She couldn't defeat the illness, and death claimed her too soon.

I won't go down without a fight.

I lose track of time. Maybe hours pass, I don't know. I wonder if I'm on the verge of delirium when the door to our shelter opens, and I hear him step inside. A hard thump sounds right outside the door, then the light in the doorway dims when his large body fills the frame.

"Sit up," he barks. It's tricky, but I manage to scramble up to a sitting position. My stomach churns with hunger, my head fuzzy. It's hard to complete a thought. He holds two bottles of water and two packages of some type of bar that look incongruous in the wild like this, as if he's just come back from a trip to the store.

When he reaches me, he kneels, looking me over to make sure I didn't do anything stupid or reckless in his absence. My mouth waters, knowing food is imminent. He takes one bottle of water and twists the top off, his huge hands dwarfing the small lid, and the little circle of plastic bounces on the floor. Placing one finger under my chin to steady me, he holds the bottle to my lips. I drink eagerly, welcoming the cool liquid as it washes down my parched throat. Too soon, he pulls it away. I whimper.

"More," I say.

"Say that again," he says with a frown.

I stifle a groan. "Please may I have more?"

He raises a brow expectantly. *God.*

"Please, sir."

"A little at a time," he says with a frown, not even acknowledging my concession to him. "You could get sick if you go too fast."

He tears open a package next. I try to see what it is. It's some sort of fruit and grain bar. He must have found the emergency food stores we had on the plane. I try to see the flavor he opens for me and frown when I see a picture of figs on the front. Gross. I hate those things.

He must notice the look of disdain, since he chuckles, opens the package further, and rips off a large portion. "Sadly, no time or space to be picky, sweetheart. Open."

I hate that he feeds me like a dog, from his own hand, and I'm tempted to bite his fingers when they come near my mouth. That would get me punished, though, and what's the point, anyway? I need food.

He places the food in my mouth. My mouth waters when the food hits my taste buds. The taste of figs is still gross but wrapped up in the nuttiness of the grains and sweetness, it's tolerable. And now that I'm a bit fortified, I need to throw him off kilter.

When he places the second bite on my tongue, I close my lips around his fingers while meeting his eyes. I begin suckling his finger. His eyes widen a bit in surprise, then darken when he withdraws his hand. Reaching for my bound wrists, he turns over my hand and places the remains of the bar. "Feed yourself, then," he says, as he pushes himself to standing. He watches me struggle with bringing the food to my mouth, clumsily and stubbornly, like a toddler, then opens a bottle of water for himself. I realize he's waited for me, to see my needs met first.

Why?

Finally, after a time, we've both finished our water and bars. My stomach still gnaws with hunger, but after a few minutes, as the food swells and fills me, I'm more satisfied.

Without a word, he leaves me on the bed and exits again, coming back a few minutes later with a large metal box.

"Emergency food stores," he says. "It floated to the shore, and I took what I could. It's only enough for a few days, though, so we'll have to find alternative sources."

I nod, not giving him the satisfaction of speaking.

"Let's get cleaned up," he says, a hard glint in his eyes giving me pause. To my surprise, he holds a yellow package in his hand. It takes me a few seconds to realize he's got my bath soap in his hands.

"Where did you find that?" I breathe. It belongs to me. And if he found that...

He shrugs. "Seems it washed up to shore," he says. But the box is still intact, not disintegrated from water. It didn't wash up to the shore alone.

"And nothing else?"

His face remains impassive. He shrugs a shoulder. "I guess time will tell, now, won't it?"

I've let him hurt me, tie me up, cuff me when I sleep and hand feed me like I'm an animal. But now, the realization that he has my things and isn't giving them to me infuriates me. I want my clothes. If he has my bag, then he might have my other possessions as well.

I get to my feet, oblivious to the fact that my wrists are still bound. "You asshole," I grit out. "You have my things. I want them! Give me my fucking possessions."

He shakes his head, my only warning before he crosses the room so fast it's a blur. I don't even have time to take a breath. He easily bends me over the bed and holds me belly down. I hear a jingle when he reaches to the floor for where his belt lies. I should've kicked the fucking thing under the bed while he was gone.

"No!" I cry, writhing under him to get away, but he holds me fast by pushing his hand on my lower back, then drawing my panties down my ass. They fall to my ankles. I squirm and kick to no avail.

"I told you your training begins today," he begins in a low, firm tone before snapping folded leather across my ass. Pain blossoms on my skin. I can't get away as he holds me in place, belting me again and again. I cry out and try to wriggle, but it's no use. His hand on me is strong, and he knows how to hold someone down for this.

Of course, he does. This is, after all, what he did to his last victim before he murdered her. The vision of her bruised and battered body assaults my memory. I close my eyes, squirming under the lashes of his belt, each excruciating smack building on the next.

"You will learn your place," he grits out, delivering another solid lash. "You will not tell me what to do, speak rudely, or defy me. You will obey me."

"No," I cry out, hoarser than before, less resistant. It needs to stop. The pain needs to stop.

He whips me again, just as firm as before.

"Apologize," he says. "Say '*I'm sorry, sir.*'"

"Is this—" I gasp out, refusing to humor him, "some twisted scene you'd do at your club? Whip a girl who begs for mercy?" He lashes me lower still, across both thighs, the burning pain unbearable. Tears clog my vision and my throat tightens but I don't cry.

I never cry. I will not cry now.

The pain is nearly unbearable, but I will survive this.

I must.

"This is no scene," he says. "You can scream a safe-word 'til you're hoarse. This doesn't stop until you cave."

The strokes of his belt slow, yet they still fall, one after another, the swish through the air and the thump of leather against naked skin.

"I can wait all…"

Thump.

"Fucking…"

Thump.

"Day."

"Ok, I'm sorry!" I wail, thinking I'm going to die. No one can withstand pain like this that doesn't let up.

"I'm sorry *what?*"

No.

A cut of the belt lands on the underside of my ass, a more tender spot than before, and I howl in pain.

"I'm sorry, sir!" I finally say, my voice choking on a sob that he broke out of me.

But still, I will not cry, even if I just forfeited my dignity to this monster. I grit my teeth and ignore my blurry vision. I learned years ago in training that tears are a response to emotion, not pain. I didn't even cry when I buried my mother, her frail frame withered down to skin stretched over bones. If she didn't get my tears, I will not allow this man the gratification of making me cry.

He drops the belt to the floor but keeps me pinned in place.

"You will obey me, Nadine," he says with conviction, the use of my name making me feel ill. He isn't someone I'm close to. He's my tormentor.

I nod, chastened and little, the pain nearly breaking me.

"Get on your knees."

He releases me and lifts me from the bed. My panties are still around my ankles, my bare ass throbbing. My stomach clenches and I wonder what he'll do next.

My knees hit the wooden floor, the pain in my injured leg throbbing. He stands in front of me, his hands on his hips. When my eyes skate down the length of him, I grimace. His cock is rock hard at attention, a bulge in his pants.

"Have you ever given a blow job?" he asks conversationally, sitting on the edge of the bed.

My stomach rolls with nausea. He doesn't know I've never let a man lay a finger on me and up until now, my plan was that I never would.

"No."

He leans in and fists my hair. "You owe me for saving your life," he says. I eye the bulge in his pants. There's no way around this. If he wants me to blow him, he can force me.

Then for some reason he seems to change his mind. Adjusting his hard on, he stands.

"The next time you decide to mouth off to me, I'll find a creative way to use that tongue of yours," he promises. "But for now, you'll come with me."

As if I have a choice.

Of course, he keeps the binding on my wrists. But I won't do anything crazy if he takes them off. Not here. Not now.

I'm well aware what happens if I do.

CHAPTER SIX

Adrian

I DON'T TRUST her enough—or, for that matter, where we are—to leave her alone. The terrain is rough and bringing her with me cuffed makes more work for me. If she stumbles, I'll have to catch her. But I watch her carefully. After the spanking I gave her, I suspect she'll be at least momentarily humbled.

I'm not wrong. She's quieter and subdued now.

I check her injured leg to see if she can walk, and though she's still in pain, it's not bleeding. We'll move slowly, but we can investigate the island.

I don't regret spanking her. I don't. She doesn't deserve aftercare like a submissive. I don't need to hold her and tell her she'll be a good girl now.

That isn't my purpose with her.

But I used to be a good man. Long, long ago, before I lost my faith in humanity, before I gave into my wicked cravings, I used to be a good man.

I blame the dehydration and lack of food for my weak-ass thoughts.

We need to explore this island. We also need to somehow dispose of the bodies on the washed-up shore. but there are other pressing needs first.

The sun beats down, hot and dry. When I planned my escape, I researched the islands in the Pacific, but there are so many I only have a rough idea of where we are now. A part of me fears that there were rescue crews sent to get us, but there is no way to tell if our communication cut out too soon.

I'm not going back to civilized life.

I'll deal with a rescue crew if the problem arises.

I have a second chance. I'll never give that up.

Though there are literally thousands of uninhabited islands where we were flying, there are some allocated to America with the specific intent of doing scientific research. It's not uncommon for research teams to travel to distant islands to study volcanic eruptions and patterns, or the flora and fauna.

I put a few facts together and have come up with a basic idea. Scientists were sent here for research. They were fine dealing with the rudimentary living conditions for the sake of their mission. While here, they were given water, electricity, food, and communication options. But when they completed their mission, the necessary supplies were cut off until another scientific expedition returns. There may never be another one.

I suspect I know how to turn the water on. Out back, I even found a small lean-to that looks like a kitchen camp: rustic but suitable with a propane stove and a rudimentary table, next to the generator. The people who were here before us were no fucking carpenters. Once our basic needs are supplied, I'll have to fashion a few things better than what we have. But before we get used to more refined amenities, we need a food source and more importantly, water.

"Where are you taking me?" she asks, a nervous lilt in her voice.

I stifle a smile.

She's with me. I'm not sure she truly comprehends how much danger that puts her in.

"We're looking for food and water sources," I explain. "The shit from the plane won't last long, so we need to see what our options are."

"They'll find us," she says, staring at me defiantly, as if daring me to contradict her.

"If they do, I'll bind you and gag you, hiding both of us and any evidence of our life here, until they leave here convinced there were no survivors," I say. She winces. I mean what I say, though. I'm not fucking leaving, and neither is she.

She's either right or wrong about rescuers, and what I think about that won't impact what will actually happen.

For a moment, I wonder if I didn't punish her well enough. But as a dominant I know better. Control isn't about brute force. She needs to know I'm someone who can be trusted. Will she be more compliant if she feels more than pain from my hand?

I stand and cross my arms on my chest, looking at her thoughtfully so long that finally, her gaze comes back to me. Her eyes are pained, shielded from me.

"Come here."

I will not soften. I'm not going to be anything but her tormentor. She's nothing to me but my captive.

But she captured *me* because of what she believes me to be. *Who* she believes me to be...

No. She can't be trusted, so she remains my captive.

I shove the weak thoughts from my mind.

I'm not really going to comfort her. I am curious, however, if she's more compliant when she's given both the carrot and the stick.

"Nadine," I say, warningly. "I gave you an instruction. Come here."

She clenches her jaw defiantly, but her gaze wanders quickly away.

She doesn't want to be punished again.

When she nears me, I put my arm around her shoulders and hold her close, then place a finger under her chin tipping her head back so I can look her in the eye. "Are you in pain?"

She blinks in confusion. "Of course I am," she says. "You whipped me."

"And you deserved it. And honestly, sweetheart, that wasn't a whipping. I spanked you with my belt. You're lucky I don't have a real whip with me." I'm so fucked up, the idea of curling my hand around the handle of a bullwhip and wielding it on her gorgeous ass makes my dick hard.

She turns away with a grimace, but I bring her gaze back to me with my finger on her chin.

"Is there anything else that hurts?" I ask. "How's your leg?"

"Of course it hurts," she says, her body wavering.

Back in the shelter, in our supplies, I have some pain relievers I could give her.

No. I push the thought from my mind.

Those will be for a real need, not for a cut on the leg and a spanking. Hell, I've spanked submissives at the club harder than I punished her.

I reach my hand to her ass, feeling the heat straight through her panties, throbbing against my palm. I knead, and she hisses, her fingers clinging onto me, but when she realizes what she's doing she releases me, trying to take a step back. She moves so quickly, and is likely distracted by her injuries, that she loses her footing and stumbles. I grab her as she falls, holding her so close it's almost intimate.

We're panting from the near fall. "You alright?" I ask her, looking at her eyes, and fuck me if I don't really want to know.

It's part of how I'm conditioned, I tell myself.

I'm a dominant. When I administer punishment, it's in my blood to see to the aftercare of my submissive, to check on their emotional and physical well-being. I spent the last year of my life in various clubs. I was never satisfied in any relationship unless I had a full-time sub.

But she isn't your submissive.

It's a constant fucking refrain in my head.

Who we are is a goddamn synthesis of our pasts and experiences, what we've done and what we hope to do. I can no more ignore the dominant training in my blood than I can ignore the fact that I'm a white male. That my father was a ringleader in organized crime. That the blood of an innocent woman will stain my hands until the day I die.

So when I hold her to me, it isn't a conscious thought.

Her eyes look at me, wide and frightened, and I don't know if the fear I see is because of what I've done to her, what I plan on doing, or that she knows where this can take us if we aren't careful.

I release her, holding onto her arm to make sure she doesn't stumble again.

"Be careful," I say, rougher than I intended. I don't want her to see weakness. She needs to fear me.

She needs to fucking fear me.

"Let's go," I say.

She walks as far from me as I'll allow, her head held high and body tight with the effort of showing me she's not going to give up her dignity. I can whip her, touch her, strip her naked and cuff her, and she won't cave. Hell, she likely wishes she'd died in the crash, with nothing to hope for.

When the thought comes to me, I shove it away. I'm supposed to hate this woman. Exact revenge.

"What exactly do we have back at our shelter?" she asks. Perspiration dots her brow when she looks at me, and it's only then I realize how fucking hot it really is. The sun beats down mercilessly, the humidity like a wet blanket, permeating the air around us. We need to be careful not to exert ourselves too much in this heat, especially since we still need to make the walk back and our water is so limited.

"Slow down, Nadine," I instruct. Obediently, she does what I say. "I don't want you falling when you're cuffed, and it's getting hot here."

"Easy solution for that," she murmurs. "Could just fu—" she catches herself. "Could just uncuff me."

"I'll uncuff you when you earn it," I tell her, but the truth is it's more than that. When she earns it, and when I can fucking trust her, which may be never.

Me, I'll stay here until the day I fucking die. There's nothing for me back in the states but vengeance and hatred. And nothing for me anywhere else in the world. I had what I needed when I'd hidden myself away but living under an assumed identity is no way to live.

Here on this island, with the sun beating down and waves crashing on a sandy white beach? Here, I can spend the rest of my life in peace.

She'll want off this island. She'll want to find a way to contact the authorities or construct a getaway boat or whatever the fuck. That isn't happening. We're too far away with too limited supplies.

A rescue crew, however... that could pose a problem.

She'll earn lots of things when she behaves herself. Cuffs off. Some of the personal belongings I found in her bag.

Orgasms, when the time is right.

But she's got a long fucking way to go.

She mutters to herself, but it's soft enough that I allow it to pass without recourse. As it is, she's sore as fuck and will be marked after that spanking I gave her.

"Oh," she says suddenly, her voice higher in pitch and losing the snark. Startled, even. She points her cuffed hands in front of her, one finger waving at a splash of vibrant color behind a shade of leafy green bushes. I squint my eyes and peer.

"Berries?"

For a moment—just one moment—we're partners in this. We walk as one, hope rising between us, when the brush opens to an enormous cluster of bright red berries. She reaches out to grab one, but I stop her with a sharp command.

"Stop! You don't touch those yet."

She turns to me, frowning. "I wasn't going to *eat* it," she says. "Just touch it."

"Poisonous berries could have you contorted in pain for hours, or kill you," I say. "We'll have to test them out first. Even touching your skin with the juice could hurt you."

Her light blue eyes look troubled as she pulls her hands away obediently. "And how do we test them?" Then she shakes her head, the sardonic edge in her voice returning. "Oh, I know. You'll have me eat them first. And if I don't scream in agony or die, they'll be good enough for you."

She deserves another spanking just for the insinuation. But not now. Not yet.

"Hold your tongue," I order. Her lips purse together tightly. "I would not do that, no. I have no intention of killing you, or taking a risk with your life."

She looks like she wants to roll her eyes, but as soon as she starts she stops herself and shakes her head. When she speaks, she's nothing but sincere.

"What's your plan, then?"

Like I need to tell her my plan.

"You're my captive," I tell her, with no remorse. "You'll be my companion here. But since you can't be trusted, you'll be trained first. In obedience. Deference to me as your authority. Only then will you earn more freedom." I shrug. "And only after I feel you've done due recourse for what you've done. The reality is, I have no intention of being here alone, and will do what I can to prevent that from happening."

"Huh," she says with a sardonic huff of breath, a humorless laugh that makes her face look uncharacteristically cruel. "Here's an idea. Knock me up, then you'll have children to keep you company. You can look after them like Tarzan of the jungle, and what happens to me after that will be inconsequential."

"That's enough, Nadine." Though my tone is soft, I know she understands I mean what I say when her mouth clamps shut, and she looks away.

"What you don't know," she says, not meeting my eyes. "Is that I can't have children anyway." She says it with both pain and pride, as if she's trying to hurt me but only ended up hurting herself.

I wonder for a moment if I should press on, demanding that she tell me more, but I decide to let it go.

In time... I'll know everything there is to know about her.

"There are ways to test these berries for poison," I tell her. "I need to inspect them closely, and test the juice on skin first, then lips, and eventually we can taste them. If they're poisonous, we'll know. Red berries *are* usually fine, though. The darker they are, the more likely they are to be edible."

"How do you know all this stuff?"

I shrug. "Researched remote islands heavily. I wasn't sure where I'd end up, so I wanted to be prepared. I needed to know how to survive in the wilderness."

"Lucky me," she mutters, but I can tell she's actually pleased.

She nods, licking her lips as she stares at the heavy branches laden with what looks like luscious fruit. The truth is, though, as important as a food source is for now, we need water more than anything. I take a strip of fabric out of my pocket, one of the remaining pieces from her shredded pants I kept in case I needed to secure her further. Her eyes widen, her body tensing as she watches. I raise a brow at her.

"Do I need to gag you?" I ask, like a stern teacher correcting an errant student.

She shakes her head silently. I will train her if it kills me.

"Answer properly, or I *will* gag you."

"No, sir," she says, her voice soft but her eyes hardened.

"Good," I say with a forced smile, watching her as I take the strip and tie it on a low, thin branch that overhangs the berry bushes in front of us. A faint flush colors her cheeks when she realizes I intended to mark our spot, not gag her. I toss her a wink to unsettle her. She looks away quickly.

"Come on," I say. "We'll come back here later and watch for wildlife, see if they consume these berries. The good news is, even if the berries are poisonous, they provide a food source to any potential wildlife. If we can draw out small rodents and heavier birds, we'll find a good source of nutrition."

She grimaces but doesn't reply. Hell, the thought of eating roasted squirrel doesn't exactly appeal to me either, but I'm not much of a fan of starvation.

"You know, there was a sound of water near our shelter," she says, as if the idea just occurred to her.

"A sound of water."

"Like running water," she says, almost shyly.

"And you're just now thinking of telling me this?" I ask, but I try to keep my tone light. I'm not angry at her.

"Well," she says. "Other things... came up."

I huff out a laugh, surprising even myself. "Well, let's go back and investigate then. It's time to have a little something to eat, too."

"Already?" she asks curiously, quirking a brow at me.

"I fed you three hours ago," I said.

"Seriously?" She looks genuinely perplexed. "How do you know?"

I pull her over to me and point to the sun above us. "That's how I know," I say, but I'm only teasing. She looks up at the sky in wonder.

"You can tell the time by the sky," she muses. "How very... Boy Scout of you."

"It is," I mutter. "I'd even know how to roast a fucking marshmallow if I had one."

She blinks in surprise and smiles.

Christ. I've never seen her smile. People should be warned when girls like her smile. Men do shit like sell their kingdoms and prized possessions for smiles less vibrant than hers.

Fuck me.

But as soon as she realizes she's smiling, she composes herself and sobers, the momentary happiness draining.

I school my own features.

We aren't friends. We're not even acquaintances.

Before we head back to our shelter, I need to explore a few more things, though. I know by my explorations this morning, my observations last night, and our walking today, that we've covered nearly half of the island. So far, I've catalogued no woodland creatures. Though I'm certain they exist, I also suspect they're hiding, unaccustomed to inhabitants on this island. Birds have flown overhead but they, too, like the animals, seem frightened and quickly take off again.

Given our limited options, I've noted all of them as potential food sources.

Ahead of us, the forest breaks out into a clearing. When we walk through the final archway of leaves, Nadine gasps, unable to stifle her surprise at what lays before us.

A small, but beautiful beach, covered in white sand and dotted with delicate seashells, stretches before us. The bright blue sky is speckled with clouds. This beach is much larger than the one where we landed, and better even than the gorgeous sand that stretches in front of us, there are dozens and dozens of sturdy palm trees heavily laden with coconuts.

I wonder why those who built the shelter chose to locate on the other side instead of here. This is the place of dreams, a utopia where people plunk down the big bucks to get to.

And it's here. Ours. Our own little private island.

"Wow," is all she says.

"It's beautiful," I agree. "Come on." I lead her onto the sandy beach and kick off my shoes. She does the same. We walk silently all the way to the water's edge, soft, hot white sand melding between our toes. "With a beach like this, I'm sure we can catch saltwater fish."

"You know," she mutters to herself. "I never really liked coconut or fish. But, something tells me I'll learn to adapt."

I huff out a near-silent laugh. "You'll learn to adapt, or I'll do the adaptation with you stretched over my lap. This is not the time to be picky."

When we reach the water's edge, she dips a toe in. "Oh, it's warm," she says. "Why is it warm now? It was so cold last night."

"Just a different part of the island," I explain. "There may have been a gulf nearby that filtered its cold water into it, and this one is more of an inlet."

"You think it's safe to swim in?" she asks.

"Hell yeah," I tell her. I fully intend on doing just that. "But we don't have sunscreen, so we'll have to wait or we'll end up roasted like lobsters or getting sunstroke. And both of those options suck."

"Mmm," she moans. "Lobster."

"Yeah, sounds good to me," I agree. "A big, fat, buttered lobster roll with a side of crispy fries. Sadly, no lobsters here."

She frowns and looks away. "I really want a bath. You said we were going to bathe."

"We will once everything else is secured."

Her eyes suddenly shutter, her jaw tensing. "We won't be here forever, you know. They heard us," she says. "They heard us call for help and knew our coordinates before we went down. They'll find us."

"Will they?" I ask. "I don't think so. Any records will show the plane's crashed. And there's no fucking way they have the resources to find us even if they wanted to." It isn't true, but I want to plant a seed of doubt in her mind. I don't want her pining away for a rescue mission that will not come, but more importantly, I want her knowing exactly how long she's here.

Forever. As mine.

CHAPTER SEVEN

Nadine

THE REST of our trip back to our shelter passes almost completely in silence. We've found berries, the possibility of fish, and there are large birds flying over the water that Adrian insists he can catch and roast. My stomach churns at the thought. Hell, back at home, I don't even buy bone-in chicken, and if I can find it already cooked, that's excellent.

Those berries, though. They looked amazing. I eye them on the return route, and even see a bird picking at them. It's a little white bird with a splotch of yellow on its beak, who nips at the ripe berries without thought of poison or shit like that, and I watch as he gobbles them whole.

If the bird can eat them and not die, why can't I?

We walk back the way we came. Adrian explains that once we find a reliable food and water supply, we'll be able to explore more fully. He estimates we can walk the entirety of this island in four or five hours, but he wants to be fully prepared for when we do.

Whatever. I just want a bath, and something to eat and drink.

Adrian holds several large coconuts he found by the base of the coconut trees. We'll need more than this, but they'll do for now. He seems proud of himself, but I am not proud of him.

He might have shown a little compassion today, but the man is still a monster.

Period.

And I'll only obey inasmuch as it'll help me avoid being punished.

I'll fool him. Let him think he's somehow broken me into compliance. And once he lets his guard down, I'll make my move.

I don't have a clue where we are, and I hope to God Adrian does. For Christ's sake, I can't tell north from south or whatever the fuck, so when he says, "Where was that sound of water?" it surprises me, as I didn't know we were so close to our shelter.

"I don't know," I say. "I do know I heard it out the

window to the left, while I was lying in bed earlier."

He nods, and heads to that side of the cabin. I follow. It doesn't take long before the sound of rushing water reaches our ears, and we both quicken our steps. We're close, now. So close. If we found another source of saltwater, we're screwed.

Please be freshwater I say in a silent prayer, something I haven't done since I was a child. We have saltwater aplenty but need to be able to drink.

The sound of running water intensifies, getting even louder still, and with it, I hear the crash of water and the rushing of waves, birds twittering overhead. The sound of the water gets louder and louder. It sounds like a lot more than a steady gurgle, though.

"I think it's around the bend," Adrian says. "Sure sounds like it."

My heartbeat quickens in excitement.

"Let's take a left here," Adrian murmurs. "Right past this bank of trees."

We turn, and when we come past the trees, we both freeze.

The reason the water sounded so forceful was because there is not just a stream, but *waterfalls*. Twin waterfalls, crashing into the deep blue water below. Sun filters down from the sky, illuminating the beautiful space with colors.

"Wow," I breathe, forgetting for a moment that I'm with Adrian. I don't want him to think anything impresses me. If he believes I'm cowering in fear or have somehow lost my ability to be impressed, it gives him less control over me.

"Wow is right," he responds.

"And I could actually swim here because the sun isn't beating down so hard overhead, with the shading of the trees."

"You could," he says, turning to me with a slight frown, "If I let you. You can't swim in restraints."

Yes. Of course. I refrain from eye rolling but barely.

"Let's see if this is saltwater."

I nod and follow him. He bends at the side, dips one finger into the water, then puts the droplet clinging to the pad of his finger in his mouth.

He flashes me a full, bonafide smile, and I grin up at him. For one brief moment in time, we rejoice together. I've never seen him smile. I can almost believe he has good in him.

Almost.

"Fresh?" I ask.

He nods. "If it's a waterfall, chances are it's freshwater."

I smile. "Excellent. And I can finally take a bath?"

The smile fades from his face as his eyes darken. "You mean now I can bathe you? Yes."

A shiver courses through me. How naïve of me to think he'd actually let me bathe myself. Not after what he did to me last night. Hell, not after what he did to me this morning. Our walk around the island made this almost seemed like an adventure. But it isn't. It's a nightmare. It's a fucking nightmare.

"Oh?" I ask, looking away, trying to pretend that the mention of him bathing me doesn't make me feel all weird inside. I'm not turned on. I'm not aroused.

At least, that's what I tell myself.

He frowns, looking around us. Pulling at his beard meditatively, he mulls out loud in his deep, raspy voice. "It's warm here, to the right, there's a little, closed off portion that'll likely be warmer than the rest, and won't contaminate potential drinking water if we bathe there."

But all I hear is blah blah blah bathe here.

His fingers reach for the clasp of his pants and I watch at the way his muscles around his neck and chest bunch. He unfastens his pants, pushes them down, steps out of them, and folds them into a neat square. He tosses the square on a flat rock, then reaches for his boxers.

My mouth goes dry. I try to look away. I don't want to see him naked. It's too awkward, and what if I get aroused just looking at him? I can't.

I can't, I can't, I can't.

But of course, I do. I watch as he stands in front of me clad in nothing but a trim pair of boxer briefs that do little to hide the curve of his lengthy erection, and the toned muscles of his ass. His legs are as sturdy as tree trunks, toned like a runner's. The flat planes of his stomach are covered in fine dark hair that runs straight down his belly to his boxers.

I've never been with a man, and I will not be with this one.

It's a virgin's torture.

"It's warm enough we'll dry on the way back to shelter," he says, with a half smirk. "Not exactly any cabana boys around here."

"I'll get eaten by bugs," I protest stupidly.

He merely gives me a stern look and crooks a finger at me, giving me no choice but to come. I know if I don't, he'll punish me.

Plus, I'm dying to get clean. I still have crusted blood along my leg, and dried sweat on every inch of my body. My hair hangs in straw-like strands, and I have to admit, I smell like someone just dragged me in from a barn.

"What if I want to wash myself?" I ask, trying to keep my tone quiet so he doesn't suspect I'm defying him.

He shrugs. "Maybe someday you'll earn that privilege." His voice hardens. "But you're my plaything and I'm your master." The words curdle in my stomach like spoilt milk, sending a tremor of nausea through me. His plaything.

Master.

He is *not* my master. But at the memory of him wielding his belt, I know my bravery means shit.

"How can you be my master?" I whisper. "We're both humans."

He stalks over to me, looming with the sun behind him casting him in shadow so I can't see his eyes. "I'm the master of you because I'm stronger, and I'm the one who holds the power here."

The asshole. He hasn't seen the best of me. He's had an advantage, and when those tables turn, he will see another side of me. My mother didn't call me *petite belette* for nothing.

When he reaches me, I'm not sure what to expect. Will he hurt me? Punish me again? Spank me?

To my surprise, he laces strong fingers through my hair, the warm feel of his touch along my scalp causing my stomach to flip, and I'm not exactly sure the feeling is altogether unpleasant.

It is, it is, it is I chant to myself in an endless refrain of denial. He won't best me. He won't seduce me like some fucking alpha lion of the jungle, claiming me as his lioness.

The tug on my scalp sends a shiver through my body, and with my wrists secured, I can't push him away. His eyes glitter at me like fragments of obsidian before he lowers his mouth to mine and brushes his lips on mine once, twice, three times, each touch making a tremor shudder through me.

I hate him. I want to maim him, cause him pain, see him bleed out until the earth is stained crimson with his blood and his eyes stare vacantly into noth-ingness.

If there's a hell, I want to send him there.

And yet... when he kisses me, it feels unmistak-ably tender. He pulls me up to his naked torso so my shackled wrists push against his belly, entwining one arm around me as he draws me near. My mind urges me to turn my head, but I'm not sure if I even move, if the protest is just internal instead of physical, because nothing changes. He's still holding me against him, his lips on mine shooting frissons of helpless arousal between my legs. When he kisses me like this, I can almost pretend I mean something to him, and he's not my brutal tormentor. I don't want him to stop.

He tears himself away from me, shocking me back into reality when he pulls his mouth off mine. Dipping down, he swings one arm under my legs and the other behind my back, cradling me against his chest. Without a word, he turns to the water and begins to walk.

"Defy me now, Nadine, and I'll punish you." The tremors intensify now that he's kissed me, now that he's touched me. I'm sick. There's something wrong and twisted inside me that my body begs to be touched. I tell myself it's just because he's so masculine, and I haven't had this kind of attention from a man before, but there's more to it.

He doesn't need to say he'll punish me, though. I know he will.

"See all those tree branches nearby?" he continues conversationally.

I don't reply. I don't need him to remind me the very many ways he can punish me if he chooses.

"You'd switch me like an old-fashioned school teacher? Or cane me like they do in Singapore?"

He smirks. "Seems someone has a fascination with getting spanked."

I sputter. "I do not! I'm just a student of history, and I'm horrified at the many and varied ways one could punish others."

We're almost at the water's edge now. He places me feet first right near the water's edge, so close to him I can hardly move, and begins the easy process of stripping me from my panties and bra. "Some people thrive under firm discipline," he says. "Time will tell if you're one of them."

"You say discipline as if it's a good thing," I say to him, hissing as the panties skirt over my bruised ass.

"Discipline *can* be a good thing," he says decidedly. "Discipline is punishment meted out with the express intent of correcting behavior. It isn't necessarily vindictive or gratuitous."

I think of how he whipped me earlier today. Was that gratuitous? It fucking felt like it.

Instead of arguing and giving him a reason to show me his methods of punishment, I close my mouth. I now stand in front of him fully naked, but I'm beginning to get used to being made vulnerable without a choice. When you're stripped away of your pride, standing naked no longer matters. People are born naked. They often die the same.

He steps toward the pool of water, right to the reaches for his folded pants and removes the bar of soap.

"What if there are alligators?"

He snorts. "Alligators? We're on an island. No alligators. No leopards or lions. There are seriously no predators here that are going to hurt you."

Except you, I think.

"How do I know you're not just pulling my leg, and as soon as an alligator comes, you won't throw me to it to save yourself?"

"Nadine," he says patiently. "There are no alligators here. But if there were, I'd gladly capture one and make us alligator soup and give thanks to the reptilian gods we were sent substantial food."

"I'd rather have lobster," I mutter to myself, but then my voice pitches off into a scream as he sweeps me back up into his arms and walks me bodily in the water. I can't flail my hands because I'm restrained, and fear ricochets through me when I hit the water, but I realize it's too shallow for me to fall under if he let me go. But he's still got me in his arms. He pulls me up against him, holds me against his chest so my ass is pressed up against his lap, and begins to soap me up. From the little pool where we are, I have a perfect view of the waterfalls, twin streams of powerful water cascading down in front of me and crashing so hard in the water below, a misty film hangs in the air. The clouds part, and the sun peeks through.

"How's your leg?" he asks.

"Hurts like hell, but better," I respond, surprised he's asking.

He nods. "Gotta rest it when we get back."

One of his arms encircles me, holding me tight against his powerful legs and erection. I hold my breath. What's he going to do to me?

He soaps me up with his right hand while holding me tight with his left, paying particular attention to my breasts. Then his hand dives between my legs and he circles my inner thighs. His touch is rough, unencumbered, and certain, and the powerful strokes of his fingers on my skin makes me shiver. He releases me just long enough to spin me out so I'm facing him now, then pulls my head back so it's in the water, just to my temples, soaking my hair. He soaps that up, too, then rinses me off, his eyes trained on me as he does the same to his large body. I think we're done, but it's not even close.

"Come here," he says, as he grabs my leg and pulls me over to him again. He turns me back around so I'm facing the waterfall and presses me back to his lap. His cock between my legs, he slowly nudges my pussy lips apart. I lose the ability to think, to move, to breathe. He's going to rape me. Right here, in the pool. There's no one to stop him but me.

Is it rape when your body is primed and ready?

I don't want this, I tell myself.

I writhe, trying to get away, but he holds me close and doesn't let me push away.

I finally realize he's not pushing into me. The thick head of his cock grazes my clit.

It's the first time he's touched me there. I try to push him away, but I can't.

"This pussy's mine," he growls in my ear. "Mine to pleasure or mine to punish."

Again and again, his hardened cock swipes against my pussy. This is different from when I touch myself under my bed sheets at night. His touch is stronger and more powerful, and there's something about him fondling me beneath the water's surface that seems private, yet wicked. Strong, powerful fingers glide to my core, and he plunges them in fully. I can't breathe. I can't think. I'm completely submerged in all things Adrian. I'm building toward climax, but fighting it, making myself remember that I don't want this. Don't want him. This is wrong, but when I remember the way he doubled his belt over in his hand, I feel myself getting closer to the release he's forcing me towards. Just when I'm on the brink, my body as taut as a string about to snap, he pulls his fingers out and shoves me away and into the water in front of him.

I blink, floating in the water, suddenly reminding myself *he is my tormentor*. I try to spin to look at him, but I lose my footing, and without the ability to brace myself I fall face-first into the water. I hold my breath, trying to scramble for purchase, but I can't get a grip. I pull my wrists so tightly against the restraints my wrists ache, but it's utterly pointless.

A large hand grasps my hair and yanks me to the surface. Pain ricochets against my skull as he pulls tightly, his eyes glaring at me as if it's my fault he just shoved me forward.

"Get out," he growls. "Get the fuck out of the water."

I do what he says, stumbling as I try to get out, but he holds me tight enough that I'm easily righted and out of the pool. He wraps one hand around my arm, grabs our neatly piled clothing and guides me back toward our shelter.

What the actual fuck just happened?

And then I know. That was no accident.

He restrains me not because he's afraid, but because it's a reminder to me that I'm dependent on him. To feed me. To care for me. To prevent me from falling. To save me when I'm drowning. And shoving me into the water was only proof of that.

The groping and bringing me to near climax was only a demonstration of his power over me.

I stumble when I get out, the pain in my leg throbbing. Without a word, he looks at me sideways and must see me wince in pain. He pulls me to him, bends, then lifts me in his arms. I breathe out a sigh of relief and let myself relax, but just a little.

I can't let him seduce me.

I won't allow him have power over me.

I have to remain on guard at all times, waiting for my chance.

CHAPTER EIGHT

Adrian

NIGHT PASSES into day and night again. Two, three, four days pass and it all blurs together in an endless stream of waking, feeding her, training her. She's responsive and intelligent, this one. She knows the sound of my voice. She calls me *sir* as she's been taught with no prompting now. She doesn't fight me when I undress or dress her and doesn't flinch when I touch her. She didn't even complain when I replaced her restraints with the cuffs because they're sturdier.

I'm no fool, though. It isn't because she's a natural submissive, or because she's given up hope. She only obeys because she's biding her time. She's nowhere near broken yet, but she will be. I prefer slower, deliberate methods.

After all, I still need her.

I sleep with her by my side, and it's all I can do not to shove my cock between her legs and thrust into her tight pussy. I want to fuck her so badly, I dream about it, my nights filled with lewd, sweaty sex. But I won't. My sexual training of her will take time, and although I'm not asking permission for anything I do, I won't fuck her outright unless she begs me.

And I will have her begging.

At night, before we go to sleep, I let my hands roam over her. I haven't brought her to climax yet, but I've gotten her to the point where she wants me to. She grinds her ass into my crotch at night, quietly begging me to touch her. She doesn't want to admit she likes when I do, but I feel the way her body heats at my touch.

I want her fearing the loss of my touch. Craving it.

I'll control her in every possible way 'til her every thought is of me. How to please me. What happens when she doesn't.

The first day, our purpose was to find food and water. I'm still not sure if the berries are edible, so Nadine's been forbidden from touching them. The fish supply is plentiful, though. She turns her nose up at it as I scale it, but she doesn't complain when we roast it over the open fire. She's eager to get to the kitchen, but I haven't taken the time to test it yet for safety, so she's still forbidden. Our meager stores from the plane, bottled water, and a few supplies are all we need for now, until I get everything else under control.

We bathe every other day by the waterfall and she's passed every test so far.

So today is the day I will take the restraints off.

Her first test.

If she passes the test, she gets a reward.

If she doesn't, I'll punish her.

After our usual breakfast of fish and half a protein bar each from the plane supplies, I help her clean-up for the day. I never allow her to wear anything but a bra and panties, but after the first day, we lost the bra, too. It's unnatural in the wilderness like this. And anyway, I like her breasts swinging free.

I managed to find a way to get the water supply working in our bathroom. It only took me that long because I had to identify the water source. It seems water is being pumped in from the larger pool, the one adjacent to where we bathe, and through pipes to our humble abode. Today, I tested them out, and they seem to work fine, but she's not allowed to use them until I know for sure the rudimentary drainage system is in good working order. I left her cuffed but free to roam about our shelter, and went out to see if I could catch some fish in a small, discarded net I found just outside the shelter, likely left over from the previous occupants.

When I'm only a few yards away from our shelter, the air rings with her high-pitched screams. I break into a run. I don't like leaving her alone and cuffed, but she isn't ready for freedom yet. Still, it puts her at a disadvantage should the need for self-protection present itself.

I come to the clearing in front of our shelter and freeze. She's cursing up a blue streak inside. The door is open, and water pours out onto the ground in front of me. Did something go wrong with the way I hooked things up?

I walk through the waves of water that course down the little steps in front of our shelter and come in to an absolute flood. Water's everywhere. Nadine's standing on the toilet seat, trying her damndest to staunch the flow of water from the shower head, but it's hard to do with her wrists cuffed. And even if her wrists were free, she wouldn't be able to do anything by adjusting the shower head. The valve needs to be shut off.

"What the hell is going on in here?" I ask, more annoyed than angry at first. It's my fault after all.

She looks at me sheepishly, but her eyes quickly cloud in anger. "Trying to take a fucking shower," she says. "Seems your plumbing skills aren't as top notch as you suspected."

I stomp through the water to the panel and yank the valve shut. It isn't possible to run more than a little water at a time. This isn't like modern plumbing at all. So we have to be careful when and how we use it.

So I know she didn't just use the shower, but likely tried the sink and toilet as well.

"This is why," I say, clenching my teeth to keep my temper in check while I grab her under the arms and sling her over my shoulder, ignoring her protests. "I told you not to use this yet. I gave you specific instructions, little girl."

I wade through the water to where it tapers off near our room and plunk her on the bed.

"Now I need to sort this out, and when I'm done, I'll sort *you* out. Your ass is mine."

She crosses her arms and stares at me defiantly, her eyes flashing, but there's a touch of fear there as well. Good. There ought to be. I haven't spanked her since I took my belt to her, keeping her in line in other ways. But she'll get her ass warmed for this.

It takes me two fucking hours to clean up the shelter, and I make her sit and watch the entire time. When it's cleaned out, I get our fish, clean them and roast them, and we eat in silence. I don't want to deal with her until my hunger's sated. I need to be in complete control.

Finally, I look up at her when we've both finished our meals.

"What did I tell you not to do before I left?" I ask.

She glares. "Not to touch the things in the bathroom."

I stand, wiping my hands on my pants, and nod. "That's right. And yet the first thing you decide to do is defy me. What are the rules here, Nadine?"

She huffs out an angry breath. "*Obey*."

"Mhm." I reach for her hair, fist it, and tug her head back so that her mouth parts open. "And what happens when you defy me?"

"You punish me," she grits out. I tug her hair to amend her statement. "*Sir*," she tacks on.

I nod, release her hair, then sit on the edge of the bed and haul her straight over my lap. Her cuffed wrists hang over the side of my lap and she wriggles, but I'm stronger.

"You should have known better than to do something so foolish," I say, not able to keep the irritation out of my voice as I slam my hand against her full ass. She yelps but can't get too far because of how I have her pinned like this. "There were reasons I told you not to touch that. Why did you decide to defy me?"

"I wanted a shower," she moans. "I'm fucking *dying* for a shower."

I've bathed her every other day in the little pool by the waterfall, but apparently that isn't good enough. I roll my eyes and smack her ass again. This is not a brutal punishment, though. But it will make her think twice before she disobeys me again. This punishment is more about humiliation, so I take my time before spanking her. There's a subtle art to discipline I've learned as a dominant, and effective punishment incorporates both the physical and emotional.

"With your hands restrained, you can't defend yourself the way you may need to in my absence, if you do something foolish," I say, then smack her harder than I had planned to punish her for drawing that confession out of me. I don't want her knowing I ran when I heard her screaming.

She's my captive. And I need her here so I don't drive myself insane with the solitary rumblings of my mind. She serves a purpose here, and it's no more than utilitarian.

I pause several long seconds before I lay more firm strokes of my palm on her ass.

"It's too bad you decided to defy me today, Nadine," I say when I let loose one smack after another, the sound of my hand hitting her ass echoing in the small, nearly-vacant room. "Today, I was going to reward you for two days of obedience by taking off those cuffs."

She slumps over my knee, and I'm not sure if it's because she's disappointed, or because she's giving into the spanking.

In any event, I'm not done. Her skin is still lightly bruised from the lashes of the belt she earned the other day. Now, the whiter parts of her ass are a scarlet red. The sight makes my dick swell. She'll learn her lesson, but hell I'm going to enjoy this.

"You'll get three more spanks for what you did today," I say. "Count."

I can feel her tense and see her grit her teeth when she turns her head to the side. I lift my arm and bring it down with a solid *smack*. I pause, waiting.

"One," she grits out.

I pause, my hand resting on her scorched skin. "But now that you disobeyed me, we'll have to continue your training. And you'll remain cuffed."

I deliver another solid spank.

"Two," she grits out through clenched teeth.

"You'll do what I say next time, or the consequences for you will be much worse."

The final swat lands with force behind it and she breathes out a strangled, "three." She squirms and makes a sort of half-sigh, half-sob sound. This is where I would normally give my submissive after-care. I've never done that for her, as she isn't my sub, and I want her to fear me. But so far fear hasn't gotten me as far as I'd like with her, so other methods of training need to commence.

I lift my leg off hers and release her hand, flip her on my lap and cradle her tight. She might hate me, but I'm going to earn her obedience no matter what the cost. She hisses when her spanked ass comes in contact with the rough fabric on my jeans. Tipping one finger under her chin, I lift her eyes to mine. "Are you going to do what I say now?"

She glares at me and I see a flash of something I've never seen in her eyes before. Is it vulnerability? Something about being taken over my lap brought out the little girl in her. Tears glitter in her eyes, her lips pointing down in a frown.

"Fuck you," she hisses.

I clearly haven't broken her. I almost put her back over my knee. But no. Spanking is only one of many tools I have.

I gently push her off my lap and let her fall to her knees on the floor. I leave her panties on. I enjoy seeing them bunched up around her ankles as I force her onto her knees in front of me.

"I told you if you didn't watch that mouth, I'd find another use for it," I say, reaching for my zipper.

The anger momentarily fades in her eyes, and they widen almost comically.

With her hands cuffed in front, still on her knees, she's given no choice. I control this situation.

My cock is rock hard after spanking her. Causing pain like that always awakens the sadist in me, the one who yearns to cause pain and discomfort. Memories flash before me when I let my mind wander, the pain I've inflicted over the years burned into my mind like a scorching brand on flesh. I'll never erase those memories from my mind.

"Open your mouth," I order, fisting her hair and drawing her head back. Her mouth parts open and she stares at me. I lean in and rasp against her ear. "And now, you'll show me how to use that mouth. Do anything funny, and I'll make you wish you hadn't. Is that clear?"

She gives the faintest nod of her head.

She knows I've left her little choice but to do what she's told. She also knows if I wanted to, I could have her spread eagled on that bed, taking my cock.

But not now. Not yet. Not until she begs.

I remove my cock, and slide it into her warm, wet mouth. Her eyes widen in surprise, then go half-lidded as she tentatively suckles.

I haven't had sex in so long, I have to stifle a sigh. It feels so fucking good.

But this is about gaining control, not losing it, and I can't let her see how her little mouth around my cock unravels me.

"Good girl," I say, guiding her head with my fist in her hair, shoving it back and forth so her head bobs between my legs. "That's a very good girl."

I reach down and tweak her nipples while she sucks, making her moan and squirm. I knead them in my hand, palm them, then give lazy little pinches that make the buds harden and peak. Her eyes close and she sucks harder. I release one breast, grab her hair, and bob her head faster, fucking her mouth with savage thrusts of my hips. She gags, and when she opens her eyes, they water.

Maintaining eye contact, I keep a hold of her hair, pulling it from time to time to guide her mouth on my cock. I'm drunk on this, and I need to come. "You like this?" I ask her. "You like being a slut for your sir?" Another sharp thrust of my hips and she gags, pitching forward, inhaling deeply through her nose. But she can't help the little moan she releases around my cock.

Fuck yes. Jesus Christ, this feel so fucking good.

When I'm just on the verge of coming I pull out, release her hair, swing it in front and wrap it around my cock. I fist my swollen cock in my hand, watching her eyes go wide when she looks at the large length.

"You stay there," I rasp. "You watch me come. I'll mark you, Nadine. Mark you as mine."

I shoot my load over her chest, watching it drip down her breasts like icing, tangled in her hair. It feels so fucking good I want to close my eyes and moan, but I don't, maintaining utter composure. I have to remain in control. I will not cave.

I keep my eyes on hers as I jerk myself off to completion, panting just a little, but not really winded.

She sits stock still, her ass resting on the heels of her feet as I've instructed her, cuffed wrists laying on her naked legs. I lean in and meet her eyes.

"Will you ever disobey me again?"

"No, sir," she says, her voice detached as if she's doing her damndest not to get sucked into whatever this is we're doing. She wants to remain aloof. Detached.

"You want to get cleaned up? Now you've earned it."

I pull up my boxers, lift her to her feet, and walk her to the bathroom. I open the door to the standing shower, and stick her in, then turn on the water. When it hits her, she closes her eyes and sighs, shoving her breasts still covered in my come under the warm stream of water. I take the soap, turn her to face me, and lather the lemony suds over her breasts, belly, then lower still, between her thighs.

I hand her a small bottle of shampoo I found in her luggage. I have all her clothes and toiletries from her luggage tucked away, and she'll earn her things one at a time as I see fit. She gasps at the sight of the shampoo but says nothing, merely closes her eyes as she lets me dip her head back and lather the sweet, feminine-smelling shampoo in her hair. Now that she's clean, I place the shampoo and soap aside so we can conserve them, and step closer to her. I run my hands down her slick body, my dick hardening again at the feel of her curves. She's beautiful. Fucking beautiful. I want to bury my cock in her to the hilt and fuck her until she screams my name.

I take my time exploring her curves and most sensitive parts, dipping my hands between her thighs and fingering her soft folds. I place my thumb on her clit, barely touching it, then plunge two fingers in her core. She arches and holds her breath, gripping the sides of the shower for support. I finger fuck her, never taking my eyes off her, until her chest flushes pink, her breath catches, and I know she's ready to come.

I pull my hands and fingers away, then clean them in the stream of water.

"That's enough for now," I say.

She slumps, defeated.

"You disobeyed me, Nadine. And disobedience brings about consequences." I snap open one of the two towels we found in the supplies here and draw her out of the shower. Holding her against me, I towel off her shoulders, torso, legs, and ass, then back up to her torso and neck. "You earned a spanking. And now you'll learn that I can give you pleasure, or pain. The choice, sweetheart, is up to you."

She scowls as I finish toweling her off and let her go back in the room where she's allowed a pair of panties. She has a few more days of training before I test her again like I did today.

She failed this test.

CHAPTER NINE

Nadine

DAYS RUN INTO WEEKS.

Hell, who am I kidding?

Every day at his mercy is a long day.

We wake when the sun rises and fill our days with the necessary means of survival. My leg's healing, though, and I'm glad for that. There's no need for things like clocks or the like here. We rise along with the sun. Collect the food we need. Clean ourselves and our surroundings. He still hasn't given me my possessions but rations them out little by little.

First a bar of soap.

Then my shampoo.

Last night, he produced a toothbrush and tooth-paste, which I'm using sparingly. I know we'll be rescued at some point, but I won't wait. I'll find a way to reach someone. Until then, I'm keeping vigil. Making sure I don't fuck up enough that he really hurts me. So far, he's whipped me, and forced me to my knees to blow him.

He can be an asshole, and maybe he's priming me because he touches me every night before bed. And I hate it, but the truth is, he makes me wet. I don't want to stop him from touching me. He's strong and powerful, and when he forced me to my knees, I felt arousal dripping down my thighs like honey.

I hate him. I fucking hate him. But I give myself over to feeling pleasure when I can.

What else do I have?

I do want these fucking cuffs off my wrists, and not even so I can get away. Where the fuck would I go? Injuring him would be a dumbass move anyway. I can't injure him until I have a plan to get away. Hurting him before then would only hurt *me* because the truth is, I'm depending on him for my survival. I can't catch those fucking slippery fish. I have no idea how to even make the plumbing work in the bathroom. If I hurt him, I'd be eating nothing but berries, and for all I know those could kill me, so I'm fucked.

If I disobey him, he'll punish me. If I hurt him, I'll pay for it.

I have no choice but to go along with him.

So when I finally climb into bed, I use my most compliant tone to plead with him.

"Sir?" It still feels weird to call him sir, but he makes me do it, so I've almost gotten used to it. "Adrian" would feel weird to me now.

"Mmm?" he asks, climbing in bed behind me. The man's got some serious self-control. I mean, he climbs into bed with me every night nearly naked. And yeah, he jerked himself off a few days ago and is likely making good use of the shower in my absence, but he hasn't done what he could have. I'm smaller and handcuffed, and there's literally no one to save me if he wanted to force himself on me.

It's this knowledge that keeps me in check.

"You said if I behaved that you would remove my cuffs," I say. "And I have."

He slings an arm around my waist, a habit that I've grown accustomed to. It would be tender, if there was anything more than hatred between us.

"So I did." I hear him yawn. He worked his ass off today, gathering a large store of fish, then fashioning some weapons that look like sling-shots and crude knives. He's been eyeing the water birds that come to feed early in the morning, and he thinks they'd make a suitable meal for us if we can catch them. We've had no luck yet, but the truth is, he's kept me cuffed since we got here. How long ago was that? The days run into each other after a while. If he let me help, I might be able to catch more than he can but he won't let me.

"You think you've behaved enough to earn the freedom to have those restraints off?"

"Yes, sir," I say, as meekly as possible. I need to play this right. I don't want him suspecting me. "And I know what happens if I disobey you. I won't do something stupid just because you take the cuffs off."

A long moment of silence passes before he responds.

"Alright, Nadine. You've earned this. But I'll warn you that if you pull anything funny, not only will you get your ass whipped, I'll find other ways to punish you, and then those cuffs will go right back on. Understand?"

Hope blossoms in my chest. "Yes," I nod, trying to keep my eagerness at bay so he doesn't see. "Of course."

He pushes himself out of bed, pads around the small room, and goes to where he keeps our supplies. I curse to myself. So *that's* where he's kept the key.

Not that the knowledge would have done me any good. I can't remove these cuffs unless he tells me to, or I'll pay for it.

He walks to the side of the bed and slips the key in the lock. My heart slams against my ribcage. I'm so close to having my arms free again, I feel almost giddy. My shoulders ache from holding this position even in sleep and calluses have formed along my wrists where the metal chafes.

With a click, the handcuffs swing open. He catches my wrists as they swing free and places them on my lap, then neatly folds the cuffs in his hand with the key and puts them back where the other supplies are. I roll my shoulders and rub my wrists, swinging my arms free happily. It feels so good to be free like this, that I smile softly to myself while he's out of the room.

He comes back in and cocks his head to the side. "You look pretty when you smile," he says, his eyes warming to me.

Oh no he doesn't.

"Thank you," I say, closing my eyes so he can't look at me like that again.

I hear him get into bed next to me, then his warm flank presses against my back. Even though he's my captor and I'm his prisoner, I enjoy the warmth beside me. I've never slept with a man before. I'm under no delusion that he's anything but what he is. This is nothing even close to companionship here. But still, his body is strong, and it feels nice pressed up against me. Every morning, before we have breakfast, he goes for a run on the beach, and I've seen him doing push-ups and crunches at various intervals throughout the day, even pull-ups on a sturdy tree branch. He likes control, and controlling his body is no exception.

So when he climbs into bed with me, I push my ass up against his pelvis. He hasn't brought me to climax. But I've grown accustomed to the way he touches me beneath the covers.

He starts slow and steady, one hand cupping my ass while the other travels up to my breasts. He palms my breast and cups my ass, never asking permission to touch me. Just touching, as if he has every right to. Slowly, deliberately, he lifts a thumb and circles it over my nipple. Just the faintest flicker of a touch, but my pussy clenches in warning.

Oh, God. God, I need this so damn bad.

"Good girl," he whispers in my ear. Now is when he starts to fondle me. Just enough to make me wet, then he tells me to go to sleep. It frustrates me, but not so much that I wish he'd stop. But tonight, he does something different.

"On your back, Nadine," he rasps against my ear. Wondering what this means, I obey.

He pulls the blanket down, revealing my pale, bare breasts, and brings his mouth to one hardened bud. I'm not breathing. I can't. I'm caught up in a bundle of nerves. His warm, wet tongue laps against my nipple, circling it softly, while his hand goes down to my pussy. Without thinking, I part my legs. I close my eyes, giving myself over to this. He uncuffed me. Maybe tonight's the night he'll let me come.

And as he starts touching me, my mind wanders.

I don't let men touch me. I never dated. My mother was a strong woman, but her taste in men blew. She dated loser after loser who took advantage of her, and I didn't get why she kept dating them until I was older. Hell, someone had to pay the utility bills. And I decided when I was old enough, that someone would be *me*, not someone with a goddamn dick.

Nothing gave me greater pleasure than to make my way in my career. I loved venturing into the darkest parts of the world and weeding the criminals out like worms from rot, coaxing them to come to light only to haul their asses to jail. I sought the basest criminals and escaped convicts. I slept well at night, knowing they were no longer threats to the innocent.

But here... here in this isolated place that should be utopia, I'm alone with my memories and a sick, twisted man who hurt innocent. When I get off this island, the first thing I'll do is see him pay for what he's done.

But I have to be patient. And I've always been patient.

It's the only way I can withstand the way he tortures me, bringing me to the brink of climax only to leave me there. I won't whimper or beg, like I know he wants me to. I can withstand more than this. So if he lets me come, I'll take it for what it is: momentary pleasure amidst endless days of survival. Nothing more. Nothing less.

Slowly tracing his finger along my thigh, he brushes the softest strokes against my skin. My pelvis wants to arch, needing him to touch me *there*, but I force myself to lie still. A sharp suck on my nipple shoots arousal between my thighs like a bolt of lightning, followed by a slap to my pussy. I gasp, surprised at the shot of pain that zings through my core, followed by the heat of arousal.

Mmmm. Yes. I can enjoy this.

I can let myself enjoy this. For now.

The pain of the spank he gave my pussy fades when he slowly dips his finger between my folds. My skin is on fire, my heart is skipping around in my chest, my breath is heavy and erratic, but I lie still. He traces the edge of my channel, just the faintest touch, before he swipes upward and skates along my throbbing clit. I cry out involuntarily, as pleasure rips through me.

He's been working me up toward climax for fucking days. I've ignored my need because I couldn't control it, cuffed like I was and under his watchful eye. But I'm slick, so wet with arousal, so ready to fly. Softly, with a touch that seems impossibly gentle for a cruel, heartless man like him, he fingers my clit while lapping at my nipple. He circles his arm around me and grabs my other breast, now working both nipples while he strokes me so expertly, I'm going to climax hard, and soon.

He takes his mouth off my nipple long enough to whisper, "You're close, you ask permission."

Then he returns to torturing my nipple with his mouth and teeth, making my need rise. Soft but firm caresses take my breath away. Pressure builds and my womb contracts, preparing to hit my peak. "May I?" I whisper, squeezing my eyes tight. I can't look at him when I come. I need to focus on the moment, and not think of who I'm with.

"Not yet," he growls. I want to smack him. I'm on the edge. I'm going to lose control, and he won't let me.

"Please," I ask, keeping my voice as steady as I can.

He laps at my nipple and releases my clit only long enough to plunge two fingers in my core. He flexes in and out, hitting just the right spot, so perfectly my hips buck. "Please may I come?" I ask him, feeling the sudden need to cry.

The asshole. The fucking asshole. He did this to me on purpose. He wants me begging.

"Not yet," he repeats.

He's never going to let me come. He's going to keep me on the precipice like Tantalus in Greek mythology, punished by the gods by being near water he could never drink and fruit he could never eat.

I open my mouth to protest when his warning stops me. "If you fight me," he says. "If you give me shit about my timing and do anything to protest. If you climax without my permission. Anything but perfect compliance will get you punished. Is that clear?"

I nod my head in desperation. Maybe if I do whatever he says he'll let me come. My mouth is dry, and my chest hurts from holding onto my breath. This is the first time I haven't been bound in any way, and he has more power over me than if I were tied up like a Christmas present. The fucking jerk knows it, too.

"Now?" I whisper. I won't say *please* again.

"No," he says, his hand between my legs stroking me faster, harder, with more purpose than before. I'm on the brink of climax, but if I come he'll punish me. Take his belt to my ass. And fuck if the idea doesn't make me want to come even harder. I hate that it does. I fight it, denying that the idea of being punished by him turns me on. It's only biology, I reason, pushing myself not to focus on how badly I need to climax.

He's a strong, attractive man who touches your body. That's it. That's all.

I force myself to focus on something else, to look away, to tell myself I don't need this. I can withstand this pressure. I don't have to climax. And hell, I can wait until he goes to sleep and do the damn job myself. I'm thinking of anything but where I am when he rasps against my ear, "Come now. Let yourself go. Chase it."

I fight with myself for a split second, then welcome the dark waves of arousal that flood me when he gives permission. I sink into the bed and let myself fly. I'm sinking, falling into the abyss.

Waves of arousal course through me. I can't breathe. My body writhes so hard beneath his hand my muscles ache, and still, it isn't enough. My pussy clenches and throbs, my breath coming in ragged, labored gasps as he milks the release out of me. I think it's over, but he doesn't stop and another orgasm builds on the first and I'm riding a second, more powerful high. My vision blurs, I feel like I'm floating somewhere above me as I come harder than I ever have in my entire life.

When I come down from the power of my release, I'm breathless and panting. He let me come. He actually did it.

I try to catch my breath. What now?

Elation morphs to fear.

Is this when he rapes me?

But he just spins me over onto my side, slings an arm around my waist and pulls me to his chest. My eyes close without conscious thought. I was tired before he made me come. Now I'm exhausted. Will he want his, though? But no. His warm breath drifts across my neck, making my long hair drift softly on my shoulder. He doesn't make a move.

I won't think about what just happened or what this means now.

I drift into a dreamless sleep.

THE NEXT MORNING, I wake before he does, which is unusual. Usually, he's up and out and going for a run before I even open my eyes. I think, being here on this island, away from everything that's important to me, has put me in a sort of depression. I sleep. Lots.

But today, I wake up first, and happily swing my wrists free. It feels so good to be able to move like this. Then the memory of the night before crashes down on me, and I freeze. God. He made me come so damn hard. He's likely proud of himself, too. I practically roll my eyes at the thought.

I listen for his sounds but hear none, just his quiet breathing. But when something hard presses up against my ass, I know he's no longer asleep.

"Morning," he rasps. "Bet you slept well."

"Hmph," I grumble.

He reaches his hand across my side and splays it flat against my belly. His hand is so big and my belly so small, his thumb grazes the top of my breast, his pinky finger just on the edge of my pussy. Already, I feel my need rising, my clit swelling. Fuck. He's got my body trained to respond to his touch. I'm not sure I like this, but as soon as I tell my body to shut the fuck up, he's on the move. Firm, powerful fingers glide along the edge of my pussy, where little tendrils of curly hair peek out. I'm bare next to him. His mouth comes to my ear.

"The next possession I'll allow you is your razor," he rumbles. "But I use it first."

Um. What?

"I want to shave that pussy."

"You have my razor and you didn't tell me?" I ask,

like an idiot. Of course he does. We'll get to the part about him shaving me next.

"Yes," he says. "Why does this surprise you?"

I'm not sure why it does either.

"A razor can be used as a weapon, so it'll stay in my possession," he says.

"A weapon? Seriously? You're concerned I might try to hack you to death with my safety razor?" The idea annoys me. "What the fuck," I mutter to myself. The idea is ridiculous.

The idea is ridiculous.

A cold shiver skitters across my skin when I realize what I just thought. Harming him with my razor makes my stomach churn. I close my eyes, trying to get a grip on what I just realized.

I don't want to hurt him.

Fuck.

I hiss out a breath when he tugs my hair back hard.

"Watch your attitude," he growls. "I don't like your tone of voice."

And contrary to what I think should happen, my body starts responding. My breasts swell, and my pussy clenches when he commands me.

"Yes, sir," I say, not because I don't want to be

punished but because I need him to leave me alone. I don't want to be touched again.

But then his mouth comes to my neck, his whiskers tickling the sensitive skin. A gentle swipe of his tongue makes my body hum with need. So soon after climaxing, I figure I haven't fully recovered, because the need to climax again builds.

"You can't—" I pant, "shave me. I only have enough blades for a few weeks. I—ohhh."

I can't keep up a train of thought since he's suckling my neck while fondling me, one large hand cupping my breast while his calloused thumb brushes my nipple, the other hand dipping between my thighs to part them.

"You were saying?" he whispers in my ear.

"Can't—shave me—with no blade refills. It'll be all stubble."

The hand between my thighs finds my folds, parts my pussy lips, and I stop breathing. So quickly, he undoes me, taking total control. I want to fight it. I turn my head away from him, squirming under his grasp. Will he even stop if I told him to?

There are no safewords here.

But... I don't know if I want him to stop. He treats me like a prisoner, but this feels nice.

So fucking nice.

I've never had a man touch me like this, and I don't want it to stop. Not now.

I need one more first. Just one more.

I'm putty in his hands when he strokes my pussy, tweaks my nipples, kisses my temple. He tugs my head back and takes my mouth with his, the roughness of his beard belying the soft touch of his lips against mine. My hips rise of their own accord. I'm on the cusp of an orgasm again, my whole body primed and tense.

"Come," he grates against my ear. At his words, I shatter, the climax tearing through me like wildfire. I gasp and groan, grinding against his hand while spasms rip through me. This time, he holds me while I come down from my orgasm. His black eyes meet mine unblinking.

"You're mine, Nadine. Your orgasms belong to me. Your pussy belongs to me. Your body is mine to do with as I will. If I want to shave you, I will. If I want to spank your pussy red, I will. If I cuff you to my bed to wait for me, then that's what will happen."

I nod, still drunk from my orgasm.

"Soon, I'll shave that pussy so I can eat you out."

I shiver. I'm oh so familiar with my vibrator. But...

that? I shake my head. No way is he putting his mouth *there*.

But there's no point in telling him that.

Adrian does what he fucking wants.

CHAPTER TEN

Adrian

TODAY, the sun beats down hot and relentless. The bodies on shore have been taken care of, and it was hard fucking work binding them and burying them in shallow graves. But at least now we can return to that beach to fish.

I'm starting out to catch our morning fish later than usual, so I have no luck. My nets remain bare despite my efforts. I frown. We'll have to find something else to eat.

Our stores are dwindling. The fish have been the easiest to catch and supply necessary nutrients. But now we need to find more resources. I'll have to catch some of those birds that flock to the shore and see if they're suitable for meals.

Something has to give.

Nadine has lost weight, and so have I, but so far, our water and food supply has kept us afloat. We need to find many more ways to sustain our diet.

I go back to our shelter empty-handed, my mind occupied with what to do next, when I hear a squeal. I tied her wrists together before I left, which she wasn't too happy about. I don't trust her enough to let her roam free quite yet. Harming me would be stupid, as she'd have to fend for herself if she killed me, and deal with my punishing her if she didn't. But the bonds were a compromise.

So it surprises me when I hear a squeal that sounds almost happy, and the sound isn't coming from the cabin but to the right of it, where the makeshift camp kitchen sits. I haven't let her touch it because I don't trust the propane, and we don't have any pots or pans anyway. So far, the open flame has proved a smarter way to cook. And now she stands just inside the little camp kitchen. When she hears me approaching, she spins around, her eyes wide with excitement.

At first, the only thing I notice is that her wrists are free.

"Adrian!" she says. I blink. I think it's the first time she's called me by name. I only allow *sir*. She's forgotten herself, but she's excited, so I let it go for now.

"Why are you out of the shelter?"

"You didn't say I couldn't come out," she says, almost pleading. "You just said *stay put,* and this is part of our little abode, so I figured it was staying put."

My palm still itches to smack her little ass for coming out of the shelter.

"Look what I found!" She points to something I can't quite see, so I walk up to her for a better look. The little camp kitchen takes up only a portion of the area. She points to a padlock, and grins at me. A key dangles in her fingers.

I reach down and grasp her wrists between my fingers. "And what happened here?" I ask.

Her eyes widen, and she looks down, as if she just realized her mistake.

"I can...sometimes get out of them," she admits, looking chagrined. She knows I'll have to punish her.

It was an act of defiance worthy of a severe punishment. I frown. I was hoping we'd have time to explore today but training her is more important.

"I'll have to punish you for this, you know."

She nods and gulps, likely expecting I'll take her over my knee, or take my belt to her ass. But there are many ways I can make her obey, and not all punishments need to involve a spanking.

"For your defiance today, you'll lose your privilege of walking free," I explain. She doesn't say anything, but her shoulders sag. A part of me doesn't like that.

But she needs to fucking respect me.

I'm not exactly sure what she was so excited about at first, until the clouds shift in the light reflects on metal. In front of us are rows and rows of canned goods.

She reaches a hand out and opens a burlap sack that sits on the floor suddenly she jumps straight back into me. Huge, hard-shelled black beetles move across the burlap. She screams and screams, covering her face with her hands. I pull her to the side twisting my body to keep her away from the insects. Gently but firmly I push her outside and turn to deal with the infiltrated supply. I take a quick glance through. I make quick work of tying the burlap and tossing the bags behind a tree.

Then I go back to Nadine. Her hands are still up to her face and she's shaking. I pull her over to me, gently pushing her face onto my shoulder. I hold her there and say nothing until her shaking subsides. Finally, after a time, I walk her inside.

"That's one hell of a phobia to have when you're living in the outdoors, sweetheart."

She doesn't look up.

"It looks like we have quite a bit of food here. That'll definitely come in handy. We just need to find a way to open it. I think it's time that we go through this kitchen. Actually, let me rephrase that. I think it's time that *I* go through this kitchen. You, young lady, are going to be punished for removing your restraints."

I need her obedience, no matter how I manage to get it. And today, it means she'll be punished.

"What are you going to do to me?" she asks, her tone sharp as flint. I know her abrasiveness masks fear.

When I get her in the bedroom I place her on the bed. She knows not to move but groans out loud when I remove the now-familiar and loathed metal cuffs.

I strip her and lay her on her bed on her back. I pull her wrists above her head and secure them with the detached precision of a physician, then do the same to her ankles so she's spread-eagled on the bed. When she's good and secured, I stand beside her and allow my eyes to roam slowly over every inch of her naked, vulnerable body, pacing the floor like I'm deep in thought. And maybe I am. She's so soft. So malleable. I want her wilting under the heat of my gaze.

My cock lengthens. I'm conditioned to want to fuck

her into obedience when she's helpless and defiant like this. Submissive.

Under my penetrating gaze, her body begins to respond without me even touching her. At first, her response is visible when the tension fades from her shoulders and the worry lines on her brow soften. Her chest rises with the deep, slow breaths she takes. My control over her permeates the air like fog at dusk, thick and impenetrable. Every breath she takes lulls her further into submission.

Pools of blue stare up at me from the stark simplicity of the white pillow, her golden hairs spilling around her like a halo. With her legs spread wide apart, the gentle breeze that filters in through the open window tickles her naked skin. The light catches a glimmer of arousal on her thighs.

She's wet for me.

I haven't even touched her. Licked her. Tasted her.

My disappointment in her disobedience fades. At first, I was afraid my training had been in vain, that she dared to defy me so readily. But no. Here, lying beneath me, completely at my mercy, her body knows what to do.

So do I.

I circle the bed, taking in every inch of her body.

"You're beautiful," I say, running my palm along the full swell of her breast but avoiding her nipples.

Swallowing hard, Nadine whispers, "Thank you."

I nod.

"I said that I would shave you." I remove my hand. She whimpers almost silently at the loss.

Her breath goes ragged, and her chest rises and falls with shallow breaths. If I put my fingers to her neck, her rapid pulse would beat against my fingers like butterfly wings.

I turn away and leave here there.

"Sir?"

I don't give her a response. She is being punished, after all.

But first, she needs to eat.

I go back to our new-found supplies and take inventory. My stomach rumbles when I eye a large tub of peanut butter. I check the dates, and it's still apparently fine. Packed with calories and fat, it will provide a very useful nutritional supplement. I take that, along with one of the few remaining protein bars, and the last of the bottled water.

From here on out, we'll boil our water from the falls for drinking. I smile at the pots and pans hidden in this small pantry as well as a small assortment of knives. This will be perfect.

I enter the room where she's still tied to the bed on her back and get to work preparing our meal. With her head tipped to the side, she watches me slather peanut butter on a chocolate-flavored protein bar. From my peripheral vision I watch her swallow.

"Do you like peanut butter, Nadine?" Still crouching, I turn my body to look at her. Her tiny tongue darts out and licks her lips. Swallowing, she nods.

"Yes. Yes, sir," she amends.

I'll feed her first. I cross the room with my stern gaze trained on her. She's still in trouble, and I don't want her to forget that.

I drop to my knees beside the bed and take a small portion of the bar in my hand. Since she's strapped to the bed, she's prone on her back. Gently, I work my arm beneath her upper back, and help her sit up as much as the restraints allow.

"Open," I instruct, but she doesn't need to be told twice. She eagerly takes the bar with peanut butter, chews, and swallows, closing her eyes for a moment in contentment at the taste.

"Drink," I order. I hold the bottle to her full, beautiful lips, and gently tip some water into her mouth. I wipe the little dribble on her chin with the pad of my thumb, then take the drop to my mouth and suck it off. She watches me with widened eyes but doesn't say a thing. After she's eaten, I eat my meal, then clean up.

"You've behaved while I fed you," I say approvingly. "Now let's see how you handle what I have in store for you next."

Though she keeps her body still, I can feel the tension between us. I've hurt her before. I intend to hurt her again. Only this time, her punishment will entail more than a spanking.

I circle around her again. I stare until I can't stand not touching her, like standing behind a large window and staring at the sea. I need to touch her. Feel her. Taste her.

Starting at her shoulders, I begin the slow, deliberate exploration of her body. I trace the beautiful, graceful slopes of her chest and hips, the sweet swell of her breasts, and the way her waist narrows. Fair hair covers her pussy, tiny little blonde curls. When I get to her pussy, I part the soft tendrils and slide my finger through her damp folds. Just by taking away her control and watching her, I've made her wet for me.

Perfect.

I stroke her sweet pussy until her hips rise, but as soon as I can tell she's building toward release, I pull my hand away. She grinds her ass on the bed, a silent protest at not letting her come. I give her pussy a sharp swat to punish her for that, but the little curlicues of hair make it impossible to really punish her there.

It's time they went.

I grab the curls and tug. The pink flush that colors her cheek looks good on her.

"It's time you were bare," I explain.

She shakes her head with terror, her eyes betraying her.

"No, sir," she says. "I don't want you to do that. Please don't."

I'm torn between wanting her to fear me because of who I am and wanting her to trust me for what I'm about to do.

Her blonde hair tumbles about her as she shakes her head wildly.

"Enough, Nadine." The head-tossing continues, so I deliver a sharp slap to the fullest part of her thigh. "I said *enough*."

My handprint blooms against her tanned skin. Her shaking stills, but her eyes follow the glint of the blade. It's a safety razor with five finely-honed blades, with a pale pink handle. I take the small bottle of baby oil I got from her bag, as well as the little bottle of conditioner.

"I need those," she whispers, but I don't respond.

"And what... what will you do when the refills run out?"

My lips twitch. I suspect she knows exactly what I'll do, as she's watched me sharpen the thin, razor-like blade I found in our supplies by the fire. But we'll deal with that when we need to.

"Part your knees," I command. The breezes stills outside our window, as if everything hinges on her obeying me.

Her blue eyes trained on mine, she slowly parts her knees. I allow my gaze to swing down her bare belly to her pussy, swollen and wet. Her body's learned to become aroused when afraid.

She'll be rewarded for that.

I kneel in front of her and place my hands on her inner thighs. Just resting, my thumbs pointing inward to her pussy. I flex my fingers and gently knead her bare skin. It's soft and supple, lightly scented like fresh lemons from washing with her soap.

"Relax," I breathe, massaging the pads of my thumbs in a circular motion. "Let it go now."

She nods, her knees falling even further apart now.

"Good girl," I approve, just before I bend and place a fluttering kiss on her inner thigh. A gentle swipe of my fingers through her slick folds heralds a promise to her: if she does what I say, I will reward her.

Eventually.

"You are not allowed out of this building without my permission, Nadine." My voice cuts sharply through the quiet. She cowers a bit, pulling back from me, but nods. "What should I do with you?"

Her eyes flash at me, a hint of steel in her voice. "Whatever the fuck you want."

I bend over the bed and cage her in, my muscles flexing as I hold my body over hers. "That's right, sweetheart," I drawl in her ear. "That's exactly. Fucking. Right." I fist her hair in one hand, the silky blonde pale against my tanned knuckles. Tugging her head back, I wait until she whimpers, and her mouth hangs open in a gasp. I take her open mouth with mine in a brief, harsh kiss that eases to gentle, and as soon as she sighs into the kiss I reach my left hand out and slap her exposed pussy. It's not as effective as it will be, but it gets my point across.

She whimpers in my mouth, and I spank her again, and again, until her eyes water. Careful not to harm her, I strike hard enough she knows she's being punished. If she's as well trained as I think she is, she'll be dripping when I go to taste her.

I release her mouth and brush mine against her ear, still tugging her tawny hair in my fist. "You do *not* disobey me without answering for it."

I let her head fall on the pillow and stalk to the foot of the bed, like a lion on the prowl. Swinging my gaze to hers, I dare her to move. Dare her to say one word of protest when I lift the blade.

"What happens when you disobey me, Nadine?"

Humbled by the spanking, she speaks in a rush of words, "You punish me, sir."

I kneel, lift the bottle of baby oil, and place the blade where she can see it, face up on the bed. I open the top of the oil and tap several drops into my palm. My eyes focused on hers, I dip the tip of my finger in the tiny pool of oil and lubricate my index finger.

"Open," I order.

Her knees fall open further and she stifles a tiny whimper. I massage the oil around her tender curls, the scent of her feminine arousal stirring my cock. I take the bottle and tip several drops of oil on her folds. She watches, bemused, a little line forming between her brows. Has she never fingered herself with the oil?

I thumb down the length of her swollen slit. She hisses and arches her back, needing more. I stroke and fondle her until she writhes, and her clit swells. She's ready to climax when I remove my fingers altogether.

A dry sob wracks her body.

Good.

"You didn't like that?" I ask. She shakes her head, eyes closed. I spank her inner thigh and her eyes fly open. "Good," I bite out. "You're being punished right now. Why am I punishing you?"

"I disobeyed you," she says through clenched teeth.

My jaw clenches, I add a few more drops of oil until she's well saturated. And then I begin. Carefully, so delicately as if she's as fragile as a wisp of spun glass, I draw the blade across her sweet curls. She closes her eyes, as if to block out what I'm doing. I clean the blade and wipe a cloth across her skin, then go back to shaving. The silence in the room is broken only by her deep breaths and the soft scrape of the razor against her skin. I continue until her entire pussy is shaved bare.

"There," I say, stroking my finger through her folds. "That's better, now isn't it?"

She blinks, and stares at me, then finally nods. "Yes, sir. I guess."

I look at her quizzically. "You guess? Well maybe it's best I show you why it is."

She watches me warily when I pat her dry. I untie her legs and position them over my shoulders so that her bare folds are in front of me. My breathing hitches. God, she's sexy.

"You won't come until I tell you to," I remind her. "If you do, I'll whip you with one of those branches outside the window." The wind whistles and the branches sway as if they're conspiring to punish her with me.

I kneel and take her pussy in my mouth, groaning when bare skin hits my lips. I grind my mouth against her, suckling her tender spot until her body tenses and I can sense she's on the verge of climax.

"Do not come," I order, returning to her pussy to lap at her so well she writhes beneath me.

"Please," she begs. "Sir. Adrian! Please let me."

"No."

I let her go and pace around the bed again, touching her breasts, flicking her nipples, palming the full slopes at her hips. I kiss every inch of her from the tips of her toes, up her thighs, across her midsection, and up her belly, then drag my tongue to her navel.

Five times I bring her to the cusp of climax, then stop.

She never cries when I spank her, not even when she was soundly strapped with my belt. But now, tears brim in her eyes.

Good. Maybe she'll think twice the next time she's tempted to disobey.

She stopped begging the fourth time. Now she's slumped in her restraints. When I bring my mouth to her pussy again, she whimpers and can't help but arch toward my mouth. I suckle and tease, holding her ass in my hands. This time between swipes of my tongue, I lift her legs and spank her. I don't say a word, just alternate kissing and licking her sweet pussy with firm smacks of my palm on her backside, until her pussy is swollen, and her ass is red from her spanking. I pull her clit in my mouth, bringing her closer and closer to climax, then release her a final time.

Her eyes are closed. Her body is boneless. This time when I let her go and don't bring her to climax, she sighs into the bed and doesn't open her eyes.

Without a word, I leave the room. She'll get a break before I return for another round.

CHAPTER ELEVEN

Nadine

I'M FLOATING, I think. Or maybe I'm sinking. I'm not sure which it is. He's taken me to the edge of bliss and back so many times, my clit is literally throbbing and swollen. There is nothing beyond my need to come. Somewhere on a distant planet, in a galaxy beyond where I am now, I'm a little hungry and thirsty and tired, but here, where he left me, I'm so ready to climax it hurts.

Of course, I can't reach myself since my wrists are still bound. Instead, I try to rub my thighs together vigorously, even clenching the muscles of my pussy, but it's no use.

He's in utter control of me.

My ass stings from the sharp spanking he gave me. I grind my pelvis against the bed, hoping to somehow make myself come, but it isn't going to happen. I have to distract myself. I need to think of another time and place.

He went out. Where did he go? We need a few things, and he likely went to go fetch them. He's been enjoying building a fire at night. Maybe he went to get some wood or kindling.

I need to come.

I gulp for air and focus on breathing. In and out. In and out. Just breathing.

I need to come.

I shake my head and clear my thoughts. No, I don't. I went for years without coming, so it's hardly going to kill me if I don't now.

But reason isn't helping me now. I have no power here. My wrists are bound, my ankles secured, and my body teeming with Adrian's touch.

What have I let him do to me?

But before I can entertain that thought, the door opens, and he enters the room.

"Do you think you've learned your lesson?" he asks.

I blink and look about the room stupidly, like he might be talking to someone else. He raises a brow.

"Yes." Maybe now he'll let me climax? "I mean yes, sir. I have. I really, truly have."

I watch as he leans against the doorframe. He's a tiny bit thinner than he was before the crash, but still large and muscular. His shoulders dwarf the doorway, and when he crosses his arms on his tanned chest, I can't help but look at his corded forearms, then my gaze travels south to the flat, detailed planes of his abs. He looks like some type of god.

I close my eyes and will my thoughts to clear. For Christ's sake, I should know better than this. I'm letting my need to climax overshadow literally everything else. I'm actually feeling *turned on* by him, and I shouldn't be.

But what, really, has he done, other than willing my obedience, and spanking me a few times?

Isn't that enough?

This. This is what he's done.

My pussy's bare like a little girl's, my wrists ache from the restraints, and my most sensitive parts throb. This is what he's reduced me to, a dependent with no privacy left to speak of. I turn my head away from him.

"Look at me, Nadine." The command from the doorway echoes like the crashing of waves on rocks.

I ignore him for as long as I reasonably can, just enough so that he doesn't punish me again, then finally turn my head to look at him.

"What have you learned?" he asks.

To be smarter when I disobey him.

"To do what you say," I parrot.

He pushes off the doorframe and walks over to me.

I don't want to do this again. *No.* I can't take it, not again.

He kneels in front of me and parts my legs, but this time I pull them together.

"No, sir. Not again."

He quirks a brow up at me. "No?" He frowns and his voice grates like sandpaper. "If I need to punish you, then I'll fucking punish you."

I know. God, I know. I only nod. I look away from him, my eyes watering. Jesus, what has he done to me? What has this man made me?

He falls to the floor in front of me and lifts my legs, draping them over his shoulders.

"Are you going to obey me, Nadine?"

"Yes. Fucking *yes*," I groan. He breathes on my pussy, the warm air making my clit throb. I'm so ready. God, I'm so ready.

"Good," he says, bending down to swipe his tongue along my slit. I groan and grind against his mouth, needing harder, longer, faster. He laps and suckles, lifting my ass so my pussy is presented to him like a feast and he's a starving man. I throw my head back, my need to climax rising so quickly I can't control it. If he tells me not to come this time, I'm not sure I can hold myself back. One hand drops from my ass and I hear the whir of a zipper. He's pumping his cock while he eats me out and fuck if that doesn't make me even closer to climax.

"Sir," I breathe. "Please. God, please." The thought of being denied again makes my throat close up. "I can't wait. Oh, God."

He pulls his mouth off my pussy. "Will you obey me?"

"Yes. God, yes. I'll obey you," I moan, grinding against his mouth. The whiskers from his beard graze the sensitive skin between my thighs, in sharp contrast to the soft, wet feel of his mouth on my pussy.

He lets me go and for one quick second I think this is it, he's toying with me again. I'm going to die. Not from starvation. Not from thirst. But this, this will be my death.

I cry out loud. I need the pressure of his mouth. The touch of his skin. I can't take this anymore. It's unbearable torture. But he's still holding me, black eyes burning into me as if he can see inside my head, inside my soul, as if he knows I'm harboring resistance and only begging for release.

"Will you?" he asks, and to my shock, he reaches for my inner thigh and pinches it. I yelp, and before I can respond his mouth is on my pussy again, working me up so fucking good he'll split me wide open.

"Yes," I pant. "God *yes.*"

He nods, his tongue probing deeper and harder when his head bobs. My body tenses, preparing to climax, but I fear he'll leave me on the edge again. Pulling his mouth away he growls, the heat of his breath warming my thighs. "Whose pussy is this?"

"Yours," I sob, my body quaking at the precipice of climax. "Yours, sir," I groan.

He responds with one slow, lazy swipe of his tongue that nearly kills me.

"Who owns your orgasms?" he rasps, his eyes going half-lidded. He pumps himself harder.

"You do," I moan, a tremor ripping through me right on the edge. I can't. I can't climax right now, or he'll whip me. Not until he says. Not until he lets me.

"Please," I cry. Who is this man, who's brought me to the cusp of insanity like this? If I don't come, I'll lose my mind. I can't take another second of this torture. "I've learned my lesson."

Lifting his mouth off my pussy again, his eyes bore

into me and his voice drops to a deep, feral growl. "Who's your master?"

"You," I nearly weep.

He nods, pleased. "You ever fucking defy me again and this will go on for days. Weeks if need be. Do you understand me?"

I believe. The goddamn son of a bitch never lies. Ever.

"Yes. Yes, sir," I nod. I do know. I've been soundly punished. I won't defy him. Fuck, if he lets me come now I'll do whatever the hell he says, and I know it.

"Please," I whisper.

He nods with the final blessedly welcome command, "Come for me."

His swipes his tongue along my slit with perfect rhythm one last time, and I lose my mind.

I thrash against the restraints, the power of my orgasm a torrent of mind-blowing pleasure and ecstasy. I come so hard I stop breathing, stop thinking, my eyes closed tight as my body is wracked with the power of my climax. Lights flash behind my eyes and I think I can't possibly take anymore, then a second orgasm tears through me on the heels of the first. A scream nearly deafens me, and I don't know until I'm cascading down the slope of that climax that it's me, losing all control in a flood of overpowering pleasure. A third follows the second, impossibly stronger and more intense than the first two and somewhere in the distance I hear him roaring his own release. I come so hard and so long when I finally fall to the bed half-dazed, my whole body aches from the tension and power that swept through me.

He's wrecked me. I'm completely fatigued. I can't open my eyes. I can hardly breathe. A few moments later, someplace far away, my restraints are undone, and I'm rolled over onto my side. Soft fabric flutters over my shoulders and thighs. A comforting warmth presses up against my back, a familiar arm wraps around my waist. I drift off to sleep.

When I wake, it's hours later. It's got to be nearly dinnertime now. My stomach growls from hunger, but my body still aches from the punishment he inflicted. I'm quiet and subdued, like a chastened child.

His rustling behind me tells me he's awake now, too. Did he sleep? Or did he lie next to me, keeping vigil?

"Are you awake, Nadine?"

I nod my head. I'm not sure if I open my mouth to speak if I can say anything.

"Come here." He rolls me on my side and to my surprise, cups my cheek in his hand. It's nearly tender. No... it *is* tender. The gentleness is somehow more disarming than when he's harsh with me.

"How are you doing?" he asks in a deep rumble. "That was a pretty harsh punishment you underwent." His eyes quickly narrow and his voice lowers. "Not that you didn't deserve it."

I try to look away but can't, since he's holding my cheek in his hand.

"I'm starving," I admit.

He huffs out a laugh that startles me.

"I'm sorry," he says. "I didn't mean to scare you. I'll get you something to eat. Stay here."

Where would I go? I'm starving and the man's bringing me food.

And I don't ever want to be punished like that again, I think.

I don't like to admit that he's subjugated me. But the thought of getting up out of this bed and disobeying him makes my stomach clench in fear.

I close my eyes and think of my mama. *Where's your petite belette now, mama?* I think. Who am I? What have I become? Am I doomed to live the rest of my life under his thumb?

In my old life, back in the States, I didn't even want a romantic relationship, much less... *this.* I can't have children. I was in my early twenties when I was told my body would never be able to conceive a child, but I didn't care. I have benign tumors that block my fallopian tubes. *Uterine fibroids,* the doctors called them. They never bothered me before, and my infertility doesn't trouble me. It was a door shutting to something I never wanted open, and I figured it was one instance when the universe knew what was best for my body, because I never wanted babies anyway.

And I never wanted a partner. Men are selfish, cruel creatures, and I don't wish to share a bed with one of them.

And yet that's exactly what I'm doing.

You have no choice, I say to myself.

Do I?

Before I can continue further, a wave of nausea rolls through me I'm so hungry. What has he done to me? The smell of something delicious wafts through the open window, and I sit up in bed. It never occurred to me to get up. He told me not to.

I hear him walking back toward me and note the way the sky's faded to indigo. Soon, it will be nightfall. I'm not sure I'll be able to sleep, after that long nap I just took.

The door to the room swings open, and Adrian walks in, wearing a pair of boxers but barefoot, carrying a large steaming pot in his hand. Hunger rolls through me like thunder.

"Oh my God," I say, pushing myself up to sitting. "What is it? What did you do? Did you finally capture that bird and make... a stew or something?"

"No," he says. "It's a can of stew I found in the stores out back. I've opened it and inspected it, and it seems perfectly fine. But I'll try it first."

I nod and sit up in bed. He walks over to the side of the bed and nestles the hot pot on the little bedside table. He lifts a spoonful to his mouth and tastes it.

"Only one spoon," he says. I'm beyond caring. I'm starving, and this man has put his mouth over every inch of my body. He dips the spoon into the pot and brings a steaming spoonful to my lips. I open my mouth to let him feed me. My mouth waters as the first taste of savory gravy and meat touches my tongue.

"Mmm," I say. "Oh God, that's delicious. I forgot how good meat tastes."

"Me, too," he says, getting himself another spoonful. We continue like that in silence, him alternating feeding me spoonfuls before he eats a few himself. A little dribbles on my bottom lip, and he wipes it with the pad of his thumb. I lick it off and smile. It's almost sweet. We eat the entire pot, and I fall back on the bed, full.

"Wow, that was good," I say. "If I never see another fish again…"

"Seriously, though," he says. "I have some good news."

"Do you?"

He nods. "I tested some of the berries. The dark purple ones on my skin didn't leave a rash. So the next step is to touch it to my lips. If it doesn't burn or hurt, I can take a small bite and see."

I nod. It's useful information.

"I found something else," he says. He lifts two small flasks.

"Is that… did you find whiskey?" I ask, incredulous.

"I did. Apparently, our studious scientists had some other resources."

"I see," I say. He uncaps one and hands it to me.

"Take a sip," he says.

I do, then nearly sputter as the liquid fire burns my mouth. He laughs, takes it from my hand, and takes a long, impressive pull from the bottle.

"God," he says, taking a deep breath and wiping his hand across his mouth. "I needed that. Haven't had a drink since before I went to jail."

"Ten years ago," I whisper. I know the dates.

They're tattooed in my mind, permanent details that were my life focus for months.

His eyes meet mine and we both sober, remembering who we are and why we're here.

We're not friends.

I reach for the flask and he hands it to me. This time, I don't sputter when I take a long pull, but welcome the flame that burns my throat and belly. I hand it back to him wordlessly, and he takes another long sip.

"Why'd you do it?" I ask. It's a risky question. He's stronger and capable of hurting me if I push him.

He doesn't ask me what, merely looks toward the door as if he's looking at a time and place that's light years away from here. He doesn't respond at first, as if he's trying to decipher if I'm worthy of a response.

Finally, after a while, he turns and looks to me.

"What were you told?"

I blink, surprised by the question. "What was I told? That matters?"

He doesn't break eye contact as he takes another sip of the whiskey. "It matters," he says.

"I saw the pictures," I say, as if somehow that explains everything.

He doesn't say anything.

"Did you?" I ask. "Did you leave those welts and bruises?" I don't know why I'm asking. I'd convinced myself he was guilty from the beginning. Do I somehow need to believe that he was innocent all along? But if I do, doesn't that make what I did unforgivable?

"Yes," he says baldly. "I was the one who left the marks."

My stomach clenches. I look away. I can't look at him the same knowing he's capable of inflicting that type of violence. For a moment... for just one moment there, I thought he wasn't the monster I thought he was.

"She wanted it, Nadine."

I huff out a sardonic laugh. "That's what the rapists say."

He shakes his head, then reaches for my chin and yanks my eyes back toward him. "It's what the rapists say," he mimics. "And sometimes, Nadine, that's fucking true."

"Fuck you," I snap without meaning to. As soon as I do, I expect him to hurt me, to turn me over his knee or even slap me, but he doesn't.

"You watch your tongue," he warns. I feel the correction halt me in my tracks, immediately subdued.

I guess he doesn't need to take it further.

We're getting off track.

He exhales and runs a hand through his hair. "She was my submissive," he begins. "And she was a masochist."

I nod. I know what that means, at least.

"She enjoyed being tied up, so I did it. I tied her up. The marks of rope on her wrists were from the session the night before. A consensual BDSM session."

I feel as if I'm going to lose my dinner when I remember her brutalized body. The bruises and welts. I nod. I don't want to inhibit him from saying more.

"I spanked her, often and hard," he said. "Sometimes I whipped her, sometimes caned her. It was rarely enough. She wanted to be hurt. Humiliated. Degraded." He turns and meets my eyes. "It's not as uncommon as you might think in BDSM circles."

I still don't say anything.

"We met at a club in NYC. She was a long-term member, and I was new. Moved there when I decided to relocate."

"Because of your father," I interject.

His eyes narrow, but after a moment, he nods. "Yes," he says. "because of my father. And my uncles. And my brothers."

I listen, imagining for a moment that maybe the history of the monster I've made him in my mind isn't the truth after all. That maybe there is more to the story than I assumed.

Isn't there always?

I'm not too proud to admit that sometimes I can be wrong.

Am I this time?

"So I met Lori at the club, and we both realized we had some things in common." He shrugs, and takes another deep pull from the flask, then wipes his mouth with the back of his hand again and sighs, in contentment or resignation, I don't know. Likely both. "We had a mutual love," he says, looking away again. "She liked to receive pain and I like to inflict it."

He doesn't say *liked*.

I like to inflict pain.

My ass burns and my muscles contract. Does that make me afraid? Disgusted?

Or turned on?

I don't know if I like how it makes me feel. I push myself to go numb and focus on his words.

"She wanted to be hurt, Nadine. You can believe it or not, but you're a smart girl. You know BDSM clubs exist, and you know at least a little of what goes on in them."

"They're consensual," I say. "And no one goes around beating people or bruising them or welting."

He raises a brow. "In the sanitized, romance-ready package presented to the world at large? Sure. In real life?" He shakes his head. "Not so much, sweetheart."

This time the *sweetheart* loses the edge. It isn't a slap in the face but something... different.

I can't quite understand that the brutal marks on the woman were something she *wanted*. It seems like a lie monsters feed to people to normalize brutality.

"She wanted to be killed?" I ask him. He flinches and looks away, then as if on autopilot takes another sip of the flask, then hands it to me. I take it from him and gratefully sip more. We should make this last. We should ration it like we have every-thing else, but it's like we can't help it. As if we need this tonight, to give us one night where we don't have to be responsible and careful. To make us brave enough to talk about this elephant in the room.

"Of course she didn't want to be killed," he says. He turns his black gaze to me, piercing me in place.

"But the people who killed her watched her. They knew who she was. They knew I was the one she came to when she wanted to be hurt, whipped, bruised, and welted, and they knew I inflicted that on her. Carefully, Nadine. I watched her, we talked, I knew how far to take her and when she needed harder."

"You liked hurting her," I say, accusing.

"I just said that," he grits out, his words like a lash across my skin. "I admit it. I did. I'm a fucking sadist, and I never said anything different."

I flinch. He is. God, he is. When he takes his belt to my ass or pinches my nipples, his cock gets hard. He's hungry for pain. He gets off on it.

He continues. Maybe the alcohol has finally spurred him on, or maybe he just needs to admit it, to say it out loud and get it over with.

"So the night before, we had a rope session. I tied her up, and she had marks that remained that I refreshed when she came to me. I tied her up tightly, and I whipped her. Caned her. And paddled her. Yes, many submissives at the club would have found it too much. Lori? She was disappointed when I didn't draw blood."

I blink in surprise. He plows on.

"Feeling the pain helped her let go. It relaxed her. That night, I brought her to subspace."

I don't know what that is and I'm afraid to interrupt him.

He goes on as if he's in court, a staunch defense of what really happened, and I hear the sincerity in his voice. "She was floating, in bliss. Couldn't even speak or move. And I was just about to give her aftercare. I untied her ropes and was going to make sure I brought her down. I'd worked her good, and she'd need attention. We had a large tub in the bathroom in a private room in the club, and I was going to bathe her to bring her back, help her come down after that high." He turns away and runs a hand through his hair. "I left her on the bed. I wanted to get an extra blanket, in case she was cold when she came down, which happens sometimes. She didn't even know I left the room. And when I came back, the door was locked."

A chill runs down my spine. I wish I could believe he's lying. I want to hold onto my innocence and his guilt, but I know in my gut what he says is true. I apprehended a man who was innocent.

He isn't a monster. Christ. He isn't.

I take a silent sip of whiskey. This time it doesn't burn.

"Then what?" I whisper.

Never looking away, he continues. "They killed her. Strangled her to death. I heard thumps and rumbles and the bathroom window being opened. I pounded on the door, but it did no good. I finally broke the door down. She was on the bed. Dead."

"And that's how they found you," I said. I know what the reports said. They found him cradling her dead body in his arms after an anonymous call to the police alerted them to her death. He was named as her murderer and the circumstantial evidence was overwhelming.

"They strangled her with the same rope I used to bind her," he continues, his voice tight. "The only rope mark I didn't leave was the one around her neck. The rope bore my fingerprints. Her entire body did. The autopsy report found my mark on every inch of her body."

I know that, too. Traces of his hair on her. His fingerprints on the whips and ropes that inflicted her bruises. His semen in her body.

He didn't stand a chance. He had no alibi. He was in the club that night, he'd been the one to mark her, and his rope choked the life out of her.

"Who did it, then?" I ask, still not giving myself permission to believe him.

"My father," he says. "I have no doubt. I betrayed the family. Death was too simple for me."

His words ring true.

Christ Almighty, it's true.

"And that's why you escaped," I say, thinking about it. In my mind, I convinced myself this man was a monster, but is he really one?

My body still throbs with what he's done to me.

Yes. Yes, he's a monster.

But is he?

Throughout his entire description of what happened, I wouldn't let myself think about my training. I know how to tell when someone lies, and I know when someone tells the truth. I've never needed a lie detector test. I'm never wrong.

He maintained eye contact while we spoke, both his breathing and voice remaining steady. He admitted his part in this, that he was the one who inflicted at least some the bruises and rope marks. His hand never drifted to his throat, and he spoke at length, in detail, and in full sentences.

He's telling the fucking truth.

I look away, unable to bear the thought of what he lost. He suffered a terrible childhood. He knows hunger and pain.

And loss. Terrible, heartbreaking loss.

"I was going to ask her to marry me," he says, finally looking away. "I even bought the ring."

My stomach twists and a lump rises in my throat.

"Marriage is for losers," I whisper.

He huffs out a laugh. "How would you know?"

I shrug. "Half of the people who get married don't mean what they say. They don't keep their vows and they break it off anyway. The other half who stay together fall out of love if they were ever in fucking love anyway. And the rest? Why do they need rings and shit? When love is real, it's real, without having to proclaim it from the fucking rooftops." I shake my head and take another sip of whiskey. "I'll never get married."

It's an odd thing to say. Hell, I don't even know if I'll be alive on my next birthday, much less ever return to a society that does things like have wedding ceremonies. I immediately feel like a total asshole. I turn away from him, tired from the drink and I wonder if that's why he brought it to me. It doesn't really matter though. I could stay up all night and sleep all day without a problem.

"Yeah," he says, shaking his head. "Me, too."

"And then what did you do?"

"You mean to escape?"

I nod.

"I made friends, had connections, people owed me favors," he responds. "I had to be discreet, since I'm positive it was my father who put me behind bars to begin with. I'd saved plenty of money and used some of it to bribe the guards. I had money, clothes, and a fake I.D. waiting for me the night I broke free. Got a non-stop flight from NYC to Honolulu. Eleven hours later, arrived in Hawaii, and from there I went to the Samoan Islands."

I can't really make the mental shift from monstrous murderer to heartbroken lover, so I don't. I tell myself that maybe what he's telling me isn't true.

But my gut knows better.

I turn away from him.

I'm sorry, I think.

Sorry for what? Everything. For fucking everything. If it wasn't for me, we wouldn't even be on this island. I'd still be in America, and he'd still be living a life of freedom on his island. And Carlos would still be alive. So would the pilots.

I close my eyes when they water, because I don't cry, and I don't really have a reason to. The bed creaks, and I can hear him moving. I don't open my eyes, but I feel him on the bed beside me. The alcohol must be getting to my head. I have the strangest, overwhelming need to cry.

I open my eyes and he's lying across from me on his belly, his arms propping up his head, which is turned to look at me. I stare into the depths of his midnight gaze and don't break eye contact. In his eyes, I see the loss he's suffered. The tragedy of death, and a past that nearly broke him. I interrogated everyone I could before I hunted him down. I know the scars on his body were inflicted by his father.

I don't know the meaning of his tattoos, though.

"Did it hurt?" I ask, pointing to the tattoo that covers him from his neck to his lower back in intricate tribal black.

His lips quirk up. "Yeah, it hurt. Hurt like fucking hell."

Well that was a stupid question.

"Why'd you get it?"

He shrugs. "I was eighteen and stupid and wanted to prove I could. My father hated tattoos, so I was pretty well determined I'd get covered."

An act of defiance, then. Because he could.

I nod, and my eyes grow heavy with sleep.

"Kids do stupid things," he says, but for the first time during this conversation, I know he's lying. It wasn't a stupid thing. It was a very strategic move.

But I'm tired. The alcohol is lulling me to sleep.

"Yeah," I say with a huge yawn. "They do stupid things. But hell, so do adults." My breathing slows. I'm so utterly exhausted.

"Adrian?" I rarely call him by his first name, and I wonder if he'll allow it.

"Yeah?" he says.

"I'm sorry." I can't look at him when I say it, so I keep my eyes closed. I feel his fingers in my hair, but they're gentle this time. He smoothes the hair away from my forehead and tucks a strand behind my ear.

But his harsh tone belies the tenderness when he commands, "Go to sleep, Nadine."

I wait for the restraints he always puts on me but fall asleep before he ties them. It isn't until I wake at dawn that I realize he never did.

CHAPTER TWELVE

Adrian

SOMETHING CHANGED when Nadine and I talked. It was the first time I ever felt free to tell her what happened the night Lori died. In my gut, I know that if I'd told her any sooner, she wouldn't have believed me anyway. She had to believe I was the monster she hunted, or she never would have been able to do what she did.

It's not like I'm an innocent. I was the one who left Lori alone. If I'd been in the room, she wouldn't have been murdered. If I hadn't left her in a vulnerable state of subspace, she might've been able to scream. If I hadn't been the one they were after... the one they wanted to punish... none of this would have happened.

And I know that a part of me *is* a monster. The part that gets hard hurting innocent, vulnerable women.

Hell, there's a part of me that wishes Nadine would mouth off to me, so I can overpower her and strap her ass again. I want to hurt her. Mark her.

Only now it's not because of retribution but simply because I fucking crave it.

She's begun marking our stay here. At first, she did it covertly, but when I told her there was nothing wrong with noting the passage of time, we began to do it together. We've now been here together one full month.

Something's troubling me this morning. I'm not sure what.

I walk to the beach and by the time I'm there I hit the beach at a full run. I need to master this monster inside me, tame it by beating it down. At home, I would lift weights until my muscles hit failure. It was the one thing in prison that kept me sane, the ability to shackle my monster with heavy, adrenaline-boosting lifting. To push my body to the extreme. To punish myself.

I have to admit, I love running on the island. There's something tranquil about running alone in the early morning. Here, it's even better. The occasional bird squawks in the air, though they keep their distance as if they know I'm ready to make them into breakfast. Waves pound on the shore and recede, the rhythmic crash and pull of the undertow better than the music I used to play on earbuds. I run before the sun fully rises, because once it does, the heat is wicked. Practically unbearable. It isn't humid here but hot as fucking hell.

Today, after I've run until my legs give way, I fall to the soft, sandy beach. This was where we landed, here on this beach. Where the others met their fate and I earned my freedom. Ironic, in a way. I turn and look up at the sky. I frown when I eye large, dark storm clouds rolling in. We haven't had more than a brief summer storm since we got here. No real storms to speak of. And there's no telling exactly what this storm will bring.

I push myself up from the beach and brush the sand off my sweaty body, then run toward the water for a quick dip. I hit the waves head-on, dip in, then turn and swim for the shore. The sun evaporates the saltwater from my skin as I head back to the shelter. We need to make sure our shelter is secured.

I don't restrain her anymore. Frowning, I pick up my pace, until I'm at a dead run.

I gave her *one* punishment after her infraction. Will it be enough to keep her compliant?

I break into the clearing near our shelter and stop dead in my tracks.

Is that... singing? I stop and listen.

It is. She's in the shower, and she's singing.

Why have I never heard her before?

She takes a short shower like she's been instructed to do but continues singing even when the water turns off. I can't make out the words, but it's in a foreign language. French? I'm still standing there dumbly when she comes out, dripping wet. She stands there in the doorway, water dripping down from her soaking wet hair, then brings a blonde strand to her mouth as if to cover herself. She's embarrassed that I caught her singing. Unencumbered by her restraints, she sings.

"It's all right," I said. "I just came to warn you there's a storm coming."

As if in cue, a massive crash of thunder cracks over the shelter. She jumps.

"Come on. Let's make sure everything's secured."

She walks to her clothes and lifts a few things up, then looks to me questioningly. No restraints. Will I allow her to dress herself, too? She hasn't yet.

I give her a nod, too occupied with what's going on outside to focus on her clothing choices. She fumbles around while I shut and lock the windows, then I step outside to make sure the wood pile is piled against the shelter, and not in the open where wind can make it fly around and become a hazard.

When I return to the shelter, she's still standing naked, staring at the clothes. This puzzles me, but I don't spend much time thinking about it. I step over, grab a pair of her panties in my left hand, then rope my right arm around her. Leading her to the bed, I sit, and almost instinctively swivel her out in front of me. I lift one foot and slide it into the leg of her panties, then lift the other foot, and slide that in as well. Then I pull her panties up her legs and give her an affectionate pat on the ass.

"Good girl," I say approvingly. "You like it when I dress you."

"Well, no," she sputters, turning as if to pull away from me, but she's bluffing. I grab her hand as she turns to go and tug her onto my knee.

"You do," I say. "there's nothing wrong with that."

I don't have time for this. I should be making sure we're prepared for the storm. But I can't help reaching my hand to the back of her neck and pulling her face down to mine. I kiss her, my lips brushing hers gentle at first, then harder as my cock hardens. She may not yield in any way but this, but that's enough. It's all I need.

She moans when I tip her head back and cradle her against my arm, her hands wrapping around my neck as if to anchor herself. A roll of thunder rumbles just outside our door, with a groan, I release her.

"Gotta get ready," I mumble, gently pushing her off my lap.

"Mmm," she says. "Can we get something to eat first?"

Shit. All the food's outside.

I look back at her, still free from restraints. Can I really trust her? Or is she playing me?

"Yeah," I say. "Let's go." I take her by the hand, not wanting to admit to her that I'm doing so to make sure she doesn't pull any moves on me.

We go quickly, just as the first sound of pelting rain hits the roof. "Move," I order, moving her along with a pull on her hand.

"Adrian, for fuck's sake," she mutters. I tug her in front of me and give her a smack on the ass.

"Don't push me now, Nadine," I say. "Just because I took the restraints off does not mean you've got more freedom. You do what I fucking say." And I mean it, too. Something's changed between us, but this isn't part of it.

"When will it stop?" she asks.

I try not to roll my eyes. "I'm not sure," I quip. "I missed the weather forecast this morning."

She narrows her eyes and frowns. "Well that's not what I meant," she says. "But you said you studied these islands and I wondered how long they usually last."

She's right. I'm being a douchebag. "Yeah. Not long. Tropical storms like this come on fast and furious but move out as quickly as they come. *Usually.*"

She nods and takes another cracker. The sound of water hitting the ground catches my attention.

"Do you hear that?" I ask her. She frowns and nods.

"Yeah. It sounds like it's... inside?"

She stands and goes to the door, peering into the main area of our shelter. "Oh," she says, her eyes widening. "It's coming in through the roof, right over the computer."

I get to my feet and go to her. She's right. It's leaking straight over the computer. It doesn't much matter, as the old thing's defunct anyway, but water and electronics shouldn't mix no matter what. And a leaking roof is bad news.

Within minutes, the clouds roll away and the sun comes out. There are four places where the roof leaked so badly, I'll need to repair it immediately.

We do a quick assessment of the damage right outside our shelter. Everything looks miraculously unscathed, just wet.

"Well, I'll have to fix that room, and immediately, before another storm comes in. It's crazy how quickly the sun comes out again. There's hardly a cloud sky.

"How are you going to fix that?" she asks.

"I found some tools in the shed. I'm going to have to make use of those with the trees around here," I explain. For some reason, she frowns and looks disappointed but I've got shit to do.

"Can I help?" she asks, which surprises me. "I mean it's not," she tosses air quotes out, 'men's work.'"

"Yeah," I say. "It is, though. But you're strong, and you can help."

She looks as if she's going to keep on frowning, but I tug a strand of her blonde hair and give her a smile.

"I just don't want you to hurt yourself, and I'm kind of a traditional guy."

She cocks her head to the side. "A traditional guy who likes to hold heavy things for girls, and whip their asses?"

"No, Nadine," I say, pulling her hair harder the second time. "The traditional guy who likes to be in charge. Now let's go."

We work for hours in the shade of the trees, but they don't do much to protect us from the sweltering heat. There was a small axe in the shed, which if I'd found even a day ago would've stayed hidden, but now it comes in handy. I chop wood until my hands begin to blister and my shoulder blades ache from the swinging of the axe. Nadine piles the neat logs and will help me fashion them into some sort of shingles for a roof.

"Doesn't really look like the people that constructed this shelter were carpenters," she mutters.

"Yeah, definitely not," I agree, swinging the axe again. "My suspicion is that they brought someone with them to build the structure when they came, but they did a basic job." I shrug. "Better than if we were here with no help at all."

"Yeah," she says. She looks off into the distance. The pile of wood needs to be a lot higher than it is now, and there isn't much left for her to do, since she's already gotten us lunch and water.

"Why don't you head to the beach for a little while? Just no more than a dip if you go in the water." I don't want her injured without me nearby.

Her eyes brighten at the suggestion. "Really?"

It will be her first trip to the beach without restraints.

"Yes," I say. "Go. Just don't be gone for too long and listen to what I'm saying.

No going in deep. Understand?"

"Yes, of course," she says. I'm surprised when she heads back to the shelter.

"Where are you going?"

"To get my swimsuit," she says.

I snort. "I can't believe you have a swimsuit."

"Well, yeah. I was living on a tropical island indefinitely. Of course I have a swimsuit with me. Did you think I was going to skinny dip?"

Snarky little thing. "I'll give you skinny dip," I growl, swinging the axe again. She leaves to change, and a few minutes later emerges in a hot pink bikini that takes my breath away.

I whistle and lower the axe. "Not sure why you brought that on a business trip," I ask her.

She shrugs. "I wasn't going to wear it outside the hotel."

"Still," I mutter. "Any girl of mine that dressed like that in public would end up right over my knee."

For the first time since I've met her, she flushes, pink tinging her cheeks.

Yes. Something changed last night.

She looks away. "Well. Okay then. I'm going." She's flustered.

"Come here," I say, crooking a finger at her before she goes. I lean on the handle of my axe, grateful for the brief break.

Slowly, she steps over to me, eyeing me as if she doesn't quite trust me. I reach for her hair and wind the blonde locks around my fingers, tug her head back, and brush a kiss across her lips.

"Be careful," I admonish her, dead serious.

She nods. "Of course, I will," she says, then squeals as I give her a hard reminder swat straight across both cheeks. She walks away, almost skipping.

I used to think of her as *the bitch*.

And now. I'm not sure what to think of her. I'm not sure exactly what to make of us.

I go back to the wood and bury myself in work.

CHAPTER THIRTEEN

Nadine

I DECIDE I don't want to go to the little beach. I don't like it, since it seems like it's haunted with dead people. I can't go to that beach without seeing the dead bodies torn to pieces on the sand and the lifeless body of Carlos. So instead, I go to the other beach. The larger one.

It's a good, long walk there but I reason he didn't tell me I couldn't go here. Hell, he takes his morning run to this one often, and maybe he even meant this was the one he wanted me to go to. And when I arrive, I smile.

It's more beautiful than I remembered. The sun beats down hot and welcoming. A beautiful blue sky dotted with fluffy clouds greets me, the breathtaking water stretching as far as the eye can see.

The large beach of white, lined with rocks that look almost as if they were placed there by hand, but just scattered enough to show they weren't. I shade my eyes as I walk along the beach feeling a lot lighter than I have in a long time. Maybe even ever. I'm used to responsibility weighing heavily on my shoulders, the weight of everything I need to do pressing in on me.

In front of me lies the most beautiful beach, my belly is full, and the fear that consumed me when I first arrived here dissipates.

I sit on the beach and bring my knees up to my chest. I don't much care that I don't have a towel to sit on, I'll go into the water in a little while. I try to decipher this feeling I have, not really understanding it at all. But as it look out at the ocean it's stretches onto infinity, I wonder… is it hope?

When sweat beads on my forehead it's time for me to go for a swim. I long to swim so deep I can fully submerge in the depths of the ocean. But Adrian didn't want me to go to deep, and I am not stupid. All it would take would be for me to get stung by a stingray, or to be caught in an undertow, or be far too far away for him to rescue me.

And when that thought comes to mind, I realize he *would* rescue me if I were drowning.

I frown, not really sure how I feel about this.

I dip my toes in, bend down and scoop the cool water into my hands and drop it on my shoulders and chest. The waves lift me just a little, lapping against the tops of my thighs before waning out to sea then back again. I want to dive in and ride those waves and let myself feel the freedom of being fully carried away. Floating. Free. And would he even know?

I don't want to die, though. Not here. Not now.

I finally walk back to shore, and suddenly I'm very tired. We worked hard today splitting wood and I did a lot to help Adrian. He didn't say I couldn't sunbathe, and he isn't ready for me to come back. I'm so tan from being in the sun every day, I won't burn if I lie here just a little while.

I find a spot on the beach partly shaded so the sand isn't too hot and lay down. Fully prone like this with my eyes closed, I bask in the heat of the sun. Clouds shift, and I'm no longer in shade. I toss one arm over my eyes, for the sun's so bright even with my eyes closed it almost hurts.

My thoughts begin to jumble. Adrian's stern face and bare chest, the tattoo on his back as he lifted the axe and swung it, wood splintering and falling, cleaved in two, falling to the ground. There's something sexy about the way his muscles ripple and bunch, then let the axe fly with surge of strength and power. His bare chest drips with sweat in my mind's eye, gliding down the valley between his defined abs. His biceps bulge with another swing of the axe.

I realize my breathing is becoming labored and heavy, a throb of need pulses low in my belly. My breasts swell and my pussy clenches as I play the memory of him swinging that axe over and over in my mind.

The axe morphs into his belt. He's looking at me with that gaze that freezes me in place from its power, and he's pointing to the bed. Then I'm over his lap, his strong thighs beneath my belly, he's spanking me and I'm begging him to stop.

Sleepy and horny as fucking hell, I moan a little on the beach and touch myself. I play the memories over in my head and work myself hard and fast until with a little cry I come, right here on the beach, the sounds of my orgasm drowning in the crashing of waves.

I blink and take my hand away. I can't believe I just made myself come with the memory of Adrian spanking me.

What the hell has he done to me? Is this fucking witchcraft?

I frown at the waves and sit up a little, looking at the waves as if they'll give me an answer. Is this how Eve felt in the Garden of Eden, surrounded by beauty and bounty, unable to have the one thing she truly wanted?

I shake my head and I slump back. I'm so relaxed after the release.

You've been chronically sex-deprived, I tell myself. I'm a woman in her sexual prime at twenty-nine.

I should be having sex.

I wonder what it would feel like being pinned beneath his muscular, powerful body while he takes me?

I'm fantasizing about sex with my captor?

But then I remember how good it was when he finally made me come, strapped to the bed and at his mercy.

My body knows how good it feels. Nature doesn't always listen to reason.

Still, I'm a little ashamed at how wanton my thoughts have turned while I'm laying here in the sun. I begin to drift, dazzled by heat and the aftermath of my orgasm. I turn to the side and nestle my head against my arms. I'll close my eyes just for a minute. Just a minute...

I wake with a start, my body aches from lying in one position.

Or is it for another reason? I sit up, and my skin feels tight, like it's stretched taut against my flesh and bones. I blink.

I hurt. My whole fucking body aches.

I look down at my legs and realize my skin is an unnatural shade of red. The realization hits me at once, and I sit up.

Oh, God. I fell asleep under the full sun. For how long? I'm burnt. Jesus, I'm totally sunburnt with no remedies here except the man who's gonna spank my ass for being so fucking careless. I groan out loud and try to assess the damage, but everything hurts. I try to turn my head, but my neck is tight and angrily hot, my shoulders on fire.

My mouth is as dry as a desert. I push myself to standing, but it hurts so badly. My skin is so hot, so dry, aching. When I get to my feet, the ground pitches up and I wobble, suddenly dizzy. Something bangs against my skull. I try to reach a hand out, but my arm hurts when I move, and I can't stop the banging. What's happening to me? I'm thirsty. I'm so fucking thirsty.

Nausea rolls through me and bile rises in my throat. I'm afraid I'm going to vomit, but the thought of holding my body in any other position is torture.

Fuck.

Something's terribly wrong.

Water. I need water.

I need to drink it though, so even in my semi-lucid state I know the water can't be the tantalizing waves in front of me. And anyway, that water's under the heat of the sun, and I need to get away from the sun because it's hurting my skin.

My breaths are shallow when I stumble back toward the forest. Where am I? If I'm on the beach, I should almost see our shelter after the little walk in this direction. But no. No, I'm at the other beach, I remind myself. I can't seem to get a grasp on my mind, can't seem to really understand what's going on or where I am. I just need something to drink.

I try to remember where I am and walk deeper and deeper into the forest. I'm convinced if I keep walking I'll see something familiar. Or maybe I'll hear his voice.

He's your captor, not your savior, I remind myself, but I can't think of that now. He would know what to do so I have to find him.

But first, water. I need a drink.

I fall onto one knee and the world whirls around me. I close my eyes to still the dizziness and open them moments later. Did I lose consciousness? Am I still awake?

A flash of vibrant red catches my attention.

Berries.

Oh thank the fucking gods. Berries. I need them now. They'll make me better.

I push myself to my feet though it hurts to move. I've dealt with worse than this. I can ignore the way my body's on fire and my muscles ache just for a taste of those berries. Fucking hell, I need them.

I get to the clearing and pause for a moment of blissful gratitude when I see them in front of me, full and plump and ripe, just begging for a taste. I pluck a few from the nearest bush. One explodes in my hand, sticky juice coating my fingers. Hell, they look so damn good I want to gorge on them. I pop the plumpest one in my mouth and bite down.

Sweet, tart juice bursts against my tongue. I sigh, welcoming the blessed relief of cool liquid, and take another bite, then another, until I've eaten a full handful. My fingers are stained with the juice and in my semi-lucid state I think for a moment it looks like blood. So much blood. I shake my head and my vision blurs.

Where am I? Sandy beaches and sunny days but pain and blood and death. Is this heaven or hell?

My limbs grow heavy, and my mouth suddenly feels funny. I frown at the pretty red berries in my hand. Did I accidentally eat a bad one? Or something mixed into the berries? I pull at my tongue. It's too big in my mouth, and it feels weird and prickly. My whole body aches. Despite feeling so hot I might die, a weird chill skates down my skin. I fall to my knees. I'm dying. This is what death must feel like. The others died quickly. Me, I've lived for revenge and hatred. So my death will be torturous and slow. My stomach contracts in pain and my lips feel swollen and bruised. I drop my head to my hands. I'm going to die, alone on a deserted island, and no one will even remember my name.

CHAPTER FOURTEEN

Adrian

I LOOK up hours later and plant my axe in a tree stump. My whole body's covered in sweat and my muscles ache like I'm some sort of fucking lumberjack. Jesus.

I wipe my arm across my brow to mop the sweat and wrinkle my nose. God, I smell. I need a shower. I roll my shoulders and neck, joints creaking and popping. I need something to eat.

Then I remember I never saw Nadine come back. I frown and stomp toward our shelter. Maybe she returned and I just missed it. But the door swings open and she's nowhere to be seen.

"Nadine?" I ask. No response.

I turn and face the forest. *"Nadine!"*

My voice echoes back to me like a slap in the face.

She isn't here.

She should have been back fucking hours ago. I grab some water and swig it down, then head to the beach. If she's still there after all this time, I'll have to make it clear I'm not okay with that. I told her to not to be gone for too long. I can't exactly give her a time to be back, but "not too long" does not mean five fucking hours. By the time I'm at the beach, I'm about to give the little brat a piece of my mind.

But when I get there, the beach is bare. She isn't here.

I turn and peer through the forest, shading my eyes with my hand. "Nadine!" I call, but no answer comes.

Jesus.

I jog back to the shelter, ignoring the rising panic that's threatening to surface.

"Nadine!"

Nothing.

For fuck's sake. She'll get more than a piece of my mind when I get my hands on her. I'll spank her ass and cuff her back to the bed if I need to.

I head back to the larger beach. Would she really be so foolish to go that far alone? But all that matters now is finding her. What could have happened to her? Where is she?

Now I really am beginning to worry.

I crash through the brush and overgrown tree limbs, calling her name. Anger fades to real concern when she doesn't respond. What if she hurt herself? What if there are predators on this island we simply haven't seen yet? What if she went deeper than I told her to and got caught in the undertow?

I shake my head. I'll find her. I have to.

Ahead of me I see the vibrant bushes with the berries. I'm just about to pass them when I notice some of the branches of a bush are pushed to the side, and there's a broken branch. I slow and come near the bushes. A low, pained moan makes my pulse spike.

And that's when I see her. She's prone on the ground, half covered under full swaths of leaves.

"Nadine!"

She doesn't move. She's hurt. She's goddamned fucking hurt.

I fall to my knees next to her and roll her over to her back. She's completely burnt to a motherfucking crisp, the tops of her arms, face, and legs lobster-red, little blisters already erupting over her shoulders, but she doesn't even flinch when I touch her. Her lips are stained red, and for a moment I think she sunburnt her lips as well, but then I realize it's berries.

I look at her hand. Her fingers are stained red.

Fuck.

Holding her against my chest, I place my fingers at her neck and feel for a pulse. I hear her moan and expect one, but need to see if it's slowed dangerous or rapid. Her pulse beats hard against my fingers, and my heart soars. Her eyes are closed. I pry one open with the pad of my thumb and forefinger, but the pupils are dilated, and she doesn't respond. Her breathing is shallow, her entire body limp against mine.

For one nightmarish moment, a flashback impairs my ability to focus or even breathe. I'm not holding Nadine but the lifeless body of Lori.

"No," I mumble to myself. "Fucking *no*."

I'll never forget how she felt, limp and lifeless just like this, but colder, more still. There was no breathing. There was no pulse. Only her broken body.

But this isn't Lori. This is Nadine, and she still has blood pumping through her veins.

With effort, I push the memory back into the deep recesses of my mind. I won't focus on that today. Not today.

If she ate the berries, I need to get them out of her system.

Quickly, I turn her over my lap face down, and pry her mouth open. It's dry. So fucking dry. I can't pump her stomach, so I have to do the best I can with what I've got. I shove my fingers to the back of her throat and hope it works, that she's conscious enough for a gag reflex. My fingers hit the mark and her body convulses. I take my fingers out just in time as she heaves the contents of her stomach on the ground in front of me.

"Good girl," I say, even though she can't hear me. "That's a very good girl. Get it all out of there." I smack her back with the heel of my hand. She gags on bile and saliva, and heaves again until there's nothing left to come up. I turn her back around on my lap and cradle her against me. Her head lolls to the side, her face weirdly pale beneath the vibrant, angry red of her skin. I get to my feet and sling her over my shoulder, my mind racing with what I need to do.

What happened? Definitely food poisoning from the berries, and a serious case. Hopefully she didn't absorb much of the berries before I evacuated her belly. The sunburn, though? Does she have sunstroke? Was she dehydrated and delirious?

Her skin is flaming hot to the touch, so hot it's painful. I place her cheek against mine, my heart tightening at the soft, silky feel of her vulnerable skin against mine. She's spiking a fever. Whether it's from the poison or sunstroke, I don't know, but it's essential I bring that fever down or she could have a seizure. Untreated, she could die.

It's a miracle we've made it this long without an emergency like this but hell what I wouldn't give for some proper first aid supplies at this point.

I have to bring her to the waterfall. It's the coolest source of water we have here. Just before I hit the water's edge, I remember. Back in the first aid kit is an ice pack, one of those chemical ones made to be activated with a hard smack that mixes the chemicals. I need to get that. It'll help bring down her fever.

But first, the water.

I hold her mouth to my ear, listening for her soft breaths. I exhale in relief. Thank God she's still breathing. I kneel at the edge of the water and strip her bikini off quickly. She doesn't even flinch when the fabric scrapes against her scorched skin. I lift her again, turn to the water, and slowly lower her body in, submerging her all the way to her neck. It's got to help.

I hold her in the cool water, then lift her up and place my cheek against hers once more. The cool water seems to be helping. I leave her suit on the shore, get out of the water, and quickly head back to our shelter. I lay her weak, unconscious body on the bed, then run to fetch the ice pack.

I smack it in my hands. The endothermic reaction of the chemicals works so quickly, the pack is freezing to the touch. I bring it to our room and kneel beside the bed, smoothing the cool pack over her flaming skin quickly, so the cold doesn't harm her.

I move it over every inch of her, over her shoulders and chest, then down her belly to her ruby red thighs. I wonder how long the cold will last when it's tested like this, flat up against the heat of her body. I don't have a thermometer but can tell she's got a dangerously high temperature.

Between the cool water and ice pack, her symptoms have seemed to subside some. I need to feed her. Then I remember the store of coconuts we've got. If I need to rehydrate her, coconut water will help. After I've felt her forehead and convinced myself she's significantly cooler than she was previously, I fetch half a dozen coconuts. I split one open with the first stroke of the axe. It works beautifully. Most of the coconut water spills, though. I need to find a way to prevent the water from spilling.

With the next swing of my axe, I bring it down just enough so that it leaves a crack, but not enough to actually split the coconut open. I stick a knife in and gently pry the two halves apart, then go to Nadine and hold the water to her mouth. I wonder if she'll be able to swallow while being unconscious. Gently, I nestle her head against the crook of my arm and lift the coconut shell to her lips. It dribbles down her lips and chin.

"Shit," I mutter. I try again, but it still skates down her chin and lips. A few drops hit her lips, but not enough. I move her down further and let her head fall back so that her mouth parts. Slowly, so I don't spill any, I pour more in.

Desperate, I growl at her, "Nadine, you *drink* this. Now. You need it. Drink it."

I don't know if it's her position that helps, or she truly hears my command, but she swallows, and coconut water courses down her throat. She sputters, so I sit her up until she's breathing steadily again, then lay her back and tip some more down her throat. This goes on for an hour, splitting coconuts and tipping the coconut water gently into her mouth, commanding her to swallow when it dribbles. I hold her until my arms ache.

The smaller, young coconuts have the most water in them. When they grow, the coconut meat takes up more space and there's less water. But this variety is small, and there can't be more than three or four ounces of water in each. At home, in sanitized cartons at the grocery, people drink coconut milk, a blended, pasteurized drink I couldn't give two shits about before I got here. But here, the pure, unadulterated water in the heart of the coconut is good for her. The electrolytes and minerals in the water will help nourish her.

When her lips no longer look parched, I lay her back on the bed and touch my hand to her forehead. She isn't as hot as she was before. Her fever seems to have subsided. I have no idea how many of her symptoms were from the berries, but I know that she's breathing more steadily now, no longer in shallow, labored breaths.

Night has long since fallen. I work with the overhead light on, but I know it's time to rest now. She needs rest, too.

I take a small paring knife, peel the hairy outer layer off each half shell, and eat the fresh coconut meat. *Like Jack Sprat and his wife,* I think. But I'll take the fat and she'll take the lean.

I'm exhausted and will have to start her on the coconut water diet as soon as I wake. I cover her with the blanket, curl up next to her, and close my eyes for a quick sleep. The slow, steady sound of her breathing lulls me to sleep. Sometime in the middle of the night I hear the whirring of wind and rustling of leaves, but I quickly fall back to sleep.

I wake early in the morning and nurse her on and off, lifting coconut water to her lips. She talks in delirious circles, mumbling about her mother and berries and sandy beaches. At first, I grow hopeful when she begins to talk, but her words quickly devolve into senseless chatter, no doubt brought on by hallucinations. She's still hot to the touch and likely still dehydrated.

When she finally falls to sleep, I nap beside her, and when she wakes talking gibberish, I soothe her.

"Sleep, baby," I say to her at one point when she wakes and cries out in her sleep in a voice so pitiful I can't help but sympathize. I frown at myself when I do. I never meant to be tender with her. And yet... what would I do if she died?

She doesn't mean anything to me. I don't even have the closeness of trust I had with the girls at the club with her, and she's nothing like—no. I can't let myself think like this.

She has to live.

I wake when the sun hasn't yet risen and know it's early. A squawk outside the window, like the calling of a rooster, has me sitting up in bed.

Is that a rooster?

Before I get out of bed I check on her. She's either asleep or unconscious, and the sunburn looks fucking awful, but her breathing is steady. I go out and gather a few more coconuts, but before I come back in the house, I listen. I *do* hear the caw of a rooster-like bird. Placing the coconuts gently on the ground, I walk toward the sound of the caw. There, not too far from the ground, sits a bird on a nest. If there's a nest... the wheels begin to spin.

I pick up a small rock and toss it in the general direction of the bird. It flutters its feathers and leaves the nest. I grab a nearby branch, swing myself up the tree, then shimmy up the side until I'm level with the roughly-hewn nest. There, nestled in the twigs, lies half a dozen huge eggs.

Those will be perfect when she's conscious and can eat them.

She's still when I reach her. Too still. I run to her side. Is she still breathing? She is. She's just in a dead sleep.

I sit her up, roll her over, and open her mouth. She needs an IV, damnit. I tilt her head back and fill her mouth with the coconut water.

"Drink," I order.

"Nadine?" I ask, but her eyes remain closed. She drinks, though, fully. My hands clench in fists, I feel so helpless. I have to rely on the coconut water.

I eat the eggs myself in silence, then keep my vigil by her side, splitting the coconut water and dripping it into her mouth, then eating the coconut meat myself for sustenance. I don't get up and leave unless I have to for the most basic of necessities.

CHAPTER FIFTEEN

Nadine

I BLINK in the bright sunlight that filters into the room. I don't remember how I got here, or what happened, but I'm dimly aware that there's been some passage of time, and I've been sick.

I sit up in bed, then freeze when my hair tumbles over my shoulder. It's in a braid. I never braid my hair. Did Adrian?

I stare at the golden twist, then look about the room. There's some banging and crashing near the kitchen area out back.

"Adrian?"

My words are met with silence for just a split second, before I hear the pounding of feet just right outside the window, so loud it startles me. When he yanks open the door, he stands in the doorframe, staring at me. He looks as if he hasn't had a good night's sleep in days, and he's lost weight. His cheeks are sunken, his eyes buried in dark sockets. His beard even looks longer. For one irrational moment I wonder if weeks or months have passed, like I've been some sort of Rip Van Winkle.

"My God," he breathes, his voice choked and tight. He comes into the room and sits beside me.

And that's when I know. I've been gravely ill.

And he actually... cares that I was.

"What happened?" I ask, sitting up in bed. I've been here so long my skin and muscles feel strangely sore. "And God, can I have something to eat?"

He shakes his head, but his eyes bely his sternness. They twinkle like stars studded in a midnight sky.

He's happy I'm alive. He's fucking happy.

He leans down, brushes the pad of his thumb down the side of my cheek, and kisses me. When he pulls away he mutters, "You are in so much fucking trouble."

What happened?

I'm suddenly nervous about him leaving, as if the absence of his presence will make me feel bereft.

"Where are you going?" I ask.

He turns and quirks a curious brow at me. "Just to get some food," he says. "I'll be right back."

And he's gone. I try to piece together the scattered parts of my memory, but I can't formulate much of anything, and it disturbs me that I can't.

Fortunately, he comes back in a moment later, with a large plate of food.

"Is that scrambled eggs?" I ask him, staring incredulously at the golden, steaming pile on the plate.

"Yup," he says. "I found a nest nearby."

"That's a little sad," I say. But I'm quickly over it when he sits next to me, takes a forkful of eggs, and lifts it to my mouth.

"I can feed myself," I say, more out of surprise than defiance, but when I lift my hand, it wobbles and shakes.

"Let me do it," he says. "I've been feeding you for days."

I sit back and let him, my hunger too strong to protest anyway. He takes small forkfuls of scrambled eggs and places them in my mouth. In between bites, he offers me a split coconut filled with water. I wrinkle up my nose. "Oh, I hate coconut."

His eyes darken. "I don't fucking care. This is what's brought you back to life, so you'll drink it."

I take a sip, grimacing at the weird taste. It's like water but mildly sweet. "Can't I just have water?" I ask.

"No. This has more nutrients and will help you recuperate."

"I guess it's medicine, then," I say.

"Exactly." His sober eyes bring me back to my question.

"What happened?" I ask, rolling over onto my side. I look about the room and see my clothes neatly folded, and a black bag next to them. I blink in surprise, but don't say anything to him. It's my toiletry bag. He's brought in my personal belongings.

He folds his hands in his lap and looks over at me, as if he's waiting for me to pass out or something, expectant and a little nervous.

"You didn't come back from the beach," he said. "You were supposed to take a quick trip, but you didn't come back. So I went looking for you, it took a while, but I found you by the berry bushes."

The memory comes crashing down on me like thunder. I exhale. "I fell asleep on the beach," I say. "I woke and was really fucking sunburned and felt sick."

"Sunstroke," he says.

"I was coming back but I was so hungry and thirsty. I stumbled over to the berries. My mind was all confused and hazy, and I thought you said they were good to eat."

He frowns. "They are most definitely *not*. I hadn't tested them all fully. It's a good thing you didn't eat more, or I never would've been able to revive you."

I look at him questioningly. I'm not sure what to make of this, to be honest. "You revived me?"

He shrugs. "I made you lose the contents of your stomach," he says, then with a smirk. "Fun times."

"Oh, gross."

"Can't exactly pump your stomach here in the wilderness, babe."

Babe? I don't respond. It's almost... sweet or something.

"Yeah," I say after a moment. "So... what did you do?"

"Carried you to the water, bathed you to bring your fever down, fed you nothing but coconut water for days."

He nursed me back to health. He kept vigil by my bedside, bathed me and fed me. God. I don't really know what to think of this.

"How long's it been?" I ask, my voice a mere whisper.

He leans down and kisses my forehead so tenderly tears come to my eyes.

"A week," he says.

"Holy shit. A week. I've been unconscious for a *week?*"

"Yeah," he says, then his gaze darkens, and his voice deepens. "You ever fucking go near those berries again, I'll take my belt to your ass. I punished you once with it, but you've not *really* been strapped yet."

I look away shyly and honestly a little afraid, since I know he means what he says. It doesn't take much to imagine him swinging that leather harder, longer.

"Yeah," I say. "I don't think I need the threat of punishment. That was fucking *awful*. So yeah, I won't." A gentle tug of my hair makes me quickly amend what I've said. "Yes, sir."

It's a reminder that though I'm no longer restrained, it's only because I've graduated. I'm still his prisoner. He's still my... master, or whatever the fuck.

But he saved my life.

"Thank you," I say.

He stands and walks to the door, then turns to face

me. "I don't want to be here alone," he says. He leaves.

My stomach sinks. I convinced myself for a short time that maybe I meant something to him. That I'm more than a body to warm his bed, that he can command at will. That I really, truly meant something to him.

He spent a full week nursing me back to health. He carried me back here. More than that? He went to find me to begin with.

But I'm just another human, so he doesn't go crazy in the near-desolation on this island.

Maybe we both will anyway.

CHAPTER SIXTEEN

Adrian

IT TAKES Nadine days to recover. Her sunburn turns to blisters in parts, and I know they've got to be painful, but she lets me treat them and doesn't fight me. Some burst, and even I wince at the sensitive skin beneath, but over time the skin begins to heal. There are parts where her skin peels away, but with rest and food, she begins to heal. Her stomach is still queasy, but I give her little bits of coconut and scrambled eggs, and eventually feed her small bowls of canned peaches and pineapple to go along with some roasted fish. This she likes. I don't enjoy using the stores in our small pantry, because we have enough food here to sustain us and those are better for emergencies. But there's only so much coconut and fish one can eat.

One day I come in from catching our daily dinner, and Nadine sits up with a smile.

"Look!" she says. She's found something wiry and cagey, likely wreckage from the plane, and she's made a sort of metal net.

"What's that?" I ask.

"To catch fish. Looks more like a lobster trap. I *wish* there was lobster here," she says. "I'm fucking *dying* to eat some lobster."

I smirk at her. She's kinda cute when she's excited about something. "We don't exactly have melted butter here, babe. And it's a North American delicacy anyway."

"Doesn't matter," she says. "I'd eat lobster any way I could." Then she frowns and tugs on a lock of her hair. "Maybe we can find shellfish. As long as you'd promise to cook it? I can't stand listening to the screams when you cook lobster."

I snort out a laugh as I begin preparing the fish. She grimaces and looks away. "A woman like you chasing down criminals gets all girly when cooking lobster? Jesus. Anyway, Nadine, lobsters can't scream."

"They *do*," she says. "Have you ever boiled them?"

"Of course," I respond. "It's the sound of the water in the shell. Crustaceans are incapable of screaming like mammals. They don't have any vocal cords."

"Believe whatever you think," she mutters, but her cheeks flush a faint pink.

"If my hands weren't all fishy, I'd give your ass a smack," I tell her, as if the threat will do a damn thing to get through to her.

"Why?" she tosses back at me.

"Because you're stubborn as fuck."

She frowns and her eyes fall on her bag in the corner of the room. "And when are you going to give me my things?"

"When I'm good and ready," I remind her. I don't want her under any illusion that we're on equal footing here. She's headstrong and defiant. We're not friends, we're certainly not lovers, and it's crucial to me that she focus on obeying me.

She frowns but doesn't respond. After a moment, she turns to me.

"Do you think the two of us could go to the waterfalls today?" she asks. "I still haven't had a proper bath since I've gotten better."

I nod, placing the fish in a bucket of ice cold water, then dunking my hands in a fresh pail to clean them. "I've gone for a run and just gutted fish," I say to her. "Damn straight I could use a bath."

She wrinkles her nose but smiles. "I was gonna say something, but…"

This time I *do* swat her ass. She runs away, squealing, while I gather up the things we need. A few minutes later, we're heading to the waterfalls.

"Did you ever go to France?" she asks.

I shake my head. "Up until I moved to my last location, I've never been out of the country."

She nods. "I haven't been far," she says, "or to many places. My mom did take me to France once when I was just a little girl, though. But I remember every detail. And one of them was visiting the Sillans de Cascade." The way she says the name sounds like butter on her lips, rich and smooth, with none of the jarring American-French accent I'm accustomed to.

"Oh yeah?"

"I mean, they're like *way* bigger. Huge. Magnificent. But still, when I see the waterfalls here it reminds me of that visit."

So the waterfalls are her happy place. They bring back fond memories. I'll remember that.

"The only memory I have of a waterfall was visiting Niagara Falls on a grade school trip," I tell her. "And they were amazing, but all I remember about that trip was how Frankie Deleanor stole my lunch money and I ended up sharing a stale peanut butter and jelly with Mrs. Grave."

"Aww," she says, but she's smiling. "Seriously. You had a teacher named Mrs. Grave?"

"I did," I tell her. "And she was so very, very... grave."

She snorts.

We reach the waterfall just when the sun is high in the sky, but it doesn't matter since here, light filters through the rooftop of trees, leaving a pattern of stippled light on the water and rocks.

Under the change of clothes, I've brought her a surprise. She doesn't know the rest of her toiletries are stored here, as well as her razor I've recently sharpened for her, and all the lotions and little bottles she brought with her. She went through quite an ordeal, and even though our latest interactions have been fraught with snarky comments, she deserves a little treat.

I place our things by the side of the water and beckon her to me. She doesn't look away shyly like she has in the past but meets my eyes as I strip her panties off. I take my time, now, enjoying the feel of her soft skin in my hands, her pebbled nipples under my palms, and the way her mouth parts with a soft little moan when I stroke the underside of her breasts.

"You're beautiful," I tell her. "Covering this body up in shit like bras and jeans and heavy, cable-knit sweaters would be an absolute travesty."

"Eh," she says with a twinkle in her eye. "You say that to all the girls."

I reach for her hair and undo the little knot she's formed at the top of her head. Golden silk cascades down over her shoulders, covering her pert breasts. I brush one length of hair aside, bend over, and stroke my tongue against her hardened bud. Her breath hitches and her eyes go half lidded. I continue to suckle her breast while I weigh the other in my hand, gently kneading her nipple.

"Oh, God, that feels good," she says, throwing her head back and widening her stance so I have full access to her sweet pussy. I release one breast while still working the other with my tongue, letting my fingers travel from her breast, down the center of her navel, to the full softness of her thighs, then slowly between her legs. She whimpers at the first stroke of my fingers, then gyrates her hips.

Someone's ready to come.

"I brought your bag with me," I say. "And today, you get almost everything in it."

"Almost?" she breathes, moving her pelvis so that she rocks against my hand.

"Yeah. You have a toy bag that you aren't getting back."

She freezes, then realization dawns on her. "Holy shit."

I found a small, velvet bag with a thick vibrator and a dildo in it.

"Didn't know someone like you would bring something like that with them, to be honest with you," I admit. "Especially on a business trip."

"I had no idea how long we'd be there," she responds. She moves her hips faster on my hand. "And if it was a long time, well... you know, I'm almost thirty."

I know she is. I found her wallet and I.D. in the bag.

"Yeah," I say.

"You're thirty-seven," she blurts out, reminding me she knows details of my life. That I was her prisoner. There are no delusions about our roles here.

"Well thirty years old is a woman's sexual prime," she chatters on while I continue to fondle her folds. Her breathing gets faster and faster.

"Yes, so they say," I respond. "But in a kink club scene, sexual prime is only just beginning at thirty."

"Really?" she asks. She reaches for my shoulders to

brace herself as she's getting closer and closer to climax.

"Yes," I grind out, my cock hardening as she gets closer and closer to release. "People wired that way find it an aphrodisiac. It's a total myth that a woman's sex drive plummets."

"And you'd know, because...?"

"Ok, well, not from personal experience," I admit, removing my hand for a split second to remind her that I can, that her tone is getting a bit snarky. "But I think that there's still plenty of sexual life left after thirty."

"Excellent," she says with a chuckle.

She tightens, just about to climax. I bring my mouth to her ear and whisper, "You don't need those toys anymore, sweetheart."

"You got rid of them?" she asks, her brows furrowed in concentration.

"I sure as fuck did," I respond. And I did. I took that bag and whipped it so far out to sea, she'll never see them again. Fucking wannabe dicks. Poser cocks? Yeah, not with my girl.

I don't regret it.

"You only needed those toys because you were never with a real man," I say, removing my fingers from her clit and shoving them in her core. She arches and braces herself by tightening her grip on my neck. I bring my mouth to her ear and breathe, "Never had a real cock."

She grumbles, "Those were really, really expensive ones." This time I remove my hand entirely.

"Please, no!"

"Please, what?"

"Sir. Please, sir? Please don't stop. I'm sorry."

Good. She's learning.

"Alright, then" I say. "Good girl. Come whenever you're ready."

She doesn't need any more time. In a scream that makes the hair on my arms stand up, she lets herself go. Her arms encircle my neck to steady herself as she screams and writhes. Jesus, it's good to give a woman an orgasm she appreciates so damn much.

When she slumps against me, I hold her until she's steady again, then lift her in my arms and head to the water. I think she likes being held. She rests her head on my chest as if this is comfortable for her. She's so small, it's easy to carry her. I like it.

At the water's edge, I place her down so she's standing next to me, and quickly strip. We use the shower some, but the showers are so short and the water cold, it's nice to come here to bathe once in a while.

We've milked this bar of soap since we got here, only bathing fully a few times a week. It's slimmer, and when it's gone, we'll have to make use of the coconuts and other island amenities. I'm fine with it, even with my longer, shaggier hair, but I wonder about Nadine. It isn't as easy for a woman to give up the comforts of home.

I go into the water first, then reach a hand out to Nadine. She stands above me, the wind rustling her hair over her shoulder, several wisps cover her face, and she laughs as she brushes them away. Her naked body, still flushed slightly after climaxing, is a picture of perfection.

When I first met her, I wanted to fuck the self-assurance right off her face. I wanted to inspire terror in her eyes and make her heart pound in fear when I neared her.

I never thought of raping her. I took what I wanted and set her on edge. It doesn't take much to turn me the fuck on, so I'd bang one out in the shower or whenever the hell I felt like it. I made damn sure she knew she belonged to me, that she forfeited her rights when she tackled my ass to the ground and cuffed me. That we were no longer on equal footing.

Were we ever?

My need for vengeance has passed.

But my need for control has only grown. Now I want to fuck her until she forgets her name, until her body aches to be filled by me. Until she breathes in my scent like a drug, chases her pleasure with my name on her lips, and falls to sleep counting her fucking orgasms instead of sheep.

We bathe on one side that's separated from the falls, in silence. I take my time lathering her up. Once she's clean, I clean myself. She watches me, her eyes roaming hungrily over the muscles in my neck, my shoulders, my torso. I worked my body hard in confinement, kept it up on the island, and the lean diet and hard labor have helped. She lingers on my abs when I soap up, licks her lips, and swallows. But when her eyes meet mine, she quickly turns away, leaps over the small barrier that divides where we bathe from the waterfalls, and swims away from me.

"Careful," I chide her, placing the soap on the shore before I follow suit. She turns over her shoulder, winks at me, then dives below the surface of the water.

"So that's how we'll play it," I say to myself, before I dive in after her. She squeals when she realizes I'm following her, and swims faster, but in five powerful strokes, I've caught up to her.

"Think you're gonna get away?" I ask.

She treads water, turns, and looks at me. I never would've pegged this woman for having a playful side at all, but the way she bites her lip and her eyes dart around me, I can tell there's more to her than I imagined.

"Nadine," I say warningly. "Don't even—"

But my warning falls on deaf ears as she dives into the water straight at me. I'm so surprised I can only blink and tread water at first until I get my bearings. She darts past me like a little silvery minnow avoiding a predator, but I easily catch up to her. She's swimming towards the falls that crash with a deafening roar. Here, it's cooler and a bit darker. I swim faster and catch her just as she surfaces.

She screams when I catch her, but without being able to stand, I can't really do much but tug on her foot. She tries to pull away, but I hold fast. Then something catches my eye, and I let her go.

"God," I mumble. "Nadine, look."

She looks at me warily. "Is this a trick? Are you telling me to look just so you can grab me or something?"

"No, I mean it. *Look*," I say, with more vehemence this time. She looks where I'm pointing, but I take advantage of the opportunity and grab her about the waist. She's too enthralled to react, though, and I'm looking along with her. Up until this point, we've only ever seen the falls from the distance. I never let her get too close, mostly because I was keeping such a close eye on her, and maybe we've never been here at the right time of day. I shade my eyes and look up at the bright sunlight streaming down from above and see that where the shade of trees was before is a large patch of sun. I squint my eyes and see there's a tree stump where there used to be a massive overhanging palm. The storm knocked it out, so sun streams through, illuminating what was dark before.

The spray from the falls masks what's behind them, but the water parts to the left, and from where we are now, we can see behind them, into the deep, blue depths. There's a cavern behind the falls.

"Come on," I tell her. "Let's check it out."

We have to swim to the side, so we avoid the powerful falling water, but there's a small opening where we're able to get through. Neither of says anything, the noise of the falls is so loud, but a short distance away, in the quiet of the little cavern, we can speak again.

"What is this?" Nadine asks, standing in the shallow water and spreading her arms out.

"Looks like a little sanctuary," I say with a shrug. There's a ledge of rock where we could sit, and above the light pours in like sunshine breaking through clouds, powerful and blinding.

I lead her to the edge, lift myself out, then lean in and hold her hand so I can help her step out as well. The ledge is warm from the sun. She joins me, and we both look around in wonder. The cavern behind the falls is small but large enough for us to stand. Beyond where we're standing now, I can see patches of vibrant green.

"Look," I say, taking her by the hand. "Let's go see."

She follows me without a word. We have to climb out of the cavern to get to the green.

"Let me go first," I tell her. She's safe where we are, and I want to be sure there's nothing lurking on the other side.

I heft myself out, then take a brief look around to be sure it's safe. My jaw drops as I see what's here on the other side of the waterfall, and I let out a low whistle.

"What is it? I want to see!" she says like an eager child, and when I turn to her she closes her mouth and looks subdued. "Please?"

I offer her my hand and help her out. She joins me, and we both look around in admiration of this little patch of paradise.

"It's like... a garden," she breathes.

"Yep. I wonder why we can't see it from above."

"Well," she says, looking around, "I think you can't see it from anywhere else, because of the stones and trees around it. It's... beautiful."

We're just at the foot of this tropical garden, and before us is the softest, lush green grass. There's something about seeing her standing there, eyes all wide in wonder as she looks around at everything, that makes me need to touch her. I tug her hand, pulling her close to me, so that she's up against my side. She blinks up at me in surprise, but before she can say anything, I lean in and kiss her.

At first, she stands rigid as if she has no choice but to let me kiss her, but when I tangle my hand in her long blonde hair, so blonde now from the sun it's nearly white, and tug her head back so I can get better access to her mouth, she softens against me. I slide one hand down the small of her back and press her flush against me. Her arms encircle my neck. Everything we've done has led us to this point, stripping each other down to the bare essentials, and in that kiss, with the sun shining down on us like a sort of private benevolence, we forgive each other.

It's an easy matter to lift her straight up in my arms. Her legs wrap around my waist. My cock presses against her and we never stop kissing, slowly exploring who we really are, now that we're stripped bare and together. I bend and lower her onto the soft grass. She doesn't let me go, still holding onto my shoulders and arms as if I'm her lifeline. And maybe I am.

I brace myself on either side of her, caging her in beneath me, and lower myself so I don't suffocate her, but I'm close enough our bodies are pressed together. There's nothing to say, because we both know.

We need this. It's time.

She told me a while ago she can't have children, and I want to know why. Eventually, I'll have her story. But for now, all I care about is that I'm going to take her now, and we don't have to worry about the outcome.

Today, it's just the two of us. Maybe there only ever was just the two of us.

I kiss her temple and cheek, then move my mouth to her jaw, planting slow, deliberate kisses along her tender skin. She closes her eyes and softly moans. My cock hardens between her legs, pressed up against the soft, silky skin there. I draw my tongue along her neck, the sweet, salty taste of her skin making me grow even harder.

"I want to fuck you," I rasp against her ear, my voice hoarse with need.

Her only response is to open her legs for me, the scent of her feminine arousal making me crazy.

I brace myself on either side of her and continue to kiss her neck and shoulders and chest.

"I've trained you well," I say, when I slide my cock head to her entrance. She's slick with arousal and ready, trained to want to come. "Even if you won't admit it, your body knows who your master is."

She flexes her hands on my back, bracing herself, but doesn't say anything.

"You've never had a man?" I ask.

She shakes her head, and I notice suddenly her eyes are wide and fearful. Is she even breathing?

I lift my left hand and brush the hair off her fore-head. "Relax, Nadine. You don't have to do anything at this point except relax."

She blows out a breath, a bit of the tension leaving her body. I kiss her neck again and suckle the sweet skin, gently nudging myself at her entrance. She's wet and swollen, and I glide easily through her folds. She's ready physically but needs a little more before she's ready mentally. Her breath hitches, but she still holds on to me.

"I'll go slow," I promise. I want to thrust into her and fuck this girl senseless, until the woods echo with her screams and I imprint our lovemaking on this little patch of earth. But she needs slow. I once thought of punishing her by fucking her, but this... this is different.

I'm the one being punished with this slow torture.

"I won't hurt you," I tell her. How is it that a woman as beautiful as she is has never been fucked? She's holed herself up, closed off from what the world has to offer. She's never trusted anyone. I'm the one who's tied her up, punished her, and kept her as my captive.

Yet I'm the one she gives this to. Her true self.

I've broken through the tough veneer. She never would have given any of this up willingly. I had to wrestle it from her, tear her open, and now that I have, I can see that deep inside is a woman so fierce she shatters me into pieces.

"Hold onto me," I whisper in her ear. My arms on either side of her, I pull her close, and as gently as I can, I glide into her. Her fingers tighten on me. She's holding her breath.

"Breathe, Nadine."

With a firm but gentle thrust, I mark her.

Claim her.

Brand her as *mine*.

I close my eyes and sink into this moment. Her pussy milks my cock as if we're meant for this.

"So goddamn tight," I growl in her ear. "Christ." I lift and thrust, slowly at first, gently building a rhythm of friction that makes her moan in my ear.

"Adrian," she whispers, her voice garbled.

"You okay?"

"Jesus, God, yes, don't you fucking stop," she hisses. With a laugh, I slap her thigh, the next thrust firmer than the first.

"Don't you tell me what to do," I order with a chuckle, but I'm swallowed up in her, the scent of lemons, her silken skin, the little moans with my every thrust, the way her head's thrown back and her mouth parts as if she's dying for air and I'm filling her lungs. I could do this for hours, for days, forever, just me and her and lovemaking.

"Am I hurting you?" I whisper.

She shakes her head and holds me tighter.

I increase the tempo with painstaking care, drunk on all things Nadine. I'm in a landslide and can't scramble for purchase; I'm the one who's conquered her, and yet she's the one that's got me in a death grip. We speak no words, but we need none. Our bodies, entwined in the quiet stillness, say what we can't, a cadence of mutual surrender.

I'm nearing the edge of release when her breath comes out in a whoosh and she throws her head back, abandoning herself to bliss. She's so fucking beautiful, I can't hold myself back, and come with a roar on the heels of her climax. Our sounds resonate through the stillness and echo, then fade as we slowly sink back onto the grass.

I move to my side, still in her. Fuck, I want to stay inside her forever.

She turns to me, subdued and humbled, her eyes downcast as she traces an invisible line on my shoulder.

"Will we be here forever, Adrian? Are we going to grow old and die here?"

"Everyone grows old and dies."

What makes her ask this?

"But what about us?" she asks.

It seems now that she's subdued and quieted, the fears she harbors surface. "I don't know," I tell her. Hell if I know.

"I'm fine being here, though," I tell her. You know... living and dying here. I'd rather die here free than live anywhere else."

She nods slowly, contemplating.

I'm not sure she agrees.

CHAPTER SEVENTEEN

Nadine

I CAN'T BELIEVE I let him fuck me.

But hell... I'm not gonna lie. It was fucking amazing.

He's brought me to climax before, many times now, but nothing... nothing was quite the same as this. With him inside me. Like I... mean something to him.

I'm not sure why I even think like that.

People fuck all the time with people they don't much care about.

Does Adrian?

I'm lying next to him on the grass, literally basking in the sun, my thighs still damp. I need to clean up, but I'm really in no rush. I close my eyes, but as soon as I do, I open them up again.

What did I just see?

"Adrian?"

"Mmm?" His head lies on his folded-up hands, and his eyes are closed.

"You have to see this," I say in wonder. "Look!"

He opens his eyes and looks where I'm pointing.

In front of us lies an array of fruit trees I expected to find elsewhere on this island. I can't identify the fruits from where I am, but suspect I'll be able to when I draw a little closer.

He blinks up, whistles, and curses under his breath.

"This is... amazing," I breathe. "But after those berries, I'm not eating a thing until we test it first."

"Damn right you're not," Adrian mutters.

"But why do you think none of these trees grows outside of this small area?" I ask with a frown.

He shrugs. "I don't know, but maybe we can find out what they are." His voice tightens. "And Jesus, Nadine, for God's sake, I mean it. Don't eat anything yet."

But it's pretty quickly apparent this is edible fruit. After some investigation, I find papaya, mango, and something else that throws me at first, as I've never seen it in person. It's a short tree with broad green leaves, and large, oval-shaped fruits the size of my hand, lightly green prickly bumps on the outside.

"Breadfruit," Adrian says when I pluck a large ripe one. "We can cook it, and it's supposed to be really good. Starchy, like a potato. Some even say bread, which is why it's called breadfruit."

I feel my eyes go wide. "Seriously? Ooh. I am so game."

We pick as much of the fruit as we can carry, and he leads me back to the small entrance that got us here to begin with. We step down and even slide a little, finally make it to the mouth of the little cave. I follow him down, and when we get to the bottom, I put the fruit down, so I can scoop up water and let it drip down my back, front, and legs. He grunts to himself, but lets me do my thing, and then we swim over to where our clothes are. My stomach growls with hunger, my mouth already watering. God, what I wouldn't give for a proper home-cooked meal.

It doesn't take us long to gather our things and head back to our shelter. We walk in amicable silence until we come to the pantry portion of our little kitchen. Adrian takes out his sharpest knife. I wince at the glint of the blade in the sun. After all, it wasn't too long ago when I wondered if he'd ever use these knives as weapons on me. I still am not sure I would put it past him, but what we shared there in that little strip of paradise makes me wonder.

Would he hurt me still? I can still see his black eyes narrowed on me in hatred, and the memory makes me shiver. I'm not sure if he'd hurt me now, but I ask myself... would I? Could I bring myself to hurt him if the opportunity for escape came up?

I take an involuntary step back when he sharpens his knife and draws it across the thick rind of the breadfruit. Frowning, he peels the green, bubbly skin, then slices the yellowish fruit into thick slices.

"Start the grill," he says. "Let's give this a shot."

I open the propane and light the stove, shoving my fears about him hurting me out of my head. It won't do to dwell on that now. And he hasn't hurt me. The way he made love to me on the grass was almost... gentle.

He holds slices of the fruit over the open flame in a way that he won't burn himself but the flesh caramelizes quickly. My stomach rumbles with hunger, and I swallow. It actually *truly* smells a little like bread.

"That's crazy," I saw, swallowing as saliva fills my mouth. "It really does smell like bread."

He nods, still concentrating on cooking it. "Supposed to taste like it, too."

The memory of bread makes me grow a little wistful. It's been so long since I've tasted bread, and I'd give anything right now for a warm slice slathered in butter.

"Here," he says, holding out one grilled slice.

I take one of the small plates we found in our stores and wash religiously every night, and hand it to him, like a starving child begging for food. My stomach growls audibly. He chuckles, takes the second, hotter slice of fruit, and pops it boldly in his mouth.

"Does that burn you?" I ask.

He shrugs. "Nah."

"What's it taste like?"

"Well," he says. "why don't you find out for yourself?"

I take a tentative nibble of mine. It *does* taste like bread. Starchy and mellow, with a subtle, unique flavor I can't quite describe but this is delicious.

"Mmm," I say. "I could get used to *this*. All I need is some butter."

He rolls his eyes. "Cows are in severe shortage, so no butter for you."

I snort out a laugh at that. "You could say that."

As we nibble on the ripe papaya and grilled bread-fruit, as delicious as it is I begin to wonder.

Will I ever sit down at a restaurant again and order a steak? Ever hit the drive-thru for a double cheese-burger? Will I ever be able to go buy myself a new dress, or a pair of earrings, or for the love of God, a pair of *shoes* ever again?

"You're a million miles away, Nadine," he says, frowning but his eyes twinkle. "What are you thinking of?"

I shrug. I don't really want to talk about it. But when he fixes me with his stern stare, I can't help but cave.

"Just... you know, modern conveniences. Wondering if I'll ever touch them again," I say.

"Miss your iPhone?"

"Mmm. All of it. Body wash and cell phones and Wi-Fi and *shoe* shopping. Don't you?"

He thinks about it for a minute, polishes off the food on his plate, and then shrugs. "Nope."

I remember what he said earlier, how he'd rather die here a free man than live anywhere else. I work my bottom lip, mindlessly reaching for another piece of fruit, when an ear-piercing, decidedly elec-tronic noise hums through the air. It's coming from the cabin. I'm so shocked, I drop the fruit and scream. Adrian goes stock still.

"What was that?" I whisper, half-expecting an alien ship to land or something.

"I don't know," Adrian says with maddening calm. "Let's go take a look."

"But it sounds like a UFO or something."

He turns, and the corner of his lips curl up. "You would know? You've heard alien ships before?"

"Well, I—" My cheeks flush. "Well, no." I frown. "You?"

He chuckles. "Nope. C'mon."

He reaches for my hand and leads me inside, but enters the shelter first in a defensive stance, as if ready to ward off the aliens if that is, in fact, who's here. But, naturally, nothing comes running at us with probes or bulging eyes. In fact, the sound was so sudden, I would wonder if I imagined the noise if he hadn't heard it, too.

"Was it coming from the computer?" he asks. But the computer was fried in the storm, and there isn't much happening. No lights or noises or really anything that would indicate it was just squawking at us a moment ago.

"The thing's dead," I say, shaking my head. "I mean it's like a big paper weight for God's sake."

Adrian turns to me and shrugs.

Suddenly, the ground tilts beneath me, letting loose a gargantuan rumble that takes my breath away. I lose my footing and stumble straight into Adrian. He tries to right me, but it doesn't do much good, as he's falling, too.

"Earthquake!" he shouts. "Get down!"

The chair in front of the little desk hurtles through the air. Adrian shoves me aside and pushes me to the floor, deflecting the chair with his forearm before it hits me full on. I scream and cover my head in a crouched position, trying to protect myself from any other flying debris. He's over me, his whole body covering mine to protect me, then the rumbling and movement stops.

"Don't move," he orders. "I need to make sure nothing's going to fall and hurt us. And there could be an aftershock."

I stay as still as I can while he slowly peels himself off of me. I can feel him craning his neck, but I maintain my position on the ground. Finally, he gives me the go ahead.

"You're alright," he says. He stands and frowns, looking around the interior. "Looks like we didn't suffer any major damage. It was a pretty small quake, all things considered." Still frowning, he stalks over to the computer and points to a rectangular-shaped object next to it with a little screen. "It wasn't the computer that made that noise," he says. "It was this. I'm no scientist but I think this might be a seismograph."

"I thought those were like attached to boards with balls and strings," I mutter.

"This one's digital."

"Ahh. Well I guess we know why the scientists were here," I say.

"Yep."

I walk over to the equipment that lies silently, betraying nothing and giving no answers, on the little desk. I'd almost forgotten it was there, as it's completely useless to us. It's nothing like the chrome computer that sits on my desk at home, connecting me to the internet and every imaginable modern comfort I could want. This thing is ancient, and I'd hardly know what to do with it.

The memory of home hits me.

"What do you think they did with my things?" I blurt out.

Adrian's frowning as he inspects every inch of our shelter. He looks over his shoulder at me. Dressed in nothing but a pair of shorts, tanned like a surfer, with his wild, unkempt hair and beard, he looks like an island native. He crosses his arms on his chest, corded forearms bulging as he looks me over.

"What things? And who's *they*?"

I swallow. I don't even know why I said it. "My possessions. At home. My... computer and shoes and the clothes and car. My... money in my bank account? What do they do with it all?"

His eyes harden. "Who the fuck cares?" he grits out.

"*I* do." I think I do, anyway. "Have they... am I dead to them?"

He shrugs, his hand on the exit. "Maybe. And if I'm lucky, I'm dead to them, too." He lets the door shut with a bang. I sink into the wobbly chair at the desk, my mind anywhere but here.

ONE MORNING, I wake up craving chicken. For breakfast. It's a weird thing to want first thing in the morning, as we usually have fruit and sometimes eggs and fish.

I guess there's only so much coconut and fish a girl can eat.

The space next to me on the bed is empty. Adrian likely went for his morning run and to catch fish. He's like clockwork, this guy. He's been trying to get me to go on a run with him. There are many things he can make me do but running on a deserted island before the sun rises is most definitely not one of them.

Outside the window, I hear a flurry of feathers, and sit up in bed. Adrian's had some luck catching the large birds that frequent our island, and I got over my aversion for them pretty quickly once he cooked them.

"Tastes like chicken," I told him the first night he stewed them. And now, it's all I have on my mind.

I'm legit crazy. Who the hell wakes up, wants chicken, and then throws their clothes and shoes on so they can chase a bird outside their window?

This girl, that's who.

The birds flutter past me, and I look about me for something to get it with. A large stone looks like it'll suit me fine. I pick it up, and without really thinking about what I'm doing, I hurl it at the large bird. Not surprisingly, I miss it, and the rock goes careening off into the woods, hitting a tree like a gunshot.

The bird turns and looks at me, and the next thing I know, it's *flying* at me. For Christ's sake, I had no idea these fucking things were so aggressive. I scream, covering my eyes, because anyone knows you cover your eyes when a bird is coming at you, and grab onto a nearby tree branch. I may not be a sunrise runner, but I *do* keep myself in shape, so it's pretty easy to foist myself up the branch and climb the tree to hide from the attack bird.

Only now the bird is nowhere to be seen.

And I'm stuck *way* the hell up in a tree.

I swear under my breath and try to look for a way to get down, but I did a really good damn job of climbing this one, as an exit is literally *nowhere* to be found. I sigh.

Adrian will either laugh his ass off or spank me silly. Hopefully option A.

I look around for an escape route and I can't quite figure out how I did this. It's like using a zip-tie, a one-way method of getting shit done that cannot be *undone* when necessary. What the hell?

I hold onto the huge branch and swing my legs down, but soon realize I'm doing nothing but dangling ten feet up in the air, and I can't just let go. With effort, I haul myself back up to a stable position on the branch, and carefully glide over to the large trunk. But here, the trunk is bare and as slick as glass, so there's no way I can grab ahold of it at all. I think I see a low-lying branch I can grab onto, and I'm just about to find a way to get to it when I hear twigs snapping, and Adrian comes into view below me.

Shit.

"Nadine?" he calls into the shelter. He hasn't seen me yet, which makes sense, of course, because I'm dangling in a fucking tree above his head. But I have to pee and I'm starving, so I can't exactly stay up here forever. I'll get laughed at or spanked, but at this point, I'll take either.

"I'm up here," I yell, my cheeks already flaming with embarrassment.

His head whips back and he looks around until he spies me. His mouth falls open. I wait for it, either the laugh or the stern look and lecture, but he only looks curious.

"What the fuck are you doing in a fucking tree?" he says.

The abundant use of "fuck" makes me wonder if I'm closer to the spanking/lecture response than the laughter, so I choose my words carefully.

"Well, there was this... bird," I begin. "And I tried to catch it. But I missed, and it got angry and aggressive and tried to attack me. So... I scrambled up this tree. But I have no idea how I did it, and definitely no idea how to get down."

He blinks. "A bird," he repeats.

I nod, but only slightly as I don't want to fall.

"You tried to... catch it... and it... tried to... attack you," he repeats, raising one brow quizzically at me.

"That's what I said," I say through clenched teeth.

He nods slowly, and circles the tree, tugging at his beard.

"Interesting situation," he mumbles.

"Are you going to help me, or just mock me?" I ask, my patience growing thin. "I am starving, and I have to pee really, really badly."

He looks up and shrugs. "I could help you, but what's in it for me?"

I blow out an exasperated breath. "Are you seriously going to take advantage of this situation?"

He nods. "Of course."

"Adrian!"

"Nadine!" he mocks, hands on hips.

I sigh. "Okay, fine," I mumble. "Help me down and I'll... do whatever you want." Already, just making this promise makes my nipples harden and my pussy clench. It's been days since he fucked me and I'm really, *really* ready.

"Mmm," he says. "Now that I can get behind. Alright, then. Jump, and I'll catch you."

He stands, feet apart, and puts his arms out.

"What? Are you crazy?"

There is no way!

He shakes his head. "I'm not crazy. Jump. I'll catch you."

"I'll kill you!"

"Didn't the first time," he mutters, his eyes darkening with the memory. I feel slightly nauseous. The first time I jumped on him he was an escaped convict and I leapt to prevent his escape. There must've been an adrenaline rush or something, because the thought of doing that now doesn't seem as feasible as it did then.

I swallow. I'm not going to focus on that now. That was a different time and place from where we are now.

"Jump," he repeats, still trying to coax me.

"God, no, I can't jump," I sputter, even though in my head I'm wondering *what the hell other option do I have?*

"Nadine," he says, using that stern tone that I can't help but obey. "Fucking *jump*. I can't come up to get you, but I *can* catch you, and if you don't jump by the time I count to three, I *will* spank your ass when I do finally get my hands on you. Understood?"

I glare at him, but he only narrows his eyes. "One."

He did this once before and I knew then I had to obey. This time is no different.

"Just... jump? And you'll catch me?" I ask, feeling like I'm going to be ill.

"Just jump," he says, in his calmest voice. "And I'll catch you. And that's two."

I close my eyes. I have to do it. How else will I get down.

"Three," he growls.

With a blood-curdling scream, I leap, straight at him, the wind whipping through the air. I close my eyes and brace myself for the inevitable crash.

I hit his arms and we both tumble to the ground, but not so hard we're injured. We land with a soft "oof."

"Oh my God, are you okay?" I ask him.

"Of course," he says, before he grabs my arm and yanks me over to him. He weaves his fingers in my hair, holding it so tight to my scalp that if I move it hurts. "Don't you ever fucking do that again," he orders. "I'll whip your ass if you do."

I know he means it. My pulse quickens and *damn him*, the threat stokes my need for him like embers in a fire reigniting. He's trained me to be aroused and a little afraid when he threatens punishment.

I can't nod with my head gripped like this so I just agree. "Okay." He pulls, making me gasp. "Okay, okay, yes *sir*." He releases my hair, spins me around, and slams his palm against my ass.

"Ow," I say, rubbing my ass with a little pout and looking over my shoulder at him. "What was that for?"

He frowns. "It was a warning because you did something stupid and reckless. I'll catch the birds. Got it? And no more climbing up fucking trees."

"It was going to attack me!" I protest, but he holds up a finger and shakes his head.

"You need to be more careful," he says, but then he spins me back around to face him. His hand comes to the back of my head and he cradles it just before his mouth meets mine. My heart flutters in my chest and I yield to him, letting him hold me. His whiskers scratch my cheek and lips, but his lips are soft on mine.

He pulls away too soon, and his mouth is to my ear. "I want you safe, Nadine," he says. I nod, a bit more subdued and honestly grateful I'm not up in that damn tree anymore. "You understand me?"

He places his finger under my chin and tips my eyes up to meet his. The near-black of his irises makes my belly flip. I can only nod and swallow hard. His stern gaze softens, then, and he brushes a stray strand of hair behind my ear. "Good girl," he says. He pushes himself to his feet and reaches for my hand. "Let's get something to eat."

We eat our usual breakfast, and I chatter on about the breakfasts my mama used to make. It's comfortable, just the two of us sharing like this.

"What about you?" I ask. He never speaks of his childhood or home life, and though I know from the research I did so long ago that he was poor, and his father was not a good man, I don't know much more.

He shrugs. "I don't have many fond memories of my childhood," he says. "I don't like to think about it."

I take a sip of water and think before I respond. "Do you like it here?" I ask him.

He nods. "I do," he says. "It's beautiful, and I like having to work for my food. I'm not sure what the weather will bring with the change of seasons, but it feels good, working for food and shelter, and living off the land like this." He smirks. "Well, the occasional can of stew notwithstanding."

We mostly don't eat the canned goods that are here, saving them for a real emergency. He looks at me. "And you?"

I don't look at him when I respond, and at first, I'm not sure why.

"I don't know," I tell him. "I miss things. I'm almost out of soap and toothpaste, and the idea of brushing my teeth with... coconut water or whatever the fuck... sort of turns me off." I sigh. "Yeah. I miss a lot of things. But there's no use of focusing on any of those things if I can't escape."

He's quiet for a minute before he speaks. "And if you could?"

My belly swoops. "What?" I whisper.

"What if you could escape? Be rescued?" he asks.

Would he let me go? Just like that?

"I don't know," I tell him. I remember how bereft I felt when he told me he'd hide me from rescuers if they ever came.

Would I feel the same now?

And I truly *don't* know how to answer the question. What would I even do now if I were rescued?

"I wouldn't turn you in," I tell him, and it almost embarrasses me to admit it. "Not anymore."

I wonder if it'll make him angry, reminding him of our roles and pasts, but he only nods and says a quiet, "thank you."

He cleans up the remains of our breakfast, stands, and stretches.

"Don't forget you owe me for rescuing you."

I stand in front of him, suddenly very, very aware of his large, muscled frame, tanned, corded forearms, and the dark trail of hair that goes all the way from his chest, down his abdomen, and into his shorts. I need to touch him.

I reach for his arm and gently stroke the fine, dark hair that covers his forearm. My eyes are on him. Is he going to push me away? When he doesn't, I continue to touch him, running my hands along the muscles in his back, then cupping his ass. He moans, and his shorts tent. My pussy clenches and my clit throbs.

"What should I do to thank you?" I whisper. I smooth one hand down his abs, and reach for his cock, cupping it in my hands. I gently squeeze. He lengthens in my hand through the fabric, making my panties dampen. I love turning him on like this. I knead his cock and palm his balls through the fabric. He hisses and moans, reaching out to grab my hair with one firm, strong hand.

"Get on the bed," he growls. He's fucked me four times since that first time on the grass, and he's getting bolder and bolder every time he does.

I get onto the bed and wait for the next command, but he doesn't say anything this time. He lifts me straight up in the air and flips me onto my belly. This is a first. My breath hitches when I remember, this man is a dom.

"Adrian?" I ask, then more tentatively. "Sir?"

He bends down and brushes a kiss across my cheek, thanking me for that. I swallow hard. In my former life, I'd have died before I'd call a man sir, but who the hell cares? It's just the two of us here anyway, and no one to come in between us.

He's arranging me on the bed by gently pressing my chest down, then taking my hands and pulling them so my arms are stretched out in front of me. "Good girl," he says. "What is it?"

I swallow. I've been meaning to ask him for a while, but now sounds as good a time as any. "What... sort of things... did you do at the club?"

I wonder if it's a sore spot. After all, he was sent to prison because of what happened at the club.

He gently swats my inner thigh to get my legs to open. God, I'm soaked already. He fingers me and grunts his approval. "Lots of things," he says. "Impact play. I like giving out spankings of all shapes and sizes. Whips, canes, paddles, straps, my hand. You name it, I've used it."

I close my eyes, and he fingers me as he tells me the things he'd do to me. "If I had you there, I'd strap you to a bench and let you really sink into a good spanking. Maybe with something moderate like a crop."

He flicks his thumb on my clit and I arch, but he quickly slaps my ass. "Chest down," he orders.

"What else?" I breathe.

"I like the furniture for a good spanking," he says. "The benches, the cross, whipping post or spanking horse." I can hear the smile in his voice. "And the sybian's a favorite as well."

"Sybian?"

He plunges fingers into my core and my muscles contract around them. I gasp and writhe. "A sybian is like a saddle, but for orgasms."

I gasp. "What?"

"It vibrates and has an attached dildo, and I control the settings. It can be used for punishment or pleasure," he explains, pinching my clit at the word *punishment*. I hiss, but when he releases me, blood flows back through my clit and I squirm against his hand. "As you're very well aware, orgasms can be a form of punishment or reward, just like a spanking."

I nod, my own need to climax building with the expert strokes of his fingers. "Mhm."

"I also like nipple clamps. They can be moderate to severe, and also punishment or pleasure. I sometimes like using hot wax, and definitely enjoy knife play."

I gasp when he flicks my clit again. I'm not shocked by what he's telling me.

"Knife play?" I breathe, my need to climax ratcheting even higher. "What... how does that work?"

He bends down and fists my hair, his breath skittering across my skin when he whispers, "I've shaved you, Nadine. Think about it. It's all about a little modified pain. You have to trust me not to cut you. And when you see that I'd rather cut off my right nut than harm you, you sink into that scene and make it yours."

He's working me up, but I'm stuck on his words. He'd rather hurt himself than harm me? Since when?

Since now, I tell myself. *Now.*

And that's all that matters.

He goes on about hot wax and hoods, blindfolds and gags, but I'm so dizzy with arousal I can barely focus.

"We can try things here, you know," he says, with a firm stroke of my clit. "We'll have to get creative, but what the hell else do we have to do?"

"I love it," I breathe. "Yes, sir."

"Come," he orders me. I'm so primed to listen to his words that at his command, I fly. My sex throbs as he works every bit of my orgasm out of me, and just when I'm on the cusp of falling down from the orgasm, I need him in me.

"Please," I whisper. He's too far away. I need him closer.

His cock slides through my folds. "This what you want?" he asks.

"Yes, *fuck* yes, please," I say. It was fine having him make me come until I felt him in me. Now, I need to finish that way. He hasn't fucked me from behind like this before. I like being prostrate on the bed in front of him with my arms outstretched, my pussy ready to be filled by him.

He anchors himself onto my hips and drives himself deep inside. I close my eyes and grasp the blankets beneath me. When he slams into me I realize he's been holding himself back, easing me into this. He likes to fuck hard, but knew I wasn't ready.

Am I now?

His cock fills my core and my walls contract around him. Every thrust of his hips sends pleasure spiking through my veins and my heartbeat crashes against my ribcage. My breath is caught in my throat as pleasure laced with pain rips through me, but I've come to like the little bit of pain mingled with ecstasy.

"Jesus Christ," he swears reverently, his fingers digging into my hips so hard I can envision little finger-shaped bruises marking my skin. His breath hitches and he growls his release just as I topple into my second harder, sweeter orgasm. I arch into him as he comes but fall back to the bed when he slaps my ass to get me back in position. I sigh. This feels so fucking good. I'm floating, my heart still hammering in my chest and my body slick with sweat.

He pulls out. I'm a mess, but I don't much care.

I still when his hand comes to my head and he rakes his fingers down my long hair.

The past is gone, and the future is uncertain. This is all we have now.

Each other.

CHAPTER EIGHTEEN

Adrian

THE DAYS RUN into weeks and then months. Her beautiful body is tanned and muscled, from her long walks on the beach and swimming. She remarked the other day that she almost doesn't need her modern beauty products, as the nutrients in the coconuts and fish and fruit sustain us. Her skin glows vibrant and her hair gleams. We're remarkably healthy here on this island, feasting on fruits and fish, getting plenty of sun, and spending every waking moment with each other.

Her razor blades have long since run out, and I've helped her shave with the finely-sharpened blade I keep by my side. She was afraid at first, but I showed her she could trust me. I lubricate her with the coconut milk and squeeze the oil on my hands from the coconut meat. It's a slow process, but by the time I'm done, she's soaking wet and ready for more.

But the razor blades remind me that our time on this island stretches on forever. No one is coming to rescue us. Or her, I should say. I wouldn't let anyone rescue me if they tried.

I'm watching her as she sleeps. When she sleeps, she's so peaceful. So beautiful. She's young and has her entire life ahead of her. If I keep her here, what's left of her life? I gently stroke her long, silky hair, and she moves instinctively closer to me, with a little sigh. Her brow is soft and untroubled when she sleeps, unlike the furrow she often wears when thinking of things that bother her, as she did today.

When she asks me about being rescued and returning to civilization, I wonder. Is she meant to be here? I'm a free man, at least for now, and I'll fucking die before I get that stripped wrongfully from me again.

But what about Nadine? She did nothing to deserve being removed from everything and anything in her life, giving up modern luxury and convenience to be here on this island with *me*.

It isn't right.

My eyes wander to the entry room of our shelter where the defunct computer equipment sits. If there's a way to send a signal to someone, some-where... I'll find it.

I take the flashlight and walk slowly into the entryway room, swinging the light around me. Even though it's daybreak, it's not too bright inside yet. The computer sits on the desk, staring at me like a time capsule, a crude reminder that we're not truly isolated in this world, but forgotten. It's a scary thought, really. Everyone thinks we're dead.

Are we? If no one knows we exist, do we matter?

I tinker a little with the equipment. It means nothing to me, so I haven't really looked at it in detail before, but I know this isn't standard equip-ment. When the earthquake came before we heard the sound, though.

And then it finally dawns on me. How could I not see it before? I've already figured out this equip-ment is meant to track seismic waves. Maybe the scientists who were here were seismologists, studying shifting plates or volcanic activity. There are only fruit trees in the small area shielded from the main island, because volcanic ash or gases could have at one time killed the others on the mainland.

If what I believe is true, the scientists could've been harmed in an earthquake or volcanic eruption, or they could've been disappointed in the results of their studies and gone elsewhere.

In any event, they were here at one point. They communicated with others. There was a way and may be still.

I look once more to the peaceful woman lying in my bed.

If there is a way, I'll have to find it.

CHAPTER NINETEEN

Nadine

I'VE BEEN KEEPING tabs on our time here, and I realize one morning, with a little jolt of shock, that it's my birthday. Instead of filling me with joy, I find the news troubling.

Adrian finds me staring out the little window in our room, mulling. He's whistling to himself after his morning run. Before he sees me, I spend some time observing him closely. He's stronger, more tanned, but a bit leaner since we arrived here. He works his body hard, running and swimming, doing pull ups on the tree branches and push-ups on the sand. I've tried, and it's fucking hard to do, so I have to admire it. He takes pride in keeping his body in tip-top shape, and I can't help but appreciate that.

His beard is thick and long, growing unhindered on the island like this, but I like it. It's sort of the hipster thing to do anyway, so much so he wouldn't even really look out of place at home.

He sees me through the open window and waves. It's been so long now since I've thought of him as my captor that it startles me when I remember. Spurred on by the memory of my birthday, I think of what future lies ahead. *Is* there a future, or am I destined to live on this little isolated patch of land forever?

I frown and sit with my chin in my hands while I think. At home now, I'd make reservations at a restaurant with friends, to toast another year of my life. We'd eat, drink, and be merry, then I'd see myself home and put myself to bed with a lighter wallet.

Do I really miss that?

I'm not so sure.

I don't like growing older here, though. Or maybe I just don't like growing old.

When Adrian comes in the room, he finds me staring off into space.

"Everything okay, babe?" he asks. We've fallen into a comfortable rhythm of things like an old married couple, and the very thought makes me grumpy. I never agreed to this. This wasn't part of my plan.

"It's my birthday," I blurt out.

He blinks, looking at me with his hands anchored on his hips. "Is it? Well, I owe you a birthday spanking then."

I glower at him. Oh no he doesn't.

"I'm good, thanks."

His lips turn down in a frown and he tilts his head to the side. "You alright?"

"Yeah," I say, looking away from him. He takes a step toward me and sits on the bed. It creaks next to me, but he doesn't touch me.

"Do you want to celebrate?" he asks. "We still have some of that whiskey. And I bet I can make some kinda cake with the breadfruit and fruits, if I get a little creative—"

"No," I snap. I don't want to talk to him. I turn away, but he doesn't let me get away with that sort of thing. I feel my chin in his strong fingers, as he pivots my head to look at him.

"It isn't my fault it's your birthday."

"Of course I know that," I snap.

"Nadine," he says warningly. He hates backtalk and rudeness. I've accepted that it's part of his nature. I'll never be like one of his submissives, but some things aren't worth fighting, especially when there's literally no one else to talk to. He expects me to behave a certain way, and for the most part I do.

"What?" I ask.

His black eyes narrow and he still holds my chin. "Your birthday is no reason to get all bitchy."

I smack his hand away. "Oh yeah? You're not the one who just hit thirty with absolutely nothing to show for it."

He nabs my wrist. "You're on thin ice," he warns.

I plow on anyway, though, "Thin ice my ass," I say. "I didn't agree to this. I didn't sign up to be tossed in the middle of nowhere with a convict who has a penchant for control and pain," I rattle on. I want to stop myself but can't seem to shut my mouth. "I didn't choose to spend my thirtieth birthday eating fish and fruit *again*." My voice hitches. This milestone of age seems to have knocked a rock loose in my mind and an avalanche of thoughts comes tumbling down. "I didn't agree to play house with hardly any modern conveniences and to drink fucking disgusting *coconut water* out of a fucking *coconut shell*. In fact, this is utter bullshit."

I try to push out of the bed so I can march off and do my little tantrum justice, when I'm lifted straight up into the air and plunked upright on his lap. Strong arms wrap around me like restraints, and even though I protest, it's no use. He'll win, every time.

"I said enough. You're cruising to get yourself punished instead of that birthday spanking you have coming."

"I didn't—"

"*Enough*," he orders, placing a finger on my lips. I huff out a breath and try to look away, but he won't let me. Damn him, he's so fucking sexy when he gets all growly and bossy, and my body knows what to do. His stern tone and firm touch makes my nipples pebble and my pussy dampen.

He told me he would train me. At the time, I was horrified and figured he meant punishments of some sort, and he did. But there was so much more to it than that.

"Look at me," he orders. With a sigh, I do what he says.

"It isn't my fault you're stuck on this island with me," he begins.

"I didn't say—"

But he holds up a finger to my lips to silence me.

"You're snapping at me, and I had nothing to do with this," he says. "And we're here. I can't send you home today any more than I can command the sun to set now, even if I wanted to."

This is true.

"So it seems the best choice at this point is for you to listen to me," he says with practiced placidity that makes me scowl. Why does he have to be so patient?

"Alright, then," I grumble.

He waits until I've settled myself quietly on his lap and holds me to his chest. "Do you want to celebrate today?" he asks.

I nod quietly.

"Good. Then we'll find something celebratory to eat, and have a makeshift cake," he says. "I'll even have you blow out fucking candles somehow."

That makes me snicker.

"But you're going to behave yourself," he says. "Or I *will* have to give you more than a birthday spanking." He tickles my side and I can't help but smile. I squirm on his lap.

I can feel his cock pressing into my ass. "It would be a *shame* to get a spanking at this stage."

We make our plans for the day, which does eventually end up with me strewn over his lap while he counts out thirty good smacks plus one for good luck, but he's so good at this it only turns me on. We make slow, sweet love, then he tucks me in bed for a nap during the hottest part of the day, while he hikes all the way to the falls to gather ripe fruit for me.

He's a good man... the man I thought was a monster cherishes me.

When did this happen? How did the tables turn?

I don't know if I can really think about it or want to. The truth is, I'm here. With him. I'm embarrassed by my little tantrum this morning. It's just hard to turn thirty in a time and place where you never expected yourself to be.

I close my eyes, lulled to sleep by the warm air that wafts in the window. I'm deep in slumber when a sound like a scream wrenches me from sleep. I wake with a start, my heart pounding, and toss the light covers off. Was it Adrian? Or was it part of my dream?

I run out the front door. That's when I hear him cursing, his growls and curses coming from behind the shelter. I turn the bend, and blink in surprise. He's standing by the propane, but the little lean-to area's caved in.

"For fuck's sake," he growls when he sees me. "Get over here and take this fucking thing off me!"

It's then that I realize the roof is on his shoulders, and he's bearing the weight of it all. With a little gasp, I run to him. He turns, trying to lift the roof off his shoulders when suddenly things happen so quickly, I can't process what I'm seeing. There's a pop, a burst of flames, Adrian screams out loud then falls to his knees. The wreckage of the roof collapses around him, the entire structure igniting.

"Adrian!" I scream, my voice cracking as I run to him.

"Stay back!" he shouts back, but his voice is swallowed in the rush of air and crackle of fire, his hoarse screams breaking me.

Shit. I try to get to him but the heat and flames lick at my bare skin, singing the hair on my arms.

"Jesus," I mutter, tears blurring my vision as I wrack my brain, trying to find a way. I remember the large bucket of water we boiled the night before for drinking, and lug it over from the corner, lift it with everything I have, and heave it at the flames. They flicker, a patch going out, and I can see him pinned in the small kitchen flames all around. With a scream, I run at him, tearing at the wood with my bare hands. My fingers grab splinters, flames scorching my skin. It hurts so goddamn bad I scream out loud, tears blurring my vision. I tear the flaming planks away as quickly as I can, throwing them behind me. Adrian slumps over.

He's not dead. He can't be dead. Jesus God, he has to be alive.

I fall to my knees, trying to get away from the smoke, and grab at him. I wrap my hands around his legs, ignoring the way the flames beat at me so badly I can smell the stench of burnt hair and flesh.

I know I'm injuring myself, but I'm immune to feeling. I need to get him out of here.

He's huge and muscled, so much bigger than I am it's like moving a rock, but I have to do it. I pull at his legs, one by one, and with a herculean effort and a scream that splits my own eardrums, I pull him away from the flames. His clothes are on fire. I tamp it out with my hands, smacking at the flames and ignoring the pain that flares on my bare skin.

I have to see if he's breathing, if he's okay. His skin is bloodied and burnt, but when I put my ear to his mouth, I can hear him breathing. I push my fingers to his wrist and feel the responding beat of his pulse beneath my fingers as reassurance.

"Thank God," I say in a choked whisper. "Thank fucking God."

I roll him over on his side, so he's turned away from the flames and can breathe in clean air, then look back at the shelter. If our shelter goes up in flames...

But the fire is apart from the shelter. Now that I've torn the planks off his body, the blaze flickers into the woods, since the entire structure of the little lean-to came apart. I turn to him and roll him back over on his back.

"Adrian," I murmur. "Wake up. Please wake up." He's badly burned and needs to be bandaged. Did something else hurt him? He wears only a pair of shorts, but his bare chest only bears the marks of burns. Nothing protrudes where it shouldn't. I reason he inhaled too much smoke and it made him pass out.

"Wake up," I whisper. "I can't lift you." He's way too big for me to lift.

I look over and the stupid flames that attacked him have almost died out.

"Jesus," I whisper, my voice shaky and choked with tears. I don't know what to do. He's damaged and unconscious, his huge, muscled frame charred and broken. "Adrian," I whisper, gently shaking his shoulder like a child trying to wake the dead, a fruitless endeavor that barely moves him. "Wake up."

I place my cheek on his chest, close my eyes, and listen to his reassuring heartbeat. He's alive, just unconscious.

I don't know how to wake him, and I can't carry him to bed to care for him, but I can tend to his wounds. I get to my feet and race inside for the forgotten first aid kit we haven't had to use in months. I fall to the floor, tear at the latch, and stare at the contents that spill onto the floor. I've been trained in first aid, so I know what I'm looking for. I grab sterile water to irrigate the wounds, non-stick bandages, and ointment, then run back to him. When I get there, he's just beginning to sit up. My heart soars with hope and my vision blurs with unshed tears. I've never been so happy to see him open his eyes.

I fall to my knees beside him, the pile of first aid supplies falling onto the ground beside him. "Oh, God," I choke. "God, I thought you were going to die."

He grimaces when he moves, but a corner of his lips tilts up. "Can't get rid of me that easily, babe," he says in a husky rasp, then coughs so hard his body shakes with the force.

"Just chill," I tell him. "I'm going to clean your wounds."

"Chill," he repeats, but he leans back and lets me tend to him. "What the hell happened?"

I shrug, speaking in short, choppy sentences since I'm concentrating on bandaging him. "There was a pop and a boom," I say. "Then flames."

"A pop and a boom," he repeats. "Makes total sense."

"Oh, hush," I say, but even I can't help but smile. I do sound ridiculous. "Something exploded," I say, shaking my head.

"Now you know why you're not allowed to touch the goddamn propane," he mutters. Thankfully, it looks like he's more damaged from falling debris than the fire, and his burns aren't as bad as I suspect. He winces while I bandage him, but says nothing. I take my time dressing every wound until he's bandaged up like a patchwork quilt.

"There," I finally say, resting back on my heels. I wipe the sweat off my brow with the back of my hand. "We'll have to keep a close eye on these and keep them clean, but it doesn't look like anything beyond second degree burns."

Frowning, his eyes skate down my arms and to my hands. "Yeah, *I'm* all bandaged up. But what the fuck happened to *you?*"

I brush off his question. "Can you get up and walk?" I ask him. "We need to get you inside." I don't want to talk about my injuries. For Christ's sake, he could've died.

"Nadine," he says with warning in his voice. "I asked you a question. Answer me."

"It's nothing. Now get up on your feet, and we'll—"

"Answer me."

Even injured and bloodied, he's bossy as fucking hell.

"Oh, fine," I breathe out. "I had to put out the flames. I used water, and that worked at first, but only a little. The rest I had to..." My voice trails off. He's not going to like this.

"What?" he barks out.

"Well I had to put some out with my hands."

"Jesus *Fucking* Christ," he growls. I ignore him and turn my hands over. The burns are pretty damn bad, blistered in parts and the skin has peeled clean away from my skin in other parts. I have a few splinters, which I pull out with a frown. he sits up and takes over the bandaging job.

"You're injured," I protest.

"Your ass is gonna be injured if you don't let me do this," he growls back.

I huff out a breath and let him bandage me up with painstaking care, though it takes him time to move, and I can see it hurts him to do so. Finally, we help each other stand, like the blind leading the blind, and go inside.

"Thank God this place is okay," I tell him.

"Thank God *you're* okay," he responds.

And you, I think to myself.

Why is it so easy for him to admit he cares about me? I just put out fucking flames with my bare hands to save him, and yet I can't bring myself to admit it.

I saved him because I need him, and it was my natural rescue instincts that kicked me into motion.

This is what I tell myself anyway.

We split pain relievers between the two of us, eat some leftover food we had from the day before, and both manage the bare essentials with our injuries. We don't say much. What could have happened looms in my mind, and I can't bear to think about it. I surmise he's thinking about the same thing.

We finally fall asleep and stay asleep until the unmistakable sounds of a helicopter wake us up.

CHAPTER TWENTY

Adrian

I'M DREAMING. At least I think I am. My body throbs in pain, my neck and arms aching from the burns and cuts. At first, I wonder if I've imagined the sounds, but Nadine's voice shakes me out of the residual effects of slumber.

"That sounds like a helicopter," Nadine says.

I open my eyes to see her jump out of bed, tossing the covers to the floor. She runs to the window and covers her mouth with her hand, then turns to me with wide eyes. "It's a helicopter. Oh my God!" She goes to run out of the room.

"Stop!" she freezes and looks at me.

"If I don't go now, they could keep on going and leave us!" she says, desperation laced in her voice. *"Please."*

"Jesus, go," I say, pushing myself to my feet. "But Nadine..."

She turns and comes to me, as we both suddenly realize what this means. This is it. I'm not going with her.

"Come with me," she whispers. "You're... we'll make something up about who you are."

"They'll find me," I protest.

She shakes her head. "They won't. They never will. I'll lie, and tell them that you were someone—"

"You did."

She blinks as it dawns on her. I couldn't hide even if I wanted to.

"I died in the crash," I whisper, watching how her eyes grow pained when realization dawns on her.

I'm not going.

"You died in the crash," she repeats, her voice cracking, then she reaches her hand out to cup my cheek. "Of course you did. Yes. You died in the crash."

She closes her eyes and a lone tear escapes. It's the first tear I've ever seen her shed. I want to capture it, hold it in a jar and keep it beside me forever like it's the elixir of life. I brush it away with my thumb, letting it soak into my skin so it's a part of me.

When she opens her eyes, they brim with tears and her lips tremble. "You died," she said. "And so did I."

I lean in and kiss her, but it's too brief, too simple, and there aren't enough words to say what I need to.

"Go," I tell her. It's an order. The last command I'll ever give her. "Fucking *go*." I spin her around and practically shove her out of the door. She could miss her only chance of escape. She gives me one final, pained expression, and runs.

It's not enough of a good-bye, but what could be? Is there ever enough time to really say good-bye?

I hear her shouting as the sound of the helicopter draws nearer and I slink deep into the forest. From where I crouch I wait for what seems like hours. Days even. Where will they take her? Are they people who can be trusted? What waits for her when she leaves this island? Will they care for her the way she needs to be cared for?

Finally, the copter lifts off the beach. Irrationally, I wonder at first if she stayed, if I'll come out of hiding and find her here. But as the sound of the helicopter fades, I don't need to look for her.

I feel the loss like I've been bled dry.

She's gone. Nadine is gone.

I can't breathe. My world is darkened, the pain of the fire the day before paling in comparison to the physical loss that draws me to my knees. I bury my head in my hands.

It's the first time since the crash I wish I'd died.

CHAPTER TWENTY-ONE

One week later

Nadine

THEY FINALLY LET me out of the fucking hospital room. I tried to tell them I didn't need it, but they wouldn't listen to me. I'm beyond really caring, though. I should be happy that I made it, that I'm still alive and back on American soil. I'm not, though. I'm numb.

I tell myself that I'm in shock. Or... something.

I can hardly even piece together the memory of my rescue.

Three uniformed people landed on the larger beach. They were just getting out of the helicopter when I ran to them, screaming like a fool and waving my hands in the air. Who could blame me, though? I was desperate.

Distraught.

One of them, a woman who looked just like I may have in my last life, her hair in a tight bun and starched uniform covering her well-built frame, stared at me and held her hands up for me to halt. She asked me who I was. Two men stood beside her.

"We're from the United States Air Force, sent to aid the scientists on the Palmyra Atoll south of here," she explained. "We were told a plane went missing in this area six months ago, and when we saw smoke, we gained permission to come here." She sobered, giving me a piercing look. "Are you a survivor?"

I answered on auto-pilot. "I'm Nadine Fontaine. I'm a U.S. Marshall who was sent to apprehend a convicted felon. On our return trip to the States, we crashed on this island."

The man standing next to her gave me a piercing look, then scanned the island around me when he spoke. "Were you the only survivor?"

Adrian is dead, I tell myself. *He's dead.* And I embraced this truth when I responded, needing to be sure I gave no evidence of a lie.

"Yes," I said.

They took my word for it, helped me onto the helicopter, and the only time I almost lost my shit was when the woman asked, "Is there anything left on this island you need to retrieve before we leave?"

I shook my head. "Nothing."

Everything.

I was taken to a hotel in Hawaii first, and treated for my burn wounds and injuries. They give me IV fluids and nutritional supplements, and even send a psychiatrist in to talk to me.

I don't talk to anyone, though.

Adrian doesn't have IV fluids and nutritional supplements or a fucking psychiatrist.

I overhear a whispered conversation, the woman who rescued me telling the others to give me space. I catch the words *trauma* and *shock.*

She has no idea.

I answer a few questions posed by some professional-looking people in uniforms, but I don't much care who they are or what they want. They explain how the island where I was found used to be inhabited by research scientists who've since relocated to the Palmyra Atoll, an island in the Pacific owned by the U.S. specifically for research purposes. It makes sense. I nod, accepting what they tell me. Do I have a choice?

After I'm cleared, I'm given a phone by someone, but I keep it off. I don't want to call anyone. I don't want to speak to anyone. Everything is too bright, too noisy. I close my eyes and sleep, until they tell me it's time to go home.

Home.

Do I still have a home?

It's been nearly six months. How can half a year seem like a lifetime?

Am I still me? Or did a part of me die in that crash? On the island?

I arrive in California at dusk. I think I may have eaten something they gave me on the plane, but I don't remember. It was only a little, though. I can't handle the processed food they serve on planes like I used to. My body's too used to fresh fish and ripe fruit. I thought I'd never want to see another piece of grilled breadfruit again, but after trying to eat the food they gave me, it's all I want.

I am not prepared for my welcome home.

I'm led off the plane by armed guards, uniformed military who keep the throes of reporters away from me. I blink at the blinding camera flashes, and wince when someone steps too close. I've never been so thankful for my brothers and sisters in the military. They've stepped up as one to defend me and keep the reporters and questions away. I'm led to a car that's waiting for me with a wide-open door. Numbly, I slide into the car.

It feels so weird to be riding in a car again, but I'm grateful for the silence when the door shuts. I lean my head back on my seat and close my eyes.

I can't think of the island.

The entire time I was there, all I could think of was how badly I wanted to go home. How I wanted to escape my captor.

I tell myself it's just a psychological game my mind is playing on me.

But I know better.

And I can't think about what I've done.

In the second hospital when we arrive in California, I'm asked an endless array of questions, but thankfully the questions involving Adrian are minimal. I repeat my story so many times, it becomes rote.

We had a fuel leak.

They tried to land our plane.

We crashed.

There's only the last line that occasionally trips me up.

I was the only survivor.

I somehow end up on some sort of news station. I'm sitting on a stool and they're doing crazy things to my hair, applying makeup with large brushes under bright lights before we go live.

"Stop," I tell the person running a brush across my cheeks. "No more."

"Just highlighter here," she mumbles to herself. It's wrong. It's all so stupid and wrong.

"I said *stop*. No more," I tell her, but she keeps at it until I finally slap her brush from her hands and it flies across the room. The team that's dolled me up stares at me in silence and I issue a command with as much patience as I can muster.

"Don't fucking touch me again."

They don't.

I sit in a stupid fucking fluffy chair with lights blinding me, and field questions from the reporter in a daze. I'm not me. I'm some dolled-up plaything they've put in front of the camera to entertain people, but what they're really doing is using me to make money. I don't want to be here, and I hate being used, so when they ask questions, I finally give them the bold truth.

"We crashed and everyone but me died. I saw body parts torn from limb to limb and strewn on the beach like the aftermath of war." The audience they've gathered hushes and somewhere in the distance a baby cries. "I pulled shrapnel from my own leg, prevented myself from bleeding out with a handmade tourniquet, and survived on fish and fruit I found on the land. After we crashed, there was blood and gore and vacant eyes that will haunt me until I die." The reporter flinches, but I meet her gaze squarely. "Any more questions?"

They don't ask me on news stations after that.

My apartment has been rented out to someone else and my things have been put into storage. It's my boss, Alex, who relays this information to me, and he's deeply apologetic.

"For Christ's sake," he says, running a hand through his hair. "Should be giving you the goddamn celebrity treatment, and instead I'm telling you we thought you were dead."

I shake my head and tell him I don't care. I had minimal things to begin with and didn't love my apartment. To his credit, he pulls some strings and gets me a nice, swanky place in the heart of San Diego, but I fucking hate it.

I can't stroll to the seashore without remembering the beaches I walked. Everywhere I go there are *people*. So many people. They talk and walk and laugh, and it makes me crazy. I end up going back to my apartment, ordering groceries to be delivered and doing everything I can online.

I find myself looking up Adrian. I find his old Facebook page, one he hasn't kept up since before he was sent to prison. A deep, abiding pain hits me in my belly when I see him. I shake so badly I have to shut off the laptop.

What have I done?

It shocks me how easily I'm forgotten. I had few friends before I left, and every one of them reaches out to me, but I can't bear talking to anyone. They don't really try after that. I never really was a people person. Thankfully, I have no family to speak of. Either my few friends understand that I need space, or they don't want to talk to a somber shell of a woman who doesn't engage in conversation or remember what it is like to laugh.

I thought I was in hell on the island. But here... here is where the real hell lies. People walk around in too many clothes and say too many words, pretending. To like each other. To care about things. They do what the others expect, and care about what others want.

It's fucking disgusting, and I can't stand it.

Three weeks after I'm back my supervisor calls me.

"Nadine, we'd like you to return to work," Alex says. He clears his throat. "But we have some conditions before you do."

"Yeah?" I say.

I want to go back to work. I need something to *do* to keep me away from this miserable existence.

I open a container of coconut water I had delivered here in green plastic grocery bags. I tell myself my body grew accustomed to coconut water, and maybe that's what I need to feel good again. I open it and stick a straw into the opening in the cardboard container, but after one sip I spit out the entire mouthful into the kitchen sink. God. It tastes fucking awful compared to the real stuff. I whip the rest of the container in the trash.

"You okay?"

"Fine," I lie. "What's the condition?"

He clears his throat. "You go to therapy."

"Oh for fuck's sake," I say, rolling my eyes heavenward. "What the hell for?"

He doesn't say anything at first. "They... think you may have post-traumatic stress from the plane crash."

"Bullshit," I say.

"Nadine..." he pleads. "Just listen."

I push myself up against the counter of my kitchen and cross my arms on my chest. Post-traumatic stress my ass.

I left the only person I've ever cared about on a goddamned island and pretended he was dead so he could live the rest of his life in peace. I left him for dead.

I was a fool. A fucking *fool*.

He goes on and on about making sure I'm okay, and the effects of trauma on performance, and blah blah blah. I don't even remember what I agree to, but I have a date and address scribbled on a post-it note when I hang up the phone. I throw the phone across the room and it lands on the couch, fortunately unscathed. It's a pain in the ass to replace a cell issued by the government.

I go to my room, suddenly tired. The walls look too white, the bed too large, and way too soft when I sit on it. A cold front has come in, bringing with it rain and lightning, and I'm suddenly cold, but I need these clothes off. I strip out of my pants and shirt and whip the clothes into the basket across the room. I left most of my things in storage and gave permission to the owner to sell it. I think I donated the money to charity. I don't much care. The place they rented for me is furnished and sparse in a sort of utilitarian, modern fashion, but it's too much. There are too many useless things taking up space in this room.

I strip out of the rest of my clothes, stand, and stare at myself in the huge, full length mirror. I'm still tanned, my body still bearing the marks of the burns, but I'm healing.

Physically anyway.

When I look at my belly I remember his hand splayed across me when he slept. I fan my fingers on my naked skin and swallow hard. When I look at my legs I remember the way they felt wrapped around his torso, how he held me in the water and kissed me like it was the last day we had. When I look at my face I remember the feel of his whiskers on my cheek, my neck, my belly, when he kissed me. I look at my lady parts I've kept meticulously bare, and remember his touch. His mouth. I take in a deep breath, close my eyes, and try to remember the way he smells, but all I smell is clean linen. I turn away from the mirror in disgust.

I climb into bed and close my eyes. I'm... comfortable. It's familiar and *comfortable* being nearly naked like this. But my bed feels cavernous and empty. So fucking empty.

I roll onto my belly, and an unfamiliar feeling wells up in my chest, my throat suddenly clogged.

I shouldn't be here. This is wrong.

I didn't belong here before I left, and I don't belong here now.

I died on that island with him, and here, I'm a walking ghost of the past that has no place to go. I pull a sheet up over my shoulder, but it doesn't stop the shaking. I think of crashing waves, sandy beaches, and strong arms around me that hold me when I sleep. And for the first time in my life, I let myself cry. Tears flow down my cheeks and I sob until I'm choking. I can hardly breathe, I'm so wracked by tears. I grab tissues from the bedside table and blow my nose, but it doesn't help. I sniff and wipe my eyes, the sadness like a weight I can't move off my chest.

"I need to go back," I whisper to no one. Back to what? Captivity? Isolation?

Is that really what it would be?

And how would I get there?

I shake my head. I know the truth now.

On the island I found *freedom*. Fucking *freedom*.

I pull the covers up over my head and cry myself to sleep.

THERE ARE two leather love seats and a recliner in the shrink's office. I was escorted in here by a receptionist and told Dr. Lynch would be in shortly.

He has a fake plant in the corner in a porcelain planter. I never much cared if plants were real or fake before, in my past life. I couldn't even tell. But now this plastic imposter makes me feel sick. I know what real bushes and plants and trees look like, clustered in verdant green, leaves reaching heavenward for sunlight. Why do we use fake plants, anyway? Isn't there enough masquerading already? Is it so hard to dump water on a living thing to keep it alive? I turn away from it in disgust and sit on the leather loveseat.

I'm dressed in simple jeans and a tank top. I feel oddly out of place, like a junior high school student at the senior prom. I don't belong here.

I don't belong anywhere, I tell myself. But I know it's a lie.

There is one place where I belonged, for a little while.

I'm alone in the room. Where is the therapist, and why is it taking him so long to get here? I glance at the pictures on the wall with gilded frames and accolades telling me that the person I'm about to talk to has somehow earned the honor of hearing my most deeply-hidden secrets.

As if a college degree gives him the right.

I scowl. I used to pay very close attention to every single detail in a room like this. In any room, for that matter. I'd observe anything that would indicate the characteristics of the person I was about to meet, cataloguing every detail. I'd know the entryways and exits, where every window and vent was, how to get to the escape routes. What floor we were on and where security stood.

I huff out a self-deprecating, mirthless laugh. I'm slipping.

What do I even remember?

I clench my teeth. I'm acting as if my days and hours are disposable and none of this matters.

But does it?

I look at the clock on the mantle and frown. He's fifteen minutes late now. I seem to remember that's typical, though, to not be on time for these things.

I need to get my shit together. First, a little observation.

The person I'm about to see is meticulous. Papers are color-coded and lined up on his desk like soldiers. He has a taste for good things, as the large, sturdy, cherry wood roll-top desk and leather furniture bears witness to. The plush carpet is clean, the glass end tables bearing coasters for drinks, and three matching frames with pictures of young adults I'm assuming are his children. It smells faintly of coffee in here, and on the mantle hums a white-noise machine likely placed there to give us some privacy.

I start when a door opens, and glance in surprise at the well-dressed gentleman who enters the room. He looks younger than I expected, certainly not old enough to have college-aged children, but I suppose some people just look young. Or maybe those people in the frames aren't his children, but nieces or nephews or something. He's fit, with broad shoulders that are visible even through his long-sleeved, button-down white dress shirt. He's clean shaven, has high, defined cheekbones and full lips, and the slightest of scars on his chin.

"Ms. Fontaine?" he says, extending his hand. I stand and shake it. It's cold and clammy, and I immediately pull away.

"Call me Nadine," I mumble, then sit back on the leather loveseat.

"Nadine," he says with a smile, but the smile doesn't meet his eyes. He looks distracted, as if he doesn't want to be here or something. And I'm supposed to be telling this guy my deepest, darkest secrets? Confiding in him?

Fuck this bullshit.

"Nadine, can you tell me a little bit about yourself?" he asks, leafing through his notebook and not meeting my eyes.

I huff out a breath. "I'm here because my boss made me come," I tell him. "I really have no interest in being here, just so we're clear."

He smiles. "Clear," he repeats. "You're here to discuss the trauma you experienced on the island after apprehending criminal Adrian Barone, correct?"

I swallow hard. I didn't expect to jump to that so quickly, and I definitely didn't expect to feel the sharp pain in my ribcage like a knife when I hear Adrian's name. It's all over the news and no secret that I was sent to apprehend Adrian. But hearing this man say it, and with no preamble, pains me.

"Yes," I say. I swallow and look away.

"I saw your interview," he says, likely referring to the interview I gave when I first returned home. I don't respond, not knowing what he really wants me to say.

He asks me a few questions about my past, if I have any family alive, friends I see on a regular basis. Do I keep up with social media? They're odd questions. I answer automatically, not meeting his eyes. I feel as if I'm going to be sick. I want this shit over with, so I answer.

"Glass of water, Nadine?"

I nod. He stands, walks over to where glasses sit on a mirrored tray, and pours a glass with his back to me. He comes back, the water in his hand. I take it gratefully and place it on the coaster next to me. He watches me, frowning, and takes his seat again.

"Tell me about Adrian," he says.

The question takes me by surprise.

"I don't know anything about him," I lie, not meeting his eyes. "He died on the plane. I arrested him because he was an escaped convict, but before I could bring him home, he died."

"How did you find his body?"

What? I blink, frowning. "He was on the shore with the rest of them," I stammer. I wasn't prepared for this, so I blunder my response like an awkward teen asking for a first date.

He frowns and puts his paper on his desk. Something isn't right here. I may have dulled my instincts, but this situation is wrong, and I need to get the fuck out of here. I get to my feet.

"Sit down, Nadine," he orders. His eyes have darkened now. He points back to my seat with his pen. What will he do if I don't do as he says?

Slowly, I lower myself onto my seat.

"Why don't you have a sip of water?" he says, gesturing to the glass. I pick up the glass and stare at it.

A few moments ago, I berated myself for not paying attention to details as I used to. Now, it's all I see. Everything is a threat. I can't trust anyone. Is my mind playing tricks on me? Will I be this fucked up for the rest of my life? Still, I can't help it. Instead of gulping down the water, I let it hit my lips and wait to see if I feel anything. Has it been poisoned? I place it back down on the coaster and look at him.

Who is this man?

"Your stories don't match up," the man says nonchalantly. I note his fingernails are longer than what's proper, untidy and dirty. My stomach churns. This is not the man who color-coordinates papers on his desk. I suddenly realize his shirt is too big, the pants too baggy.

"In one interview, you said one body was in the cockpit and he'd likely drowned, but now you're saying all the bodies were on the shore. What was it, then? Who died?" He pierces me with a look. "Who *didn't?*"

I get to my feet. This isn't fucking therapy, it's torture.

"Sit," he orders again. And then my gaze wanders to the closed closet door, and I see the stain of something red on the carpet, barely visible under the door. Reality dawns on me like a flash flood, cold, blinding, chilling.

"You're not a doctor," I whisper. "Who the hell are you?"

"Of course I'm a doctor," he says, his voice calm. "Now tell me about Adrian," he repeats. "Did he ever make it off the island? Did you ever have him on that plane at all?"

What?

"Excuse me?" I whisper.

He reaches for the waistband of his pants, folds back his suit jacket, and pulls out a gun. "I said *sit*, *Nadine*," he repeats.

What the fuck is this? Who the hell is he?

"Who are you?"

"Answer the question."

"I *did!*" I shout.

The man is on his feet and his hands are on me, the gun pressed up to my temple. "I saw you on that show," he grates in my ear. "I heard everything you said. I could tell from where I was you were lying, and you know exactly where Adrian is. I doubt he was ever even on that plane heading back home and that somehow, he escaped, didn't he? You'll tell me where he is or I'll pull this trigger."

The hell he will. I have information he needs.

"Fine," I say. "I'll tell you about Adrian, but only if you put the gun down."

He lowers the gun and glares at me, nodding.

"Adrian was not on that plane," I tell him. "We thought we apprehended him, but I lied to my superiors because I didn't want to fail the mission. Our sources say he escaped to Fiji but has now relocated to Australia." It's close enough to the truth that if he's recording me, he might believe it.

His lips twist into a sadistic grin when he thinks I'll give him what he wants. I wait until he lowers the gun, then drop to the floor and yank him behind the knees on my way down. The gun goes off and glass crashes, but I keep my head, duck low and tackle him to the ground. We wrestle, me pinned under him.

"You bitch," he growls. "I just needed answers, but you'll pay for this shit." He reaches back and backhands me. Light turns to stars and pain shoots through my jaw. Anger floods through me, and I know then that I'm not going down without a fight. There was a purpose for my return home.

My mama called me her *petite belette* for a reason. He reaches back to hit me again, and I roll out of his reach, twist hard so he's off balance and shove him off of me. He roars his fury and strong arms come at me, but I grab his wrist, bring it to my mouth, and bite down until the wet taste of copper hits my tongue and he screams like a rabid animal. I take the chance to flip him on his back then knee him hard in the groin. He howls with his hands between his legs and growls, "I'll fucking kill you."

I don't give him the chance, though.

I lunge for his gun, the familiar cold weight against my palm, turn and pull the trigger.

I haven't shot a gun in a very long time, but my aim is perfect. Crimson stains him just above the bridge of his nose. He falls back to the ground, lifeless. I close my eyes and pant, willing the bile that rises in my throat to abate, for my nerves to leave me the fuck alone so I can make the right calls.

I check his pulse to make sure he's good and dead, though I know the chances of him surviving that gunshot are slim to none, then haul myself to my feet and go to the phone on the desk. I open the door and sigh when the lifeless body of the real Dr. Lynch falls to my feet.

I need to call Alex. I dial the numbers on the phone and wait for help to arrive.

But my decision is made.

CHAPTER TWENTY-TWO

Nadine

ALEX and I sit in a dive bar right at the shore's edge. I'm sipping my gin and tonic and he's taking a long pull from his beer. We're in civilian clothing, and both off duty. In jeans and a black Oakland Raiders t-shirt, he looks younger than I remember, though I know he's old enough to be my father. I stare at the pirate emblem in gray and white on the black background on his t-shirt and take a long drought from my drink until ice hits my lips.

"Haven't lost your touch, Fontaine," he mutters. "Right between the eyes, eh?"

I hold my hand up to the waitress and order another. I miss the island and dislike being home but ordering alcohol from someone who serves it to me on a tray with little white napkins is a decided benefit of returning to civilization.

"Guess not," I mutter.

"Proud of you," he says. He looks out over the water. Sailboats glide in and out, and a small crowd dances to live music to our right.

"Thank you, sir."

I've always been proud of what I do. I've worked hard to land this job and have assisted in arrests for some of the most notorious crimes on the West Coast.

"You're different since you came back," he says, sitting back in his chair.

"I am."

He nods slowly, as if contemplating the impact of what he needs to ask me. "Question for you."

I wait. After what happened yesterday, I'm prepared to face fucking anything.

He looks at me, and in his eyes, I see sympathy. Understanding. It surprises me, so I swallow, but I don't look away.

"Sir?"

His jaw tightens before he speaks. "Why would anyone attack you for information regarding a prisoner you captured who died in a plane crash? It doesn't make sense, Nadine."

It doesn't. He's no fucking fool. The man hasn't hunted wanted fugitives for a full decade and not learned a thing or two. I take a deep breath and let it out slowly, then decide to tell him. But before I do, he speaks up.

"He didn't die in that crash, did he?'

I look at him sharply, my response answer enough. He nods, confirming what he knows to be the truth. The waitress brings me my second drink, which I sip slowly before I answer.

"I was the one who died in that crash, Alex."

He arches a brow but doesn't respond.

"I'm not who I was anymore. And the man who survived that crash is not the one responsible for the death of the woman he supposedly murdered."

Alex nods slowly. "I see."

I think there's almost nothing I can say that will shock him, but I'm wrong, as the next thing I say makes his eyebrows arch so high it's almost comical.

"Send me back, Alex."

He tilts his head at me. "Send you back?" he asks, tracing the condensation on the outside of his beer absentmindedly.

I nod. "You can do it. I know you can. You have contacts in relocation programs. With the swipe of a keyboard, Nadine Fontaine died in the line of duty." My voice lowers. "And it wouldn't be far from the truth."

"I could," he said. "And I could make a good case for your relocation. But can you tell me why?"

I wave my hand at the ocean in front of us, the sea of people dancing below the blinking lights hanging from the ceiling like stars in the sky. "Because who I was died in that crash," I tell him. "There's nothing left for me here anymore." I look at him, meeting his eyes. I'm going to give him the bald truth. "And because I love him."

"Jesus Fucking Christ," he mutters. He looks out at the sea and is silent for several long, agonizing minutes. Alex has been married to his wife, Shirley, for thirty years and I hope he thinks on this as he decides. Finally, he turns to me. "We've done this for lesser people than you," he says with a sigh. "And I believe every word you say is true."

Hope blossoms in my chest even as fear makes my hand on my glass tremble. I've just asked for something monumental and it's been fucking granted. A lump rises in my throat when I think of returning to Adrian.

"Tomorrow morning, seven sharp, meet me in my office," he says. "The details of this are too important to speak of in public."

"Thank you, Alex," I say, my voice thick with emotion.

He reaches for my hand and shakes it soberly. "You're welcome," he says. His voice catches at the end. "It was nice knowing you."

I SIT in my seat on the helicopter Alex has arranged, kneading my hands. I'm never nervous while flying, but I've never flown away from what I'm leaving now. Though I've told myself it means nothing to me, it's sobering to read your own fucking obituary, and watch as your body is buried with honors.

"So brave," the newscasters say. "Escaped near-death only to meet her end so soon after coming home."

I feel mildly guilty. But I've served my country. What happened to me on that island changed me forever. And though I'll miss the relative comfort and luxury of home, I'm eager to get back to the island. To feel the warm sand between my toes. The sun on my bare skin.

To see Adrian.

I tremble a little when I think of our reunion, and part of me worries... will he welcome me back? Does he feel the same way about me as I do him?

Will he forgive me for what I did?

There's nothing normal and regular about our relationship. I can't write to him or expect a letter in the mail or go out on a date. No. We've had to get to know each other without the trappings everyone else has to navigate. There are no dating games or rules to follow.

Just us. Alone. Surviving.

I packed one small bag of essentials, but even those seem nearly superfluous now.

Alex was more than generous with how he orchestrated this. My death was staged, my body buried. He was able to obtain an I.D. for me to use if I decide to travel, and even contacted a scientist friend of his who was able to determine where our island is located. He enabled a small communication device to be connected to the power source and has insisted on weekly communication. I can also contact the witness protection program should the need for anything arise.

I'll think of all that later, though. For now, I just need to get back to the island.

I couldn't even enjoy my visit to Hawaii, though I tried. I ordered food in a restaurant and stocked *way* the hell up on razor blades that cost a fucking fortune. I took the longest, hottest shower I could stand and lathered myself up in fragrant soap. But my thoughts were elsewhere.

I'm exhausted from all the travel and have been on this helicopter now for hours and hours.

"Twenty minutes to landing," the co-pilot says to me.

I nod.

The pilots flying me here have been amply compensated. They flew a private jet to Hawaii, and now we're on a helicopter to prepare for a water landing.

The pilots work closely with the witness relocation program, so they ask no questions. My name is Janet Dole, a pretty lame variation on Jane Doe, and they're flying the coordinates given to them from a superior. Alex obtained the exact coordinates from the rescue team that found me. I even have I.D. for Adrian for when the time comes for us to travel off the island and pay a little visit to Hawaii, Fiji, Australia, or New Zealand. My husband John Dole now has a passport as well.

Alex set it up so we'll received dropped care packages twice a month, with basic luxuries and supplies from home, and anything else we request. I'll be able to contact him when I need to, and can travel whenever I like.

But I'm not sure I'll want to often.

When the island comes into view, I peer out the window. I'm looking for Adrian, but it's silly to look when I'm so high up. And if he's consistent, he'll hide from the sound of a jet.

We've arranged for my things to be dropped, then a water landing for me as there's no room on the island for a landing.

The helicopter bobs on the surface of the water. My stomach churns with nerves when I bid them farewell, leap from the aircraft, and swim to shore. Shortly after, I hear the deafening sounds of their take off.

With shaking legs, I swim toward shore. Though the jet takes off with a deafening roar, the ringing in my ears continues even after the jet is long gone.

Tears blur my vision. I'm a bundle of fucking nerves.

Did I make a mistake? Who the hell leaves civilization to return to a place like this?

Things look about the same as they did before. The shelter still stands there, the roof repaired with clean white shingles made from bark. I need to get this over with.

"Adrian?" I yell out, but my voice echoes and there's no response. A light breeze rustles the palm leaves above my head. I look to my left and right, and note neatly-stacked logs, a pile of coconuts, his knives and axe leaning against the shelter. Has he gone fishing? Well, no. It's way too late for that.

I place my things down and strip down to my shorts and tank top. I smile. It's the first time I've smiled since I left here.

I yell his name, but again nothing but the sound of my own voice comes back to me. It's when I get to the second, larger beach, that I begin to grow worried. When I left him, he was recovering from terrible injuries. Did he not recover from them? Did he grow sick, with no one to care for him and no real medicine to speak of, unable to call for help in anyway?

What have I done?

But no. I shake my head. I haven't exhausted all the possibilities yet. And the pile of coconuts outside the shelter are evidence that he is indeed still alive.

Then where is he?

I go back to the shelter to look once more, but he's still nowhere to be found. I pause when I get to the bedroom. The bed is neatly made. Beside it stands a roughly-hewn side table. It looks as if it were carved from solid wood. On the table lies a small bouquet of fresh flowers, like a memorial of sorts.

A memorial for *me*.

I really, truly *have* left my life behind.

I leave the shelter and head to the waterfalls. Maybe he's gone for a dip, or to gather more fruit. "Adrian!" I call but still, I get no answer.

I slow when I get to the waterfall, as my body suddenly begins to do some strange, unpredictable things. My belly dips and clenches, my throat clogged with emotion.

He's here. I can *feel* him before I see him. Adrian's here.

But when I come into the clearing and look at the water before the falls, I don't see him. I let out a little involuntary whimper. I need to see him so badly. I gave up everything, traveled across the world, and I need to see him. I made a horrible mistake leaving him.

Was it unforgivable?

I strip the remains of my clothes off and step into the water. It's warm and welcoming, and envelopes me like a hug.

Welcome home.

Home. I'm more at home here than I was anywhere in California.

"Adrian?" I call, but no answer comes. I fear the worst, but I need to see.

I swim toward the falls, and get to the cave, the water cooling when I swim into the shade. I heave myself up and onto the floor of the cavern. If he's not here, I'm not sure where else he could be. I'll have to go back to the shelter and wait for him, but if he's injured somewhere on this island...

I pull myself up onto the grass, and peer around, my heart hammering in my chest. My intuition speaks to me before my mind does, my heartbeat kicking up now that I know he's here.

He's standing by a tree, picking ripe fruit. He wears nothing but shorts, tanned so that his skin looks like dark caramel. His muscles ripple as he reaches for the fruit, his tattoo stretched across his back. To me, it's like the most beautiful artist's canvas. He's bigger than I remember, rougher and rugged, his hair long and unencumbered, like some sort of Greek god.

I open my mouth to call him, but I can't make the words come out. I can't speak. My hands shake, and my body vibrates with the need to touch him, to hold him, to feel him. I stumble toward him on trembling legs when he turns.

He drops the fruit in his hands and freezes. "Nadine?" he whispers. He walks my way slowly, as if I'll vanish like vapor if he goes too fast. When he reaches me, he extends his hand toward me and gently touches my hair. "Am I dreaming?"

I shake my head, take his hand in mine and pull him toward me. Without a word, I kiss him. I say with my lips what I can't vocalize, not yet—*I missed you. I never should have left you. You made me realize who I am and what I want, and what I want is you.*

I'm sorry.

I love you.

He cups my face in his hands and holds me close. I breathe in and fill my lungs with him, my chest expanding as he breathes out. I'm enveloped in the smell of lemons and coconuts, focused on the feel of his coarse hair beneath my fingers, warm from the heat of the sun. Releasing my face, he rakes his hand down my body, still wet from the swim, and cups my ass. He lifts me up, and my legs wrap around his body. A thousand words are spoken in that kiss, the past and future collide and all we're left with is right here, right now. Stripped down to nothing but our mere essences, we kiss with fervent wonder.

He holds me up to him and gently lowers me to the ground. My back is against a soft blanket of green grass. He lowers his body on mine and I sigh into his mouth. He pulls away and whispers a heated, tortured, "you came back," against my ear.

"I never should have left," I say, my voice choked with meaning. "I don't belong there anymore. I belong here." I spread my arms out wide then bring them to rest on his shoulders. "Here."

"It rained for six straight days after you left, like the island wept for you."

Tears prick my eyes.

I'm home.

He leans down and flutters kisses along my temple and cheek. I close my eyes and let myself feel the roughness of his whiskers and silk of his mouth. My breasts swell and my belly dips with need. This. *This.*

He quickly strips and lowers himself down on me. "Baby," he whispers. It's the first time he's ever called me that.

I like it.

I spread my legs for him, my eyes focused on his as he slides into me. We don't speak a word, our bodies silently saying what words can't convey.

You're mine.

Welcome home.

I love you.

At the first thrust of his hips, I cry out. At the second, fresh tears dampen my cheek. He stakes his claim, making sweet love to me like we're the only two people on earth.

And maybe we are.

EPILOGUE

Adrian

We sit by a little fire I've built outside. It's a little cooler now that the sun has set. I've built a small fire pit with large rocks I've found around the island. I like to sit here at night. The fire keeps pesky bugs away. There's something soothing about the flickering flames and gentle heat the fire gives off.

But tonight, Nadine sits on my lap. I sit on a roughly-hewn chair I made in her absence. I've been giving myself projects to do to occupy my mind, and even considered building a boat and making my way to another island somewhere. That's just plain stupid, though. I have no idea what they're saying about me in America, and there's nothing like some loon with wild Tarzan hair and burn marks to arouse suspicion. And for all I know, with no real navigation or sailing equipment I'd just sail to my death anyway.

So I stayed here, and I've been working on crude carpentry. I have a few chairs, a stack of plates and bowls. She's proud of the work I've done and admires it. I don't let her talk much, though.

So after we built the fire, I sat down and pulled her onto my lap. She turned and burrowed herself into me, her cheek against my chest. She was so still, her breathing so soft, that I thought she'd fallen asleep.

"Nadine?"

"Mmm?" she asks.

"Thought you were asleep, baby."

"Nope. I'm just soaking this up. Jesus, I missed this so damn much. I was an idiot."

Without thinking I give her ass a good slap. "I don't want to hear you say that again," I warn. "You were *not* stupid. And anyway, I was the one who told you to go."

She nods and smiles. "You know, that's true. It's actually your fault, then. Why'd you let me go?"

I wrap my arms around her and hold her even tighter. "I decided I didn't want you as my captive," I tell her. "I wanted you to be free."

"I am," she whispers.

We sit in silence until a log falls over in the fire. The crackling sound makes her jump, but my arms tighten around her and she quickly settles.

"Are you going to tell me what happened?" I ask.

She nods, lifts her head, and looks up to me. "There's actually a fucking *lot* to tell," she says.

I smile at her. "I'm not going anywhere."

She grins at me. "Yeah. This is a good point," she mutters. "So I got back home. When I got back there, they'd sold my apartment and gotten rid of my things because they thought I was dead."

"Seriously?" I'm mad on her behalf. Jesus Christ.

"Yeah," she says with a sigh. "Seriously. And then I get off the plane, and there are like all these reporters and flashing lights and so many goddamn people."

"God, I fucking hate people."

She laughs and sighs and buries her head on me again. "*Me too.* And this is why you're mine."

I nod. "Likewise. Go on."

She goes on about her new apartment and how she couldn't stand how it looked and felt, and how she longed to get back here, to our little patch of paradise in the middle of nowhere.

"Where there's no beeping phones or trucks or text messages to answer or bills to pay." I say softly.

"Yes. Where there's none of that. And where there's... what I really, truly *do* need."

I look at her quizzically and lift her chin in my hand. "What's that, baby?"

She looks shy, ducking her chin against my hand. "*You,* Adrian. I... well, maybe I got used to the way you are with me."

"You missed getting your ass spanked," I mutter. God, I missed teasing her. "You girls are all the same. You're all *ow, ow, ow, sir, that hurts!* And then you go for a week or two without it and you need to be brought back to heel."

She smacks my chest. "Brought to heel!"

I nab her wrist and drop my voice. "Damn right."

Her pupils dilate, and she bites her lip. "Well maybe I *did* sort of miss it a little. And I really did miss the island. The serenity. Calm. And..." she pauses. "You."

I have no qualms about the bald truth. "I felt like someone died when you left. Sorta wished I would. The bed felt lonely, and I thought I was gonna make myself crazy talking to myself. But I missed you, too." I take her chin back in my hand, forcing her to look at me. "Because I love you, Nadine."

She swallows, licks her lips, then whispers. "And I love you."

I let go of her chin and let her burrow into me again.

"I hated being back in America. There's so much fucking *pretense* about things."

I nod. I agree. It's why I never did play the goddamned games, and never regretted not playing them. The games I played with my family took on a whole other fucking meaning, too, so I was mired in layers and layers of goddamned deceit.

"Yeah, I hear you there. But didn't you like your... hmm, how did you put it... body wash and cell phones and Wi-Fi and shoe shopping?"

Her shoulders shake with laughter against me. "Not as much as I thought I would."

I sigh. "I could go for a steak, though."

She sits up on my lap. "Well, now it's time for you to hear the rest of the story..."

She fills me in on her interview and the insistence from her work that she get into therapy. She quiets when she gets to arriving at the therapist's, though.

"Why did you stop?" I ask, weaving my fingers through her hair.

"Because I know you," she says.

"What?"

"I know that what I'm about to tell you is going to make you so furious you'll probably want to kill someone, and since I'm the only one on this island..."

I grip her arm and force her to look at me. "Don't even joke like that."

"Okay," she says. "But I wasn't joking about the other part."

"Tell me."

"Just don't overreact."

"For God's sake, tell me before I have to spank it out of you."

She sighs but smiles a little and nods. After she tells me every detail, I lift her off my lap and place her on her feet. She was right. She was fucking right. I *do* want to kill someone, but the person I want to murder is already dead, and by her hand.

"They're total fucking *leeches*," I fume, marching around the fire and running my hand through my tumbled hair.

She's on her feet. "But they're gone now, Adrian. And thanks to Alex, I am, too."

I freeze. "Who the fuck is Alex?"

She grins at me like I just gave her a goddamned diamond. "You're jealous," she says. "You are *so* jealous."

I cross my arms and glare at her. "You *really* need a spanking."

She laughs out loud and shakes her head. "Alex was my *boss*. My very old, very happily married boss."

I breathe out a sigh of relief.

"So Adrian... when I say it's over, I mean it. You don't exist anymore to any of them. And I don't, either." She walks over to the bag she left on the ground outside the shelter that I didn't notice before and pulls out a navy-blue folio. "You are *now* officially Mr. John Dole."

I tug out the one behind it and look at both of them. "And you're Janet Dole?" I grin at her.

She nods.

"So... neither of us exists to anyone else in the entire world?"

Her eyes light up like little stars at night. "Exactly."

I tug at my beard. "So we don't have to get married or any shit like that, right? Our I.D. says we already are. And there's no one to do the job anyway. I can just drag you by your hair to my cave and call you woman?"

She tosses her hair as if to tempt me and grins. "Perfect."

THE END

CHAPTER ONE

Aria

"Today, you are going *down*." I shove my glasses up the bridge of my nose for the umpteenth time with a little smile, blinking at the screen in front of me. Although it's cramped in this small, makeshift home office which consists of a tiny desk I rescued curbside nestled in a corner of the room to give me the best access to my computer screens, here's where I do my magic. While I don't really mind teaching coding at the little community college outside of Coney Island, I don't like the red tape and long hours. I long to get back to my little haven, where my fingers fly over the keys and I truly come alive.

Today, in the most boring white conference room under harsh, fluorescent lights, tepid coffee in hand, I longed to get home to unwrap what I discovered last night: *the* motherlode of all encrypted goldmines. Way too complex for me to delve into before school, but now, when the night is young and the moon rises, I get to play.

Professor by Day, Hacking Goddess by Night.

At least that's what I like to think.

I glance at the time and stretch. I can out-code anyone in the world, bar none. One day, I'll no longer be known as Aria Cunningham, the nobody, barely scraping by at the local community college. I'll actually make a *difference* in this world.

I blink and stare at the screen.

Wait.

My heart beats faster. Is that...

No.

My mouth dry, I click the little icon indicating my download is complete. I scroll down, my hand covering my mouth as I'm seized with two conflicting emotions.

Elation — *I did it!* I successfully hacked into the most notorious database of criminal activity I've ever seen in my life.

And gripping, terrifying fear.

No one has ever done this before. And unearthing something this massive comes at a cost.

I stare, my mouth agape.

Names. Dates. Locations. Pictures.

Evidence.

Politicians and celebrities, CEOs and religious leaders, military icons and monarchs. I stare in both horror and glee as I realize…it *worked.*

I scroll past pages and pages of information that should be encrypted but reads clear as day now. Oh my *God.* This is worse than I thought. If this got out to the press…if anyone knew what these people have done. *No.*

And worse? If the owners of this information ever realize I've hacked into their database…

"Good thing you covered your tracks," I whisper to myself.

A blinding yellow light flashes. I stare for a second too long.

I leap to my feet. I smack the button on the surveillance camera that overlooks all entryways to my apartment. My blood runs cold at the sight of six armed men at the back door. I might be in an old, mostly unoccupied house that was nearly condemned, but there are still *three* access points, not including windows, and I don't take risks.

Shit.

Oh God.

My heart beats so fast I feel nauseous, bile rising in my throat as I quickly assess my options even as my mind whirs. *How?? How did they discover where I am so quickly?*

I'm so damn careful, sweeping *every* digital footprint as thoroughly as possible. I leave no trace behind and cover every possible angle. I don't have time to unravel this.

I kick my keys into the trash bin and grab my laptop. I have seconds as I scramble to my hideout in the tiny attic. The trap door glides into place at the same time my front door opens.

I slide into position, my heart beating so rapidly I feel like I'm going to be sick.

I listen. It's just as I imagined. I told myself I would never actually *need* a hideout. And yet here I am.

My mind races.

The type of information I discovered was under high profile lock and key. The people responsible for this set up an immediate alert in the event of a security breach and absolutely had the funds and resources for high security measures.

Oh God.

Footsteps sound on the floor below. How long will they look for me? How thoroughly will they search? With a pounding heart, I wait in the corner of the attic, well hidden. If whoever's here had the foresight to bring a search dog, I'll be fucked, but I'm mostly invisible to the human eye.

Glass shatters amid loud, commanding voices. Though I can't make out clear words, I know they're trying to get me out of hiding. I swipe at the tears that fall and clutch my laptop to me at the sounds of my meager possessions being destroyed.

I listen for words but can only hear muffled voices. From my perch in the attic, I crawl on my belly to look through the tiny, triangular-shaped window that overlooks the driveway. Three unmarked luxury SUVs.

Shit.

I hold my breath and pray the camouflaged trap door remains hidden.

The footsteps come closer. Someone bangs a heavy hand on the closet walls and ceiling. I slap my hand to my mouth to stifle a scream. The voices come nearer.

I hold my breath until I'm dizzy.

I wait until it sounds like every single one of my belongings has been obliterated and the cold, angry voices retreat. I stare out the small window and watch the SUVs reverse onto the street and leave.

I can't go back to any place that's familiar or home.

I have to run.

CHAPTER TWO

Aria

I clutch my laptop to my chest as I stand outside the towering door. The imposing estate alone almost makes me want to flee, but I didn't get where I am by running when I'm scared.

My finger hovers over the doorbell, my hand quaking. I will myself to push it. No turning back now. Loud chimes sound inside the elegant house.

What am I doing? Why am I here? I wish I didn't feel so out of place. I wish I had another option.

My heart's racing when the door opens and Tatiana, my old college roommate and former best friend, stands in front of me.

She blinks. She's barely aged the past few years and looks as beautiful as ever with her pale skin the color of cream, and her ice-blue eyes, a mass of thick dark curls framing her face. "Oh my God. *Aria?*"

"Tatiana," I say with a forced smile as I look over my shoulder. "Please. I need to come in."

The quick snap of her gaze tells me she understands. With a nod, she steps back and slams the door behind me.

"Come with me."

I follow her to a small room that looks like a study, complete with a sideboard and gleaming mahogany desk.

"Sit." She points to a chair. While I never bothered with small talk, Tatiana never bothered with formalities. Without another word, she takes a glass from the shelf, opens a decanter with amber liquid, and pours. "Drink?"

I normally don't drink. It's too expensive and I like to stay in control of myself. But this is good stuff and God, has it ever been a week. I drink what she gives me until ice hits my teeth.

Tatiana gives me a half-smile. "How've you been?"

I swallow. "Been better. You?"

With a sigh, she nods. "Same. I knew you'd eventually come to claim your dues. So let's hear it."

Claim your dues. So that's what we're calling it now. Ah, well. She isn't wrong.

"I need to know that we're safe here. I cannot be overheard."

"We're alone."

My mind whirrs and clicks. I can't help it.

There were two cars in the driveway, four pairs of shoes in the entryway when I entered, and two sets of keys on hooks by the door. Either she likes duplicates, or she's lying.

I know her well, and I think it's the latter.

I give her a look with a pierced eyebrow. "Really?"

"It's recent," she says, clearing her throat, and looking away before she drags her eyes back to me. "I kicked him out. That's all you need to know, Aria. Spill."

At one point Tatiana and I were best friends. Eventually, as our college days passed, we had less and less in common. No one really liked me — I was too honest, too direct. I didn't play well with others. My clothes were never the right style, I didn't know how to drink, how to fit in, and my grades surpassed everyone else's. But we both know I'm the only reason Tatiana graduated from Suffolk Law.

She stares at me. "You've finally done it, haven't you?"

I wince and nod.

A slow grin spreads across her face. "I knew you'd do it someday. You're fucking amazing."

She would know. Whereas others might ask for help with homework or essays, I was the one people came to when they needed hacking skills. She was the one that came to me, tearfully begging me to hack into the school grading system when she was at risk for failing. I did, with the promise that one day she'd pay back the favor.

"Tell me everything you can."

"It's huge," I tell her in a whisper. "The more I tell you, the more danger you're in. You're in danger just being with me right now."

Her brow furrows, and her lips press together. She nods.

"Listen, Tatiana...The stuff that I found...if it ever got out to the press...it would destroy institutions across the world. You remember the Epstein scandal? Think bigger. Multiply it by a hundred, drag in every major institution you could think of, and you'll be getting closer."

"Holy *shit*."

I nod, my belly churning.

"World," she repeats, her eyes wide. I watch her swallow before she clarifies. "Not just the country?"

"*World.*"

"My God," she mutters. "So if you're found..."

"I'm fucked." One of the people implicated could have me killed with a simple command, hiding all evidence laughably easily given the lack of contacts and influence I have. I lick my lips and nod. "Even the good guys can't help me this time." Because even the "good guys" are on that list.

"Are you in danger right this very minute? Do you have a place to stay?"

"Yes, I am and no, I don't."

I pull out my phone and tap the article I saved. Wordlessly, I hand it to her.

Mysterious Campus Attack Unleashes Panic as Authorities Hunt for Missing Professor

In a chilling turn of events, the tranquil campus of West End Community College is reeling after a brutal attack last night, sending shock and horror through the community. The assault, which authorities suspect was aimed at locating a missing professor entrenched in a high-profile investigation, has left students and faculty in a state of fear and confusion.

At approximately midnight students and campus security reported masked assailants arriving on campus. Some believe the assailants suspected Professor Aria Cunningham was hiding on site.

The attackers managed to evade capture, disappearing into the night as swiftly as they had arrived.

West End Community College has been placed on high alert, with classes suspended indefinitely, and students urged to stay safe. Officials are urging anyone with information on the whereabouts of Aria Cunningham or the attackers to come forward immediately.

Finally, she blows out a breath and nods. "My God. *Officials.* And you're telling me you found information on said officials that would destroy them."

I blow out a breath in relief. "That's exactly what I'm telling you."

She nods and smiles wanly. "I knew when you came to me it wouldn't be to set you up on a blind date or to borrow some gas money. How much do you need?"

I exhale. "I need more than money."

She stares at me as reality dawns. "You need

protection," she says in a whisper. "Someone outside the law."

"Exactly," I whisper back.

She rises to her feet and paces the room.

"Holy shit, Aria. *Girl...*" Her voice trails off as she thinks over the implications of what I've told her. "This is too big for me. You'll need someone who can give you protection and money. You need someone with power. I have money, but money will only go so far." She mindlessly tugs at the delicate gold necklace she wears. "You could — no, no, that's too much. Hmm. That won't work," she says, as she mentally sifts through ideas. "Could send you to — no. Not this time of year, it's too busy and they'll be looking for those records anyway." She blows out a breath. "You can't show me what you found?"

I shake my head. "I don't want to involve you. The more you know, the more dangerous it is."

And honestly? I don't know her. Not really. What if she decides she wants to turn me in herself? Suddenly, the thought of coming here in the first place was the worst thought I ever had.

My heart is beating so fast I'm dizzy. I can't wait any longer. I can't stay in one place.

I stand up.

"You know, I'm good. I think that I—"

"Aria! I've got it!" She reaches for my arm and grips it tightly, her eyes so wide she's scaring me. "There is someone who can help. I mean…he's…vicious. He's scary as fuck. But if you go to him, okay, *them*…and offer your skills…it just might work. I mean, you've got information that law enforcement doesn't want you to have. Your only choice is to go to someone who's *above* the law. Who doesn't care about niceties or following the rules. Who hates the Feds and would likely love fucking them over."

I eye her skeptically. She's right, but…"Okay?"

"The Romanovs," she says in a whisper.

The hair on the back of my neck stands up. "They rule The Cove and they despise local authority," she continues. "They're the only ones *above* local authority."

I lick my lips. "How?"

"Organized crime. You know? *Bratva.*"

Bratva. I do know. When you do what I do, sifting through the vast network of connections and people and places…you know exactly where the most powerful people live.

The Romanovs own The Cove, the large, sprawling "Little Russia" smack dab between Coney Island and Manhattan. That's all I know.

But I have no safe place to go. I could form another identity, uproot everything, and flee the country. I know enough that I could fabricate a new ID and start from scratch.

But I'd have nothing. No one.

"I've lost everything, Tatiana. I'm willing to pay the price of anything at this point."

She stares at me unblinking. "Anything?"

I swallow. "Anything." My small apartment is gone. My identity has been leaked. I don't have a job anymore and had no money to begin with. For the first time in my life, I'm thankful I have no loved ones I could lose.

"The Romanovs are in charge of everything in The Cove. I can tell you right now that whatever you ask of them, it will come at a price. A price you may not be willing to pay."

My mind goes over every possible price. Debt collection. Forced involvement in crime. Unpaid labor, human trafficking...sexual favors.

What would they demand of me?

"I have what they may find to be a...marketable skill," I say, my voice trembling.

She blows out a breath, and relief floods me when she smiles. "Of course you do. What do you know about The Cove?"

I shake my head. "Honestly, not much." I want to hear what she has to say.

Tatiana's family is Russian, so she's a lot more familiar with it than I am.

"So it's this neighborhood known for having a lot of Russian influence. The shopkeepers speak Russian. There are restaurants, grocery stores, cultural centers. An Orthodox Church. There's like a beach, and a boardwalk. It's really popular in the summer, because people sunbathe and swim, and take walks. In the winter it's less crowded because of the drop in tourists. But that's when the Romanovs come. That's when they set up shop, or whatever the fuck they do. I don't know. They own everything. Literally everything. The restaurants, hotels, venues. But they also have apartment buildings and single-family homes, you know, residences. They own those, too."

"Wow. Okay."

I can do this. What do I have to lose? I've already lost almost everything. Almost.

She bites her lip thoughtfully. "This just might work."

CHAPTER THREE

Mikhail

"My condolences, Mikhail."

I stand a full foot taller than the old man in front of me, but despite Fyodor Volkov's smaller stature, no one ever mistook him for being weak.

Volkov reaches to pour me a shot of vodka, but I shake my head.

"So soon you forsake tradition, son?"

"Call me son again and I'll remind you who I am."

Volkov's bodyguards come to attention at the challenge in the air, but I don't fucking care. "Don't try me," I tell them. "This conversation is between your *pakhan* and *me*. If any of you dare to defile my father's memory, you'll wish you were buried with him."

Other than staff, a few of my guards and Volkov's men are the only ones present for this impromptu meeting in one of my restaurants. I chose this one for the security of its location – the beachfront at my back and only one access point. The secluded room is located deep within the walls of the building.

Though from the outside it appears to be an ordinary restaurant serving Russian cuisine, it's only a front. The atmosphere is thick with the rich aroma of Russian foods, the walls decorated with paintings of Russian landscapes and art, all underscored by the threat of unspoken violence. If these walls could talk...

A muscle twitches beneath the old man's eye, but before he can respond, I lean in closer. "Some men respect the elderly, cousin. Don't make the mistake of assuming I'm one of them."

"If you think—"

"I don't *think*," I snap.

One of his men starts. I know for a fact the last man that interrupted Fyodor Volkov lost his tongue. My fingers itch for his guards to come at me, but they don't.

Volkov holds a hand up, a silent gesture to hold them at bay. I'm done with the formalities.

"I know why you're here, old man. I'd like to remind you that by law we're in our days of mourning. If any of your number breaks that law, retribution will be swift and merciless. The only reason I've given you permission to be in my presence before now was out of respect for my father." I reach forward and adjust Volkov's lapel. "Is. That. *Clear?*"

We have ten days left and he knows it.

Muscles twitch in the old man's jaw, his watery eyes narrowed. He pulls away from my grip on his collar with effort. Though his men outnumber mine, the sheer strength of my cavalcade would overpower them, at least in this moment. My father trained us to be dynamite in human form, veritable panthers.

Volkov would be wise to hire more muscle.

"Ten days left," he says, before playing his final card. "But you know our traditions."

I need no reminder.

I wear the knowledge of my duty like a noose around my neck, tightening with each day that passes. The dissolution of my first arranged marriage agreement on the heels of my father's death was no accident. Volkov is notorious for hitting hard when a man is down, for striking the Achilles heel with no mercy.

My first fiancée went missing, and while we hunted for her, Aleks discovered their financial stability was fabricated. The second arrangement ended as swiftly as the first when my second fiancée was found dead. The third was much harder to secure after my history of arrangements, but we were finally able to. Money talks. And then my third fiancée was found dead this morning.

I nod my head to my cousin's men. "You've outstayed your welcome. You have three minutes to leave before I consider your presence trespassing on our territory and treat you accordingly." My guards practically vibrate with excitement, rabid dogs who smell blood in the air.

I take out my phone to send a red alert.

Krasnaya trevoga

Unlike Volkov's men, greater in number but languid under the leadership of their aging *pakhan,* my brothers obey on command. All are eager to show obedience and homage to their new *pakhan.*

Volkov stares around the room with those narrowed eyes of his for a few beats before he eyes me carefully and gets to his feet. Without another word to me, he gestures for his guards to escort him out. I've already dismissed him as I turn to my phone and send another text.

I tap the computer screen in front of me and wait, drumming my fingers on the mahogany table.

"Another drink, sir?"

I nod without looking at the waiter, scrolling through my notes in front of me. "A bottle of *Stolichnaya Elit* and a platter of appetizers. And send all staff out unless I signal you directly."

In my peripheral vision, I see him nod. "Right away, sir."

Quietly, he evacuates all staff from the room. I pay my employees well to be discreet and obedient, so they know the routine.

Aleksandr is the first to arrive. I wave a hand to greet him at the door, wordlessly point to the seat beside me, and turn back to the computer.

"Heard the news. Bad fucking luck."

I grunt in reply. "Luck has nothing to do with it. Sit."

Aleksandr takes a seat, leaning back and opening up his cell phone. While the rest of the world uses their phones to scroll social media and take selfies, Aleks runs an empire.

He scowls at his phone, his fingers dancing over the screen.

Aleks is younger than I am and in impeccable physical condition. Like all of us, he battles demons, but Aleks schools them under the weight of a barbell. The combination of brilliant techie and sheer brutal strength is useful in our line of work.

He looks nothing like me, which sometimes comes in useful. All of the Romanov men were adopted, a part of our father's intricate plan to build an empire.

It worked, for the most part.

Aleksandr sits brooding, as his fingers fly over his phone screen. He mutters to himself and stifles a groan. Today's news fucked up our plans. But the Romanovs always find a way to prevail.

I tap my computer monitor and pull up the video feed. Viktor is the first that shows on screen, followed swiftly by Kolya, Lev, Nikko, and the rest.

"We have a situation." I quickly bring them up to speed.

"This morning, I got a call. Irina Smirnova was found dead, strangled in her sleep. Of course they have no fucking leads, but we know who was responsible."

Nikko scowls at the camera, his arms crossed over his chest. He's glistening with sweat and I can see the walls of his home gym behind him. Nicknamed "The Steel Serpent," Nikko's our head assassin. "Volkov."

Kolya finally breaks the silence. "Being engaged to you's a fucking death sentence."

Kolya, our group mastermind, served with my father in the army. Though younger than my father, he's older than I am. I respect his brilliant strategic mind.

Our laughter quickly dies because it's true.

He shakes his head at the camera, running his fingers through his short hair streaked with silver. "We don't have much time to arrange another marriage, Mikhail." Kolya's voice is grim. "If we hit that deadline and you're still unmarried, we know the consequences."

The destruction of our assets, the possibility of attack from our enemies, the potential threat they could use leverage against the few people that mean anything to us. Even my tribe of panthers isn't enough.

We're on the cusp of war if I don't have a wife, a war we're not equipped to win.

Kolya continues. "No one in our circles will agree to another arrangement, Mikhail. We'll have to find someone else."

I nod, stroking my chin as I think. The waiter brings our food and pours vodka into shot glasses.

"You have our support and protection, brother," Nikko says, his sober, earnest eyes meeting mine on screen.

I nod. "Thank you."

"We'll find you a wife," Aleks says. "Secretly, of course. We have a network of contacts and resources that can help."

The rest agree.

My phone buzzes with a text. I feel my eyebrows rise with surprise.

The timing couldn't be better.

Would you like to read more? Scan the QR code below to order your copy of *"Sovereign: A Dark Bratva Forced Marriage Romance"* now.

Fueled by dark chocolate and even darker coffee, USA Today bestselling author Jane Henry writes what she loves to read – character-driven, unputdownable romance featuring dominant alpha males and the powerful heroines who bring them to their knees. She's believed in the power of love and romance since Belle won over the beast, and finally decided to write love stories of her own.

Scan the QR Code below to receive Jane's Newsletter & be notified of upcoming new releases & special offers!

Be sure to visit me at www.janehenryromance.com, too!

www.ingramcontent.com/pod-product-compliance
Lightning Source LLC
Chambersburg PA
CBHW070407310726
48977CB00003B/595